Anne Marie

By
P. Nelson Byrd

Airleaf
Publishing

airleaf.com

ISBN: 1-60002-026-7

ABOUT THE BOOK
(ANNE MARIE)

"Obstacles are those frightful things you see when you take your eyes off the goal."—taken from "God's Little Instruction Book II, Special Gift Edition, 1994, Honor Books, Inc, Tulsa, Ok 74155.

"Anne Marie" is the life story of a once very innocent black child, who with great determination struggles to become a successful business woman, college graduate, lover, family member, friend, and Christ-like person.

The story begins in a small town just after World War II and is viewed through the eyes of Aunt Boo (Billie Forman); a loving friend of Anne Marie and one of the main characters in the book. The tale also charts the life of two same-gender-loving-males, a wise and witty black woman, a pride filled community, and new insights. Anne Marie also cites individuals who are sexually abused, religious hypocrisy, souls motivated to succeed, victims of jealous behavior, sufferers of betrayal, victims of lost love, and other familiar and not so familiar human feelings.

DEDICATION

THE ALL, my mother; Ms. June Byrd, Geneva, Fardia, Wayne, Marcha, Roxann, Vanessa, and Glennis. Thanks B.J. Hale, Edward Sullivan, Eric Woods John Nelson, Ola Linda and Derrick C. Dawson. Also, thanks to a host of other family members. Thanks Kerry.

Dear Diary, I am writing because I have to tell the real story of my Anne Marie. As a God-fearing woman, I feel compelled to shed the real truth about the life of Anne Marie Palermo. While I am not a cursing type of woman, I will do my very best not to use those worldly words in telling my Anne's story.

"Anne Marie. I don't care if the bitch did die, better her than me," Sara Mae said.

"She's been a headache every since I brought her into this motherfuckin' world."

"But she was not the cause of most of her problems Sara Mae. You were the main cause of my good friend dying!"

"Will you and Jerome stop your confounded fighting and have some respect for the poor old dead," I said. "Please let our little Anne Marie rest in peace?"

"Sweet home, I've got a beautiful home, sweet home, Lord I know, Lord, I wonder, will I ever get home…"

Pastor Newbreed, a dark-brown skinned, fifty-nine year old, six foot four man with salt and pepper close-cropped hair, walked into the waiting room. He requested that we prepare to walk across the hall into the sanctuary where Anne Marie Palermo's body was lying. Her remains were in one of the most beautiful caskets this town had ever seen.

Sara Mae couldn't get Anne Marie's two children to attend their mother's home-going. Minnie, Sara's youngest daughter would not attend either. Other close members of the Turner family (you see, that was Sara Mae's married name before, but I'm getting ahead of myself) would not come to the burial of Anne Marie for that matter. So, the only people there who could possibly be considered "family" were Sara Mae; Anne Marie's mother, Jerome Goals, Anne's most trusted child-hood friend, my husband and me, Billie Mae Forman—Ant Boo.

As we marched into the church's sanctuary, my eyes caught sight of the many town folk who had the decency to come and pay their last respects to Anne Marie. Most of the folk loved Anne Marie, but found they were as helpless to *stop this human train wreck, as was her "family." They could only stand and watch the tragic end take place.*

Proceeding down the aisle toward the casket and the seating area, I noticed Miss Peach holding on to the back of a pew with both of her small hands. Miss Peach was a ninety-eight year old Negro woman. Her white hair was parted in the middle of her head. She wore two braids that were pinned up on the back of her tiny head. Her face appeared as though she had a thousand and one wrinkles that spoke volumes about her life. As we passed her, she smiled, nodded her pea-shaped head and said in very faint voice, "May the "All" bless you Sara Mae, God bless your family."

Sara Mae appeared not to hear Miss Peach and continued her walk forward staring at the beautiful mahogany casket.

Slowly closing in on the casket, Jerome, holding back what few tears he had left, began to softly hum a slow bluesy type song. You know, one of those songs that today's young people are singing in these, what you call them…oh yes, community choirs. No one had ever heard that song until now.

"Lord you have been a way maker when no one else was around, Lord you have been a way maker when no one else was around, Lord, do not leave me now…"

"Child, Jerome could really sing a gospel tune or any song for that matter."

Reaching the casket and before we took our seats, I noticed a white man leaning over the balcony railing. The stranger was tall and had mixed gray hair. He wore sunglasses. He appeared to have an air of "good living" about him. When he saw me looking at him, he immediately turned his head and re-focused his gaze on the casket.

I was so taken up with the stranger in the balcony, I did not hear Pastor Newbreed's request for the family to view the remains of the body. I was somewhat startled when the good pastor placed his large wide hands on my shoulders and said, "Mrs. Forman."

P. Nelson Byrd

"Mrs. Forman, are you okay? Would you like to sit down?"

"No, pastor, I'm alright, I just got a little distracted. I'm a wee bit tired from the week's events," I managed to say.

With Sara Mae leading, Jerome and I followed the family as they began to file past Anne Marie's rich, dark-brown mahogany casket. My mind was flooded with the sights and sounds of sweet Anne Marie Palermo's past life on this planet. "How could such a wonderful person as she, lose her life so soon and in such a manner? God, what could have been done to save her?"

Looking around the church, I spotted my good friend Donna Jean Moore; she was signaling me to look at the obituary. Anne Marie was born March 14, 1940, at St. Marks Hospital. At that time, the hospital was just beginning to allow Negroes in as patients. Sara Mae was fifteen at the time she brought Anne Marie into this world. Rumor had it that Sara Mae was fooling around with some white boy at the high school. Being that her mother did not believe in abortions, Sara Mae was made to carry Anne Marie until the day she was born.

Mr. and Mrs. Pitts, Anne's proud grand-parents, were considered by most to be very religious people. On the one hand they viewed the birth of Anne Marie as punishment for Sara Mae's being so contrary to God's will. But no one could ever doubt the overwhelming love they had for their grandchild. Sara Mae did not want to give birth to Anne Marie. Eventually she agreed with her parents over the matter of Anne's birth and resigned herself to carry to term and give birth to the girl child she would name Anne Marie.

The obituary cited Minnie Turner as Anne Marie's youngest and only sibling. Anne's two children, Roger and Rochelle were also mentioned. Also named, was Sara Mae's brother, Ishbosheth; we all called him Ish for short. My husband Henry and I were listed as close friends of the family. Henry wanted to attend but had the arthritis so bad he could hardly stand-up. But child, near the ʼ very end of the obituary, an Alphonso Palermo, was named as the father of Anne Marie. Hence the question, who was Anne Marie's father? Alphonso Palermo, again pardon the expression, who in the blazes was or is Alphonso Palermo?"

Secrets.

Nearing the end of the obituary, my mouth fell wide open. My eyes began to water and my heart began to pound loudly-or so I thought. My head slowly turned toward Donna's direction. Donna nodded her head at me and gave me that, "wise and otherwise look." You know the one indicating I had come across that which she and others in the sanctuary had already reached. Anne Marie was going to be buried in St.

Catherine's Cemetery. Well, integration of the races was finally upon us and we were alive to see it. Anne would be the first Negro to be buried there. Why who in God's green earth arranged for Anne to be buried at St. Catherine's Cemetery, who, indeed!

In all my dealings with Anne, that's what I called my beloved Anne Marie, neither Anne nor her trifling Ma, ever mentioned Anne's father to me. Well sir, what you won't learn in a day's time...*Alphonso Palermo! Indeed.* "Who was Anne Marie's father? Alphonso Palermo? "I'm just at a loss for words on this one all this time and..." in the blazes was or is he?"

The home-going service first called for the African Baptist Church Choir to sing two songs. After the choir sang, Deacon Moorhead read some of the many condolences sent to the family. Jerome was then called upon to present a solo. You could feel the anticipation among those in attendance. Everyone knew that if anyone could get a tear out of you when a song is sung, it was going to be Jerome and his baritone voice. Of course, the fact that Jerome was tall, dark, smart, and just plain good looking added to the suspense of the moment. As soon as he raised his head and began to sing *"Sweet home, I've got a beautiful home, sweet home, Lord I know,"* Miss. Peach began to raise her tiny head and shout out, "Sang Jerome, sang for Mama Peach!"

As evil as Sara Mae was, even she began to tap her feet to the syncopated sounds coming from the piano and Jerome. About three minutes into the song, more than three fourths of the choir was shouting, crying, and giving praise to God. Every other person in the pews forgot about the summer heat and the four large noisy fans blowing from each corner of the room. People began to follow the choir's lead by shouting, crying and giving vent to the Holy Spirit. Jerome had ended his song and slowly began to take his seat. He had drained himself and those of us in the room of all emotions, slowly began to take his seat. The tranquil, yet regal smile on his face as he sat down could only mean one thing…*"That was for you Anne Marie."*

Next, the choir sang another song, this time it was one of Anne Marie's favorite, "Yes Jesus Loves Me." After the song, Pastor Newbreed invited those who wanted to view Anne's remains to follow the ushers lead down the aisles.

In what seemed liked an endless parade of people passing the casket, the family members were showered with such comments as:

"Keep the faith family."

"It's going to be alright."

"She is now in a better place."

"Don't cry."

"I know how you feel."

"Child, I thought if I heard one more stupid thing coming out of another person's mouth-well..., I just wasn't going to be responsible for my bad Negro behavior."

The whole time this was taking place, Sara Mae sat quietly with a cold empty look on her overly made-up face. Lord, that woman still does not know how to apply make-up and has the nerve to think she is *let me stop, I'm in the House of the Lord.*

"Alphonso Palermo? In all my dealings with Anne, that's what I called my beloved Anne Marie-no one ever mentioned Anne's father name to me! Well, yes we all knew Anne's last name was different from Minnie's, but still and yet..."

Finally, Pastor Newbreed began to read the eulogy. Child, why do people read the eulogy at funerals, can't people read now-a-days? Afterwards, the good pastor began his sermon.

The sermon was taken from Ephesians, the Sixth Chapter. The first six verses. Basically, Pastor Newbreed was saying that children should obey their parents, but more importantly, he seemed to be saying that parents should lead by example. You know, children following their parent's lead in being good individuals. Then he got to the part about "fathers not provoking their children to anger." Pastor Newbreed paused at this point, then said, "I don't think the Lord will mind if I paraphrase a little at this juncture."

"And ye mothers provoke not your children to wrath, but bring them up in the nurture and admonition of the Lord."

Baby, when the good pastor said that, a resounding AMEN could be heard throughout the whole church. Why, I bet most of the folk in the room have never gotten that far into Ephesians and at best, they were only signifying when they were loudly saying AMEN at that moment. At any rate, Jerome and I felt good about what Pastor Newbreed had said at the home-going of our Anne Marie.

Then came the hard segment of any funeral, the pallbearers were called into place. Pastor requested the congregation allow the family and the casket to pass before we exited the church.

For the first time during the proceedings, Sara began to show some kind of motherly sentimentality. She really did appear to be suffering from the loss of her beloved Anne Marie. As we got to the exit of the sanctuary, Sara Mae cried out, "bye baby, see you later." I guess that was Sara Mae's way of saying she thought she was some-how going to HEAVEN!

Jerome and I rode in the limousine with Sara Mae. That was the longest twenty-minute drive I have ever experienced in my life. Jerome and I used the occasion to catch up on what had taken place in Spring Oaks since he left to become a well-known attorney in Detroit, Michigan. Sara Mae did not say one word the whole ride to the gravesite. She just looked out the window with a blank stare on her face.

As we arrived at the gravesite, dark clouds began to form and a fine mist of rain began to cover us.

The family was escorted to some folding chairs, in front of Anne Marie's casket. *It was about time Wellborn Funeral Home got some new chairs; those old wooden ones were falling apart.* As the casket was being lowered into the ground, Pastor Newbreed began to pray. Well, child, it was at that moment all h—began to break loose. Sara Mae jumped up and screamed to the top of her voice. She lunged toward the casket, so quickly that she was a blur to me.

"Oh God, why did she have to die, I tried to stop them from hurting my baby, but, oh Lord, please, please, forgive us, and please, please, please, forgive me.

It took four big men to restrain Sara Mae's large frame from falling into the grave on top of the lowered coffin. Jerome, who was sitting next to Sara Mae and who could have easily helped the four men hold Sara Mae, sat motionless with the same peaceful look on his face as when we had left church. Others, who had followed us to the gravesite, began to murmur among themselves. Some of the comments were loud enough to hear and were meant to hurt Sara Mae more than to help her. EVIL, JUST EVIL FOLK!

Nurses from the church took Sara Mae aside to care for her. As the remains of Anne Marie Palermo were being lowered into the cold, black wet ground, the sun started to break through the gray and purple clouds. And while the fine mist of rain continued to fall, the sun caused what at first appeared to be sad faces among those attending, to now beam with sheer relief.

"The devil is beating his wife," Miss Peach, was heard to mutter under her breath.

Walking back to the limousine from the grave, I heard some residents of Spring Oaks, voicing their approval of Pastor Newbreed's sermon. Others were too busy exploring around the grounds of St. Catherine's Cemetery to say anything to Sara Mae, Jerome or me. As Jerome and I were about to be helped into the limo- *that's hep talk for limousine-,* the white gentleman, who was sitting in the church balcony, beckoned us to wait for him. As I turned to wait for him to reach the limousine, Jerome and I could walk no farther- for escorting Sara Mae to the limousine, was, not one, but two white men. One of the men was the one seen in the church's balcony. He walked up to us and tipped his hat to me.

"Good morning Ant Boo; my name is Rocco Palermo."

ANNE MARIE PALERMO

I knew everything there was to know about Anne Marie, almost everything. I used to live a couple of doors north of her grand-parents, who in turn lived one door north of Anne Marie and her mother; Sara Mae. When Sara Mae was not with Anne, her parents; the Pitts were looking after her. And when the Pitts where not caring for Anne Marie, I was keeping an eye on her. Lord, how I loved that child.

Sweet Anne Marie Palermo was born on a cold 14th of March, 1940, at St. Marks Hospital, in picturesque Spring Oaks. She weighed six pounds even. While most babies are not all that cute at birth, Anne was the exception. Her hair was very thick and full of large shimmering black curls. She was the color of coffee, with rich whole cream in it. Child, Anne Marie was the most beautiful baby born at that hospital in a long time.

It appeared that all the nurses on that floor of the hospital just could not complete their work unless they were doing something for or with this lively baby. Sara Mae appeared very proud of her new-born when she first brought baby Anne home. Sara Mae could often be heard around the hospital asking about her lovely Anne.

"Where is my baby, don't y'all get my baby mixed-up with the rest of those"?" Let me see my baby? What is that on my sweetie pie?"

"Mother, Annie Marie will be fine, please relax, we will take care of her!"

The nurses would cater to Sara Mae's every wish and command as it related to our Anne.

At first, the folks in Spring Oaks were none too pleased with Sara Mae having a baby out of wedlock. A teenager having a baby at fifteen was unheard of in this neck of the woods. Some of the neighbors on the block felt she should have been "more child-like and kept her panties up." The fact that she was rumored to have been impregnated by an Italian boy from the next town didn't help matters either. Why, in all the years of recent and past history, no one ever remembered a Negro and an Italian from the next town ever co-mingling! Mind you, there were many Negroes in Spring Oaks who took too much pride in their parents and grandparents being anything but-Negro.

"I'm part this and that, with a little of the other mixed in me!"

Mr. and Mrs. Pitts, though "religious folk," weathered the negative talk coming from their neighbors about Sara Mae. On the day Sara Mae was allowed to come home from the hospital, the Pitts proudly brought Sara Mae home in their new car. As they slowly got out of their car they held baby Anne high in the air so all could see their daughter's new-born. This was indeed a great day for the Pitts family.

The school district didn't allow Sara Mae to return to high-school with her classmates. She attended classes during the evenings instead. While going to night-school, Sara Mae began to pay less and less attention to her Anne Marie. Mrs. Pitts was often found fulfilling most of Sara Mae's motherly duties.

"Sara Mae, I wish you would take more time with that baby. Dear God, have mercy!"

Sara Mae's response to Mr. Pitts during these encounters was the usual, "I have home-work to do, or I'm too tired to do"

After graduating from high-school, Sara Mae began attending college to become an elementary school teacher. Anne Marie was mostly cared for by her grand-parents. The Pitts began to care for Anne as though she were their child. They could be seen every where with that child. Anne could be seen in the neighborhood, either at the Pitts home, or attending church with the Pitts. People said Sara Mae was going around town saying things about Anne that could only be interpreted as she being jealous of her own baby. Can you imagine that?

One bright August day, while the Pitts were attending a church convention, Sara Mae brought Anne next door to sit with me on the porch.

"Ant Boo, I just hate I had this d—baby," I really wish I could make her disappear and I could have my old life back again."

"Well baby, just do the best with what you have." "Anne is a beautiful and good baby, why just look at her beautiful smile, she can light up any room with that smile of hers." "And look at the way you and the Pitts dress her, why she is the best dressed baby in town."

Sara Mae just sat on the steps with a cold, blank, tight smile on her face.

Baby Anne Marie could be heard cooing in her mother's arms. Oh what price false safety brings us!

When Anne became age three, the Pitts and I were in sole care of her. Sara Mae was often no where to be found and when she was around, Sara Mae would rush by Anne as if Anne had some kind of disease. Anne at this stage in her life was calling Mr. and Mrs. Pitts, "mama and daddy." She called me Boo. Anne never did call me Billie-I wonder why that was? On rare occasions, Sara Mae took the time to feign "motherly interests" and demand that Anne call her "mother." With the brightest of smiles and that most innocent of expressions, Anne Marie's only response to her mother's demand was a cute- "S A R A!"

At age four, Anne was still a lovely looking and bright eyed baby. She was full of laughter and was most talkative. Sara Mae, ever the "mine is better than yours type of individual," enrolled Anne Marie in Mrs. Tilly's Nursery. The Nursery was situated in Mrs. Tilly's home. The Pitts and I protested this move, but Sara Mae held fast to her word and informed us in no uncertain terms...

"This is my child, I will do with her what I d—well choose to do with her!"

Sara Mae didn't figure on having someone bring Anne home from the nursery while she was in school or at work. After all, Mrs. Tilly closed the nursery at 3:30p.m. Sara Mae's week-day work schedule was 8:30 a.m. until 4:45p.m. So, either the Pitts or I would bring Anne Marie to our homes until Sara Mae arrived. I still think the only reason Sara Mae placed Anne in that nursery was so she could hurt the Pitts and me.

At the age of five Anne was enrolled at Spring Oaks Grade School. Anne appeared to really like her kindergarten classmates.

One day when I went to meet Anne to bring her home, Anne said to me, "Ant Boo, this is Jerome, he is my friend. Jerome lives on Taylor Street, behind us."

"Hello Jerome, what is your last name and where do you live?"

"His parents are Mr. and Mrs. Goals; they just moved here last week," Anne quickly said.

"Oh, your folks live across the alley from Anne."

Just as I said that, Mrs. Goals approached us and introduced herself to me.

"Good afternoon, I'm Mrs. Goals, you must be Ant Boo. Anne and Jerome have told me so much about you." "I am so glad Jerome has a playmate living so close to him."

Mrs. Goals and I began to talk and walk toward our respective homes. In that exchange she informed me that both she and her husband worked for the United States Government. Mrs. Goals, though, was taking some time off from her duties to care for Jerome. As we neared my home, Mrs. Goals asked if she could take a short cut through my yard to her house. She and Jerome said their good-byes, and then walked through my yard and down the alley to their home.

By the time Anne reached first grade, Sara Mae began dating a man by the name of Sam Turner.

Sam Turner was born and reared in Compton, California. He was the second of two children born to Ester and Fred Turner.

Fred Turner was rumored to have been a very intelligent man, but was always flirting with the women in town.

When Sam was six years old, his mother remarried. Sam did not like his step-dad; he often spoke of his step-dad's SPECIAL TREATMENT to his older sister. Sam hated that man with a passion.

Sam was a very gifted student; he skipped a couple of grades while in elementary school. At age twenty, Sam graduated from one of the state universities in California with a degree in accounting. A few years later, he was hired by a firm in the "city." Sam Turner moved to the Westside of the "city," where as he said; "the real people lived." Shortly after his move, his mother informed him she was seeing a psychologist because Sam's step-father had left her for another woman. Sam's older sister! The two of them were living in Houston, Texas, and were planning to have a baby soon. Sam's mother made him promise not to do harm to either his step-father or older sister. This affair broke Sam's heart and he began to drink alcohol quite steadily. This "dysfunctional mess" caused Sam to have three counseling sessions. While he was advised to continue with the session, Sam stopped going to his "head-shrink" and "He was becoming more and more disturbed about his tragic child-hood being ever present, hence, he made attempts to bury the past with whatever it took.

Sam and Sara Mae met at a party given by a mutual friend. It was at this gathering that Sara Mae fell in love with her "Sammy."

Child, they were both running away from their pasts.

Yes, Sara Mae was in love with this five foot nine bother. She loved his skin, which was a light brown, his almond shaped eyes, his "pointy nose," thin lips, his "good hair," and the fact that he was well spoken, well, almost drove her wild. She was always bragging to her friends about how handsome Sam was and her plans to one day marry him.

That old adage of being careful of what you asked for readily applied to Sara Mae.

At first Sam was kind to Sara and Anne. Though, for my money, he was a might too attentive toward Anne Marie. He was always hugging and kissing on Anne Marie. He played a little too rough with her to suit me. Why, on one occasion, I remember seeing him kiss Anne on her lips and his hand placed on that child in spots where-well, I just think he is a little too strange to be a father to a girl child in first grade. I brought this matter to the Pitts; they shared the same concern I had regarding Sam's relationship with Anne. Mrs. Pitts spoke to Sara about the matter. Sara Mae reproached Mrs. Pitts about the matter and she began to act strangely towards me. At first, Anne appeared to like Sam. Anne would often smile/laugh and play with Sam. However, it was when Sam convinced Sara Mae that, "Jerome was visiting Anne too much and should cut-down on his visits to Anne that we noticed a change in Anne feelings toward Sam." There after we noticed Anne's mood start to become more somber around the house. Anne's teacher notified Sara Mae of a decline in Anne's school work. The teacher suggested Jerome be allowed to continue his frequent visits to the house. For appearance sake, Sara Mae, heeded the advice and allowed Jerome to continue his visits. Sam, put up a mild fuss, but soon stopped challenging Sara Mae. As soon as Jerome was allowed to resume his visits, Anne's spirits began to lift and all was well again- or so it appeared.

Near the end of second grade, Anne was still considered an outstanding student. However, she began showing marked changes in her appearance. She began to eat more, especially sweets. As a result of such cravings, she began to gain more weight. Sara Mae said the gain was "childhood growth!" Anne began to withdraw from Sam and he began to exhibit signs of anger about Anne's *polite show of rejection*. Sam began to berate Anne about her "chubby little face."

One day when Anne and Jerome were visiting me on the front porch, Jerome said to me, "Ant Boo, I hate Sam."

Anne sat motionless for the moment, and then she requested to be excused to use the bathroom.

"Jerome, why do you dislike Sam?"

"Ant Boo, I did not say that I disliked Sam, I said I hated him!"

About this time, Henry was coming from the back yard onto the porch.

He had overheard Jerome and said, "What is this I hear, Jerome, about you hating Sam?"

As Jerome was about to reply to my husband, Anne returned from the bathroom. I motioned for both Jerome and Henry not to continue their discussion regarding Sam.

A few minutes later, Sam appeared in front of the house. He spoke to Henry and me, but did not say a word to Jerome. He then requested Anne Marie to come home.

As they turned to walk away, Henry said, "Hey Sam, you forgot to say good afternoon to Jerome."

Sam just kept walking toward the house without responding. Anne followed awkwardly behind him.

Curious to know what Jerome meant earlier, when he made the statement about Sam, both Henry and I called out Jerome's name at the same time.

"Jerome, what did...?"

Just at that moment, Mrs. Goals came from around the hedges of my yard and called to Jerome, "Jerome, it's time to come home and get ready for bed."

As she held out her hand for Jerome to come with her, she asked us if Anne were all right.

With the eagerness only children could express, both Henry and I said, "yes, why do you ask?"

Mrs. Goals sensing she had said too much to Henry and me, continued, "oh, I just get a sense that Anne is not happy these days, don't ask me why, but...well I must be heading home, have a great evening."

With that, she and Jerome disappeared behind my hedges and through my yard to their house.

Henry and I just looked at each other and shrugged our shoulders. I gathered some clothing material, and followed my husband into the house. Henry went upstairs to wash and retire to bed. As I walked into the bathroom downstairs, my eyes immediately caught sight of the inside of the toilet bowl. Anne had not flushed it. As I began to reach for the handle, I noticed that the water in the bowl was pink and the tissue had what looked like blood on it. *"Could this be blood? Had Anne been bleeding?* I wanted to call for Henry to come and look in the bowl, but thought better of it. I flushed the toilet and began to run water for my evening bath. Needless to say, the whole time I was bathing, my mind was on Anne and that toilet bowl.

"What was I to do? Who was I to share this finding- the Pitts, Sara Mae- Anne Marie?"

The next day, Sara Mae brought Anne to my house bright and early. I walked Anne to school. Sara Mae then drove across town to work. Sam went to work an hour earlier than Sara Mae. Mrs. Goals and I walked our charges to school together every morning for about a year. Having walked Anne and Jerome to school, I took the occasion to ask Mrs. Goals about the comment she made yesterday about Anne.

"Mrs. Goals, yesterday, you asked how Anne was doing, did you have any special reason for asking," I said.

Mrs. Goals appearing defensive, then said, "Well, Ant Boo, I was cleaning the house the other day when Anne came to visit Jerome. She appeared to have been crying."

"Crying!?" I said.

"Yes, crying!"

Crying about what?

"When I asked Anne Marie if she had been crying, she denied doing so and swore all was well. Later on that day, Jerome told me Anne Marie had indeed been crying and that her father and mother were the cause of Anne's crying."

I politely informed Mrs. Goals that Sam was Ann's step-father. I asked Mrs. Goals to continue with what else she could share about what may be taking place in the Turner's home.

While I thought that there was more to the story, it was clear that nothing more was going to come from Mrs. Goals this day. We then proceeded to walk back to our homes. Walking from the school, we talked about everything else, but Anne Marie.

As the summer was about to end, news that Mr. and Mrs. Pitts were both in the hospital battling cancer reached Henry and me. This event marked a significant emotional change in the lives of all who knew the Pitts.

Rumors were starting to circulate about Sara Mae and Sam separating from each other. Sara Mae was two months pregnant and was working over the summer months so she did not have to spend too much time at home with Sam. Miss. Ruth Peach lived one-door south of Sara Mae and Sam. Miss Peach was much aware of the loud arguments Sara and Sam were having.

One evening as Mr. Goals was parking his car in the garage, he told me of his having seen Sam chasing Sara Mae out of the house onto the back porch. Sam was beating her with his belt. Now don't get me wrong, Sara Mae was putting up a rough fight, but her fighting proved no match against Sam's strong arms. When Mr. Goals peeked over the Turner's fence to see what was happening, Sam, seeing Mr. Goals, stopped beating Sara Mae and returned to the house.

"Mrs. Turner is everything alright, "is there anything I can do for you?"

"No Mr. Goals, me and Sam were just funning, everything is fine." Sara Mae's hair was standing straight up on her head and she was breathing heavily.

Wiping the blood from the corner of her mouth, Sara Mae cautiously walked inside the house. Anne was visiting Jerome at the time and was not aware of the fight between Sara and Sam- at least not this fight.

Miss. Peach, the Pitts, the Turners, and I lived on the 400 Block of Church Street. There were six churches located on Church Street, from one end to the other. African Baptist was located at the end of our block, south of Miss Peach. One evening I happened to pass by the Turner's house on the way to church. Sam was sitting on the front steps drinking something that was covered with an old brown paper bag. As I got in front of the house and was about to say good after-noon, Sam spoke to me.

"Good after-noon Ant Boo. You know, I wonder why so many people always want to get in my business!"

"Sam, folk can't get into a person's business, if that person doesn't put his business in the streets."

Maintaining my same stride and smile, I continued walking toward the African Baptist Church.

Late that evening, Miss. Peach told me she overheard Sara Mae questioning Sam about my finding blood in my toilet bowl after Anne had used it. No doubt my previous encounter with Sam was his futile attempt to signify on me for telling Sara about my discovery. But, what was I to do, let the matter go unnoticed?" "I don't think so!"

Sam separated from Sara Mae when Anne was in the lower grades. Some how Anne began to drop some the weight she had gained when Sam Turner was in her life. Some how she also managed to maintain excellent grades while in school.

When she and Jerome were not playing in each other's yard, they loved to play in my yard. They would not play anywhere else on the block.

Anne could be found doing her home work either at her house or Jerome's. She could also be seen at African Baptist Church participating in the many activities held for children in her age group.

Ishobosheth, the Pitts' youngest child, was asked to care for the Pitts during their illness.

Miss Peach did not trust Ishoboseth. She called him "Ish" for short, mostly because she did not want to take the time to pronounce his full name. The neighbors followed Miss Peach's lead, and began referring to him as "Ish" from that time until he died. Miss. Peach would always say to me, "Billie, I don't care for that boy, I don't know why, but I just "can not" seem to put too much faith in him."

Folk around here deemed the Peach as a type of "reluctant mystic," someone who could see into the future.

The Pitts were the prime example of doting parents when it came to rearing Ish. They use to give him everything a child could ever want. Oh don't get me wrong, they use to do the same for Sara Mae, but it appeared to most of us, they did a *tiny bit more* for Ish.

The neighbors were never quite sure of Ish's where-a-bouts. He would disappear, then show up on the block all of a sudden. Strange, strange, strange!

When Ish was about twenty-one, he returned to the Pitts' house. He began to take an immediate liking to

Anne. At first, Anne would laugh and smile at Ish's silly mannerisms, but by the end of the school year, she began to shy away from his attempts to get her attention. Ish used to always speak to Anne from his parents porch as she passed by the house. And that's another thing, we never saw Ish enter Sara's home while he was caring for his parents. Hmm!

Whenever he wanted to speak to Sara Mae, he would either telephone her, talk to her from the porch, or send messages to her by Anne.

Sara Mae had another baby in March of that year. She began to shower this newborn with most of her attention. Anne began to spend more time with Henry and me.

One day I asked Anne what she thought of her baby sister, Anne with all the indifference a child her age could bring together, replied, "She's o.k."

Whenever Anne came to visit me and upon her return home, she would either run or walk rapidly past her grandparents' home. She would have nothing to do with Ish.

On a warm summer day when Jerome and Anne were playing house, I over heard Jerome say to Anne Marie.

"Let play house, I'll be "Ish.""

He then stuck his tongue out at Anne and rolled it around his mouth in Anne's direction.

"Stop that Jerome, I don't like that."

Anne Marie turned her head away from her trusted friend, Jerome. The scowl on her beautiful face caused me lean forward in my chair and take notice of what the two of them were doing.

"I'm sorry Anne. You know I wouldn't hurt you." They then moved on to some other children's game.

Children, what they won't think of next.

Little did I know then, what would become of that simple childhood act and what an impact it would have on Anne in the years ahead?

Mr. Pitts died near the end of that summer. We all wondered how much longer Mrs. Pitts would last without her husband. They had been such an ideal couple for nearly fifty years.

One day Anne and I were walking home from church, we spotted Miss. Peach sitting on her steps eating homemade ice cream. Icky Boo, her one-eyed dog was sitting next to her. Miss Peach made the best homemade ice cream in the world- well just about the best.

"Good day Miss Peach, how are you?" I said.

Anne Marie extended a similar greeting. Miss Peach, always eager for guests to visit, returned the greeting.

"Hey Forman, hey Anne, stop by and sit a while." What was going on at the church? Stop that Icky Boo, child this dog "sho" loves it when Anne comes around. Sit Icky Boo, sit!"

"Oh, the NAACP held a meeting in order to deal with the whites controlling the down-town shops," I said.

"So what are the colored folks going to do about that situation, asked Miss Peach?"

"Stop buying down-town and set-up our own stores somewhere," I said to her.

As we sat with Miss Peach on her spacious porch, we noticed that "Ish" was walking past the house. Upon seeing Ish, Anne moved closer to me. Why she almost knocked me into the side-post with her quick movement. Icky Boo began to growl.

"Good morning everyone," Ish said.

"Morning," Miss Peach and I said in unison.

Anne just sat there with her head down. She did not say a word to him. Miss Peach looked at Anne. No doubt she was going to ask Anne to speak to her uncle "Ish," but before she could get a word out, "Ish" said.

"Hello Anne, aren't you going to say something to your favorite uncle?"

Anne dug her face into my lap and very softly said, "Good evening Uncle "Ish."

With that, "Ish" walked past us.

Miss. Peach's eyes followed Ish down the street until she could not see any signs of him.

"You know Forman, I just can't...oh well, I must be minding what I say in front of this child." "That red head, tall demon, ain't good for...shut-up Icky Boo, stop that noise; he's gone now!"

"Anne, honey, I guess we must be getting you home and me to bed," I quickly stated.

I knew how well Miss Peach could express her feelings on topics like this. I then took Anne home. After I walked Anne Marie home, I headed home and prepared for bed.

THE BIG CHANGE

Not much occurred around here that I did not soon know or learn about. As things continued on, there were major changes in the affairs of my Anne Marie.

Upon Anne entering the fourth grade; Mrs. Pitt's health declined for the worst. She called Sara and me to her bedside late one evening. She informed us she had obtained Fred Black as her estate lawyer. Fred was a good Negro man. Most of us trusted him. He was also the president of the local NAACP.

Mrs. Pitts appointed me as the executrix of her will. Child, you should have seen the evil look on Sara Mae's face when Mrs. Pitts said that I was granted this privilege. At one point during that session, Sara Mae looked as if she was going to state her disapproval regarding my appointment, but seeing her poor old ma was dying; she opted to keep quite about her disapproval.

During the late evening, Mrs. Pitt's voice began to fade more and more. She motioned us to step closer to her bedside.

"Billie, I do not want Ishbosheth to have my home. I'm leaving it to the African Baptist Church."

"Sara Mae, I do not want Ishbosheth to take your children should something happen to you."

Again, Sara Mae was about to voice her disapproval, but again she let her concern go unsaid.

"Should something happen to you, I want Billie to take the children." I have taken care to see that Ishbosheth will be well cared for in the future."

"Sara Mae," Mrs. Pitts said, "I have paid off the mortgage on your home, so it is now yours and baby Anne Marie's."

"Thanks Mama," Sara Mae said, with tears streaming down her rounded face.

Sara Mae didn't loose weight after her pregnancy with Minnie, her second child. As a matter of fact, she gained more tonnage than needed. She was no longer wearing the size eight she use to be so proud of after she had brought Anne into the world. *Child, before Sara Mae got pregnant with Anne, Miss Peach used to say that Sara Mae had a shape that the whole world should be in!* Now, it appeared that Sara Mae was wearing a size fourteen – at the very least!

A few hours later, Doctor Dear entered the bedroom and requested we let Mrs. Pitts get some rest. I placed my arms around Sara Mae and walked her into the living room. Ish was asked not to enter his mother's bedroom, but was to wait in the living room.

Poor Ish, all his life, he had been given anything he wanted and now the one thing he dearly wanted and needed; his mother- was about to be denied him.

Early that next morning, Sara Mae brought Anne to the house for me to keep while she and Ish accompanied Doctor Dear and Miss Pitts to the hospital.

"Ant Boo, mama is dying, what am I going to do without her?" Sara Mae said.

"Well baby, just remember the good things your mama taught you. Sometimes, when people are as good as the Pitts are, memories are enough to carry you through this mean old world," I managed to say without crying.

"But what is Ish going to do now that mama and daddy are gone?" Sara Mae said, with a look of desperation on her face.

"He will have to grow up and trust God to lead him. He will have to start being his own man I guess." I said.

After the burial service, the family returned to the Pitts' home. Half the folk; who had attended Mrs. Pitts' home going, had come to her home to extend comfort to her two children. Others were more concerned about the well-being of poor Anne Marie.

Although she was still a child, Anne Marie seemed to sense what impact Mrs. Pitts' death would have on her life. Anne Marie was such a very cute little girl sitting in her grand-mother's house. She was dressed in a very pretty light blue ruffled dress that I had made for her when she read her Easter Speech this past spring. She also wore a pair of white strapped shoes. Two white satin ribbons were tied to each one of her shoulder length braids. Most of the folk in attendance were giving Anne much more attention than they were giving to Sara and Ish. I knew this would not sit well with Sara Mae.

As the after-noon wore on, Sara Mae, never able to hold her liquor, became quite the wild bovine. She yelled at Anne Marie, who was sitting in a chair in a far corner of the dining room.

"Anne, it's past your bed time, get your ass upstairs to bed. "After all, it wasn't your mama who died."

Well, child..., you could have heard a pin drop in that room at that moment. Anne immediately jumped to her feet, and ran upstairs.

Remembering Mrs. Pitts asking us not to allow Ish to get close to Anne Marie, I said to Sara Mae, "Sara Mae if you don't mind, I'll take Anne home with me."

"No, Anne has to learn to obey her mother. She can stay here for the evening," Ish immediately said.

35

Ish's sudden outburst brought to mind a large hairy well fanged white slobbering wolf leaning over a helpless little girl. The little girl began to cringe, cry out, and run into the misty nowhere.

Sara Mae upon hearing Ish then said Anne Marie could spend the evening with me. Child, you should have seen the look of relief on the face of Miss Peach at that moment. Ish, who had a look of total frustration on his face, then fell back into the Queen-Ann Chair.

Within a few moments after that frightful scene, many of the guests began gathering their coats in order to leave. I gathered Anne's things and began walking to the door with her. Suddenly, Ish said to Anne, "Have a good night little niece, think of me when you go to sleep tonight, okay?"

"Shut-up Ish, let my baby alone, good night mama's little baby."

Child, as I walked Anne Marie to my house, I noticed how much her little hands were trembling. She had gripped my hand so tightly; I began to feel a slight pain in my left hand.

The next day, Miss Peach called and told me that Ish was moving into Sara Mae's home as we spoke.

I immediately phoned Sara Mae and asked her if Ish was moving into the house with her.

"Look, Ish is my brother no matter what he has done in the past. The past is just that, the past. Besides I will keep an eye on Anne as long as Ish is in the house."

That school term, Anne's teacher reported Anne as not showing interest in her schoolwork. She often would not cooperate with the other children when it was playtime. She became withdrawn from her peers.

Miss Intellect also said Anne could often be found crying in class. Anne refused to share her problems with the teacher. On one occasion, Jerome was caught fighting two of Anne's classmates. Jerome had caught them groping Anne in the coatroom. When the teacher asked Anne what had happened, Anne refused to corroborate what Jerome had told the teacher.

It was around that time I noticed how Anne's eating habits had changed- and for the worst. She seemed to crave sweets. Sara Mae, not being the greatest cook, would oblige Anne's "sweet-tooth" by letting her eat all types of candies, fried foods, snack foods, and only God knows what else.

I tried everything I could to get Anne to eat nourishing food. She would only pick at those meals.

Child, Anne was gaining too much weight for her own good.

While I knew it was not proper for me to question someone else's child about such delicate matters, I knew Jerome had some insight into Anne's problem. I also knew I had to do something more than *pray* about this matter.

One bitterly cold January day, I telephoned Mrs. Goals and asked if I could visit her. Arriving at her home, I asked if she noticed or knew anything about Anne's recent "acting-out" behavior.

Reluctantly, Mrs. Goals informed me that Jerome was not allowed to visit Anne Marie any more. When I asked her why Jerome was not allowed to visit Anne, she suggested she and I go into the front room to talk.

On a late September evening, Jerome was taking a break from his home-work assignments. As he was looking out the kitchen-window with his telescope, he could see Ish and Anne walking to the garage. Anne appeared resistant to enter the garage. Icky Boo was barking very loudly over in Miss Peach's back-yard.

Jerome said both Anne and Ish stayed in the garage for a long time. When they came out, Jerome noticed that Anne was crying and appeared to be hurt or in some pain. I asked my husband to phone Sara Mae and let her know what Jerome had seen.

"When my husband got off the phone, he had a very surprised and helpless look on his face. He said Sara Mae insisted Jerome made a mistake in the matter and that Anne was in bed sleeping. She also informed my husband that Ish was not in town that evening.

Sara Mae said Jerome was not to visit Anne any more and that we mind our own business!?

When I asked her why she didn't tell me about this before now, she said Mr. Goals demanded that we adhere to Sara Mae's request, that -"*we mind our own business!*"

Feeling as though I had participated in a four-mile race, I began to feel completely exhausted. I thanked Mrs. Goals for her time and I slowly walked home in the chill of an unfriendly evening. I told Henry what Mrs. Goals shared with me. Henry responded by shaking his head from side to side.

"What can we do? After all, Anne is that woman's child." Sara Mae has the last word on what happens to Anne Marie, right?"

Having informed Sara Mae of Anne's lack of academic progress, Anne's teacher told Sara Mae she had no other recourse, but to have Anne repeat the fourth grade. Both Jerome and Anne were baffled and saddened by this move. Sara's solution to the matter was to berate Anne by calling her foul names and comparing her to other children in the neighborhood. What Sara should have known was that none of this would have happened had she honored her deceased mother's request of not allowing Ish to move in with her.

One late summer noonday, Miss Peach came by to visit me. She said her niece told her that Anne was taken to the hospital three times this year for some kind of problem with her "private area!" Miss Peach said that Doctor Dear warned Sara in no uncertain terms, that if Anne had any more problems with her "privates," he was going to doing something- something Sara Mae would regret for the rest of her life.

Ish moved out of Sara's house the day after Miss Peach told me about Anne's hospital visits.

Child, I was so angry with Sara Mae, I wanted to beat her on sight.

Lucky for Sara Mae and me, Henry, having the cooler head in the family, got me to calm down. He convinced me that Anne and I would suffer if I carried out my plans of whipping Sara Mae's b—.

With Ish removed from the house, Anne resumed her normal child-hood play. Her superior academic skills in school began to reappear. Although things looked "back to normal" in Anne's life, her teacher said Anne began to show a more than normal fascination with the boys in her class playing inappropriately with her.

By the end of the spring term, Anne's teacher reported Anne's academic performance was such, that she felt Anne could move on to the sixth-grade.

Sara refused to allow Anne to enter the sixth grade. The teacher contacted me about the promotion. I, in turn gathered Miss Peach, Henry, the Pastor, and The Lord Almighty together to convince Sara to allow Anne to receive such an advance. Sara Mae could not defeat all of us and so Anne Marie was allowed to enter the six-grade.

At one point during our discussion, we almost lost that battle.

"Besides, the promotion, Sara Mae should allow Jerome to visit Anne again," Miss Peach said.

Noticing Sara's response was less than positive when that remark was made, Reverend Starter piped up with, "Praise the Lord Sister Turner, Anne will be placed in her rightful class again."

WHEW!

Appearing weary of so much fuss about Anne Marie, Sara finally complied saying, "If this is all people, I have some papers to grade. I must finish some other chores around the house also."

A few minutes later we filed out of Sara Mae's house. As I walked slowly to my house, I could not help sighing- *"SARA MAE, SARA MAE, SARA MAE!"*

ANNE MARIE/SCHOOL DAYS

Anne Marie's adventures during her school days were periods that caused us great concern. They were times of heightened anxiety and frustration for poor Anne.

For the most part, Anne did well in school. While she didn't exhibit the sharp mind she once possessed a few years ago, overall, she did manage to keep up with the class.

One hot steamy day, Sara Mae "got on her high horse" and said she wanted to place Anne at St. Augustine Roman Catholic Grade School. As soon as Miss. Peach got wind of this, she reminded Sara Mae of our neighbors' children's tales of the unnecessary beatings by those white nuns and priests at St. Augustine. Some Negro parents were withdrawing their children from that school as a result of excessive punishment. Again, thanks to divine intervention, Anne remained in the public grade school system.

While Sara Mae did not allow Jerome to enter her house, she did allow him to sit on the steps. She did allow Anne to visit Jerome.

On those blessed days of visiting Henry and me, Anne would read, play with her dolls/toys, converse with Jerome, or sit at the kitchen table and have some of my "down home cooking."

Anne did not attend too many social gatherings unless she was with Jerome. Jerome was a well- liked child. He was a very independent thinker. Jerome was a very talented young man also. Not only could he sing well, he was very creative when it came to artwork. His name could often be found on the honor-roll throughout his grade school years.

Jerome was an excellent dancer; despite some church members discouraging our young people to dance. They said dancing was a form of devil worshipping – can you believe that mess! Whenever a party was given by his peers, Jerome was the first to be invited. Jerome always took Anne along with him to these parties. Even though Anne was not the best dancer, she was very much liked by the boys. One Saturday Morning while Jerome and Anne were sitting on our porch, I over heard the two of them talking.

"Anne that wasn't a very nice thing you did the other day! You know Butch Mc Gee is no good and only wants to play with your privates!"

For as long as I have known little Jerome, I've never seen him show so much anger. Anne did not say a word; she just looked straight ahead.

Folk began to share the many rumors regarding Anne's precocious sexual behavior. Why one of the neighbors even informed Miss Peach and me about Anne being caught with their sons in their back yard *pretending* to have sex. Some of the neighbors no longer allowed Anne to visit their homes after that incident. When these same neighbors attempted to share their stories with Sara Mae, they were quickly rebuffed. Sara Mae then told them not to return to her home again. *Poor Anne Marie!*

Miss Peach and I would often purchase clothes for Anne. Most of the clothing Sara bought Anne looked like they were best suited for a middle aged woman. Anne would often leave her house and change into the clothes Miss Peach and I purchased for her. She would then happily sashay off to school.

Besides the clothes issue, Miss. Peach and I often found ourselves arguing with Sara Mae about Anne being given too many household chores.

"After all, she is just a child," Miss Peach and I would say to her.

Because of Anne's many chores, she was often too tired to attend some of the parties or church services for that matter.

As of late, Anne seldom smiled or laughed. She could often be seen sitting on the porch in over-sized dresses attending to her younger sister, Minnie. Sara Mae was seldom home on the weekends. "She was always "visiting her girlfriends."

Though Anne appeared tired at the eighth-grade graduation ceremony, she looked like a princess to Miss Peach and me. I noticed that I had to purchase more material for the dress I made for her, but Anne did look beautiful.

The party was held after the graduation ceremony. Jerome took Anne to the party in spite of being teased by many of his classmates and peers. Just after the DJ played *"The Hokey Pokey,"* sweat began to pour down Anne's forehead like a waterfall. Jerome ran and got Anne some water. A little while into the party, Anne said to Jerome, who was sitting next to her tapping his feet to the sounds of a Ray Charles' tune.

"Jerome why don't you go and dance, I'll be alright, Go and enjoy yourself."

Jerome forever the gentleman, said, "Okay, but only if you promise not to get sick on me."

With that Jerome walked over to Mary Joy King and danced with her for about three dances before someone screamed, "Someone get a doctor, Anne Marie just passed out."

Jerome almost knocked Mary Joy King to the floor trying to get to Anne Marie.

Sara Mae asked Mr. Goals if he would take Anne to the hospital. Mr. Goals was one of the chaperones at the party. Sara Mae and I followed them in my Ford Coupe.

When we arrived at the hospital, we found Mr. Goals' and Jerome sitting in the emergency room waiting for us. "Where is Anne, is she alright, what is wrong with her?" Sara Mae yelled.

Mr. Goals nodded his head in the direction of Anne's bed, where Dr. Dear, the attending physician, was examining her.

Sara Mae and I walked to Anne's bed. As we arrived to the area where Anne was lying, I noticed Anne's head was turned toward the windows. Before Sara Mae and I could say a word, Dr. Dear asked me to step out to the hallway, so that he could have a word with Sara Mae. After what seemed like an eternity, Dr. Dear asked me to return to Anne's bed. As soon as I opened the curtain, Sara Mae, whispered to me, "That slut is having a baby, a g—d—baby."

"Mama, please, please!" Anne Marie cried out.

Dr. Dear asked Sara Mae to calm down. He then gave her a list of things to do for Anne.

I gave Sara Mae my- *"don't you even try it look; you have to remember when you were in her shoes not too long ago look!"* I then walked over to Anne. I was sure she needed a hug by this time. I held her and then rocked her to sleep.

When we came out of the room, the Goals were standing in the hallway anxious to hear about Anne's condition.

"Mrs. Turner is there anything I can do?" Mrs. Goals nervously asked.

Sara Mae gave Mrs. Goals a very mean look and said, "no, I think you and your son have done enough already."

Mr. Goals pulled Jerome to his side, gave a polite, but cryptic smile, turned, and walked away.

"Sara Mae, why in the name of God were you so rude to the Goals?"

"So what? For all we know, Jerome could be the daddy of my daughter's baby," Sara Mae said as she slowly turned and walked away from me down the hospital halls to go home.

Anne was allowed to come home four days later. When she arrived home, the poor dear had the look of a frightened deer standing in front of an oncoming car's headlights. The doctor said she needed lots of rest and should not do heavy house-work. Sara Mae turned the sun-porch into a temporary bed-room for young Anne. She was told not to allow Anne to do a lot of stair climbing.

Days and months passed, Anne began to experience problems carrying that baby. We discovered that Sara Mae had Anne returning to heavy housework. Sara Mae expected Anne to clean the house by herself on the weekends. Though old enough to do "some" house work, Anne's younger sister Minnie, was not expected to lift a hand in cleaning the house.

Most of the neighbors were supportive of Anne. While on occasion some "smart little boys" would pass Anne humming or singing the Hank Ballard tune, *"Work with me Annie or Annie had a baby,"* Those who knew of Anne's situation, supplied her with anything she needed. All of the church folk were equally as kind to Anne.

Sara Mae often repeatedly questioned Anne about Jerome being the baby's father, but Anne never did say who fathered her "sweet little Roger." Finally, Sara just gave up and stopped asking about the matter. Against their better judgment, matched with Jerome's persistent pleas, the Goals allowed Jerome to visit Anne Marie. Sara Mae, for whatever her reason, began to let Jerome inside the house. She even began to offer him food, to which Jerome would always say, "No thank you, I will have dinner later on, thank you again."

Anne was rushed to the hospital twice after her initial visit there. Her doctor said she was bleeding too much, plus, the doctor felt the baby was dropping too fast. Dr. Dear suggested that if the baby dropped any further, Anne might lose it. When Miss Peach heard what the doctors had said, she called Sara and me to her house. Miss Peach informed us not to let these new fangled doctors tell us what to do. Sister Peach told us to take a bed sheet, place the broad part of the sheet around Anne's stomach, then tie a knot around Anne's neck. She suggested that we adjust the sheets to Anne's level of comfort. Miss Peach and her neighbor Miss George took care of the intricate aspects of Anne's pregnancy. They took care of Anne as though she were their own child. Sara, ever the ungrateful soul, never said one-day of thank you to anyone.

Anne was not allowed to return to school. She was informed that when she gave birth to the baby, she would have to attend night school to complete her education.

Anne gave birth to a healthy baby boy in March of 1954. When we went to visit her in the hospital, we found her in a private room. The hospital had just built a new wing adjacent to the old hospital. Some of the nurses who doted over Anne when she was born were still employed there. These same nurses catered to Anne ever time she graced that building. Time had not eroded their love for my Anne Marie.

Anne named the baby boy Roger Palermo. As we walked into Anne's room, I couldn't help but notice how the room was filled with expensive looking flowers. For some unknown reason, Sara pretended not to be affected by the aroma wafting through the room and feigned ignorance as to who gave Anne the flowers.

As time progressed, Anne appeared to have recovered her great smile. She even had those two long braids hanging down her back. The poor dear looked a little paler, but she also had the appearance of great relief. The baby's complexion was much lighter than Anne's. He looked as though he was going to be tall and thin. His eyes were light brown. Though not as cute as Anne when she was born, Roger Palermo was a good-looking baby none the less.

When Roger was born, Sara Mae held the baby for a brief moment then abruptly announced she had to attend an emergency meeting somewhere.

Child please, everyone this side of Georgia knows that Sara Mae has never attended a meeting of any importance in her entire life. *Why of all the days in her life would she now have to leave her child?*

"Sara Mae, do you have to leave now, you've only been here a short while." Anne said.

Sara continued walking toward the door, opened it, and began closing it to leave. She blew Anne a "goodbye kiss" and vanished.

After about a week, Anne was allowed to bring the baby home. Miss Peach said she would look after Anne, Roger, and Minnie while Sara Mae was out of the house. I agreed to help also. Miss George, who lives across the street, made herself available to help Anne with the baby on the weekends.

Now that Miss Peach was in the house on a regular basis, Minnie was expected to do chores around the house. Miss Peach began to teach Minnie how to wash dishes. She expected her to make-up her bed and to maintain a clean bedroom. If Minnie showed the slightest sign of insolence, Miss Peach would give her that "peach eye" and Minnie would quickly be about her assigned tasks. She did have the presence of mind to know when Miss Peach gave an order; that order was expected to be obeyed-*pronto!*

When Anne was strong enough to walk around, she and her baby accompanied Miss Peach, Henry and me to church. Jerome was to sing a solo on the morning she returned to church. To the delight of all the grown-folks, Jerome led us in an old favorite church tune.

"Father I stretch my hand to thee, no other help I know."

The congregation began to follow Jerome's strong lead.

"If thou withdraw thy help from me oh where shall I go?"

We would again repeat after Jerome until the whole song was completed.

As Jerome continued to sing, Miss Peach began shouting and running around the church. Mr. and Mrs. Goals both sat with smiles on there faces. Mrs. Goals began to stand up while the song was being sung. Mr. Goals sat quietly with his head appearing to be in the clouds. Others in the church were shouting and praising God. Child, Jerome was some singer, even at such an early age.

The pastor preached a most uplifting sermon from Psalms 34.

After church, folk began gathering around Anne, Miss Peach and me. They extended their well wishes to Anne and offered assistance to her if she needed it. They also surrounded Jerome, showering him with praise for the solo he presented.

The four of us began to walk home, many of the young folk Anne's age playfully passed by us extending a polite greeting to us. They were singing, laughing, and playing among each other. Anne looked at them with a look of longing to be with them, but knew she could never recapture that aspect of her life again.

Noticing that look on Anne's face, Miss Peach, gave Anne a kiss on her forehead. She then took the baby from her.

"It's going to be alright Anne Marie, you'll make it through this time, just you wait and see!," I said.

As Anne's baby grew, it appeared as though Sara Mae had by some miracle, discovered her maternal instincts and began to shower a great deal of attention on Roger. Mind you, Anne was a good mother to her Roger, but Sara seemed to have taken an immense liking to Roger. Sara Mae began to perform all her "grandmotherly" duties on Roger.

Seldom did she allow Anne to care for Roger. If Sara was not holding Roger, Minnie was. Baby, you would have thought Anne was no where in that house at times.

Why if Anne even so much as looked at Roger, Sara would find some sort of excuse to prevent her from holding him.

"Anne don't you have some homework or housework you forgot to do," Sara would say.

The look on poor Anne's face at that moment was enough to make any one cry.

If Anne put up the slightest resistance to Sara and Minnie's keeping her away from her child, a verbal rebuke would come her way. Anne said there were times when she wanted to feed Roger, Minnie would often gently push Anne's hand away from Roger and perform the task herself. *Child, please!*

While attending evening school, Anne seemed engrossed in her class-work. She was determined to graduate and attend college. After evening classes Anne would immediately walk the half-mile to her house. She seldom caught public transportation home.

"I have to save money to care for my baby," Anne often declared.

When Anne arrived home from school, she would address her daily chores-of which there were many. She would complete her homework, briefly share time with Roger and then she climb the stairs to her bedroom for a well deserved sleep.

Just before Anne was about to enter her second year of high school, the District's School Board decided not to hold evening school. Anne was terrified of the prospect of attending high school during the day. How could she face her peers? How would they react to her returning to school after having a baby? Fortunately, that semester, the school-board set-up a "last minute" special afternoon-evening classes at the high school for young people who had situations similar to my Anne Marie. These classes were intended to help girls and boys adjust to re-entering daytime classes.

With the added support of Jerome and others, Anne found herself attending high school during the day with a spirit of comfort. She quickly found herself placed on the honor roll along with Jerome. Although she could not join the many extra school activities, Anne was pleased to have rejoined the members of her former eight-grade classmates. She appeared at peace during this time.

One crisp spring evening, I began walking toward Evening Prayer Meeting. Just as I stepped in front of Sara Mae's house, I happened to see Sara and Minnie running out of the house. They were both in their bathrobes. They had rollers in their hair and were screaming for help at the top of their lungs. Anne was just behind them with a large stick in her hand.

"This is my g—d—baby and don't you two tell me what to do with my baby ever again," Anne yelled loudly.

I thought, "Billie d—n, that girl sure has a big mouth when she gets angry,"

Sara Mae was as angry as a wet hen about the matter, but after much cursing at Anne she decided to let the matter rest.

After prayer meeting, Miss George, Miss Peach, and I walked toward our homes. As we neared Sara's home, we could see a light in Anne's bedroom window. Sara and Minnie were sitting on the porch eating their evening meal while the sound of Sonny Till and the Orioles' *"Crying in the Chapel"* came from inside the house. Right behind that song, I could hear Etta James singing "*Sunday Kind of Love.*"

I didn't want to engage in too much conversation so I tried to quietly walk past Sara and Minnie.

"Did you see what that heifer did to me, the ungrateful bitch?," Sara Mae asked. "Why I ought to throw her big ass out of here!"

"Look what that bitch did to poor Minnie. Now she'll be scared for the rest of her life," Sara Mae said to me, as if she thought I was going to give her some sort of sympathy.

"Ugh," I thought. Sara Mae, Sara Mae. Poor Sara Mae!

I think you should be glad Anne Marie did not send the two of you to the hospital.

The next day, as Henry and I were getting in our car, we noticed Minnie on the porch shaking some floor rugs. Sara Mae was preparing to wash the porch and steps. Henry smiled at me and asked, "When have you seen those two doing anything around that house like shaking rugs and washing the porch and some steps?"

I hadn't told Henry what Anne had done to Sara Mae and Minnie. No wonder he was surprised at what he saw. Of course others and I were aware of what had prompted the supposed change in the hearts of Sara and Minnie. Child, we lived for this very day to get here!

The next evening, the local chapter of the N.A.A.C.P. held a progress meeting at African Baptist Church. Mr. Parker, the newly elected president of the N.A.A.C.P., reported that the credit union, which was sponsored by three of the Negro churches in town, was now a huge success. More Negroes were now saving at the credit union. Only a hand-full of folk were still saving at the down-town bank.

Henry's Tailor Shop was doing well also. Our new councilman was about to make a bid for the position of mayor of Spring Oaks. Mr. Parker also announced that more Negro businesses were being established downtown. Child, but the best news of the evening was when the president of the school board reported that more Negro teachers were being hired at the grade and high school levels. Why, we had elected two Negroes on the district's school-board-Hot dog!

As the summer approached, Anne announced she was pregnant again. Sara Mae, though showing sighs of disgust, continued to play the mother and grandmother role to Anne, Minnie, and Roger.

With Jerome now visiting his uncle and aunt in Detroit, Michigan more often, Anne refused to attend church. She would often retreat to the back-porch to read or play with Roger. Miss Peach and the Goals said that on any given day, they witnessed poor Anne alone, staring off into space on the back porch. Miss Peach said Anne frequently played loud music on the back-porch. It seemed our Anne was especially fond of Percy Mayfield's *"Please send me someone to love."*

One real hot summer day, Henry and I invited Sara Mae's Family to our house for dinner. Sara said neither she nor Minnie could come because she was "entertaining company," meaning she was "courting" again and Minnie was at some-kind of after school practice.

To our pleasant surprise, Anne said she would come for dinner. I asked her to bring Roger also.

On the evening of the invite, I walked to the door to meet Anne. As I opened the door, I noticed that Anne Marie had cut her hair very short. She had only combed it back, giving it a kind of "wild-woman look." She looked rather large for a girl her age. After all she was only five feet six inches tall-CHILD PLEASE! She had on one of those dresses Miss Peach and Miss George wore; you know the kind that looks like an oversized apron. Her face was as pale as a ghost. As she entered the house, she kept her head held down. She only raised her head to care for Roger. Her feet looked as if she had not washed them in quite a while.

After dinner Henry and I walked Anne Marie and little Roger home. As we were mid-way the block, we noticed Miss Peach and Icky Boo rapidly walking towards us.

Placing her hands to her small breast, and heaving a lot, she managed to say, "Y'all, the pastor was just found dead in the church. The doctor said he had a heart attack."

As the summer ended, Anne was informed she would again not be allowed to return to high school. No one appeared willing to champion her cause this time. People were too involved with Miss George's illness at the time. Sara Mae was too busy dating a new man each time you saw or heard from her. The church members were busy trying to find another minister to replace Pastor Starter. Jerome was much involved in school and church activities.

Anne did have another baby, despite her doctor's warning. She stayed in the hospital much longer than usual. Rochelle, Anne's baby girl, was delivered as "a breach baby,"

This pregnancy, did very little to boost Anne Marie's self-esteem. It appeared she was sinking fast into an abyss of depression.

Sara Mae refused to help Anne when Rochelle was born. She said that she had her own life to live and "could not be tied down any more!"

Miss Peach and I went to visit Miss George the day Miss George died. When we walked into the hospital-room, we over-heard Miss George softly speaking to herself, "Look at them babies at the foot of the bed, there's smoke coming from under them...they, they, smell, get them out of here!"

Miss Peach said that Miss George had aborted two pregnancies and was now smelling death coming to get her.

Child please, have you ever heard of such mess?

Miss Peach and I sat in chairs close to Miss George's bed-side. Miss George's voice became ever so faint as she requested Miss Peach to move closer to her. Miss Peach stood up, leaned forward, and placed her left ear to Miss George's mouth.

"What baby, where are they, are they in this drawer?" Miss Peach asked softly.

Still looking at Miss George, Miss Peach began to walk towards the top drawer of the nightstand. She opened the drawer and pulled out an old decorative leather covered book. The craftsmanship on it was stunning. You could tell the book was very old and meant a lot to Miss George.

Opening the book Miss Peach began to read through some of the many faded letters it contained. Tears started streaming down her face.

"Hula after all these years, you saved these old love letters?"

"Love letters, what love letters, from whom were these love letters sent-what!? What was going on in this room?"

At that moment, the nurse walked into the room and asked Miss Peach to accompany her to the front desk.

Noticing that Miss George appeared to be sleeping, I walked over to the leather book that was filled with letters. As I approached it, the book fell to the floor- I swear it did! As I began to collect the letters that had fallen to the floor, I noticed that one of the letters was dated 1946.

The letter was from Miss George expressing her love for Miss Peach and how happy she was to finally be moving to Spring Oaks to be with her "Peachy? She thanked Sister Peach for all the support she had shown throughout her husband's illness and eventual death. The letter continued by saying that had it not been for Miss Peach, Sister George couldn't have made it through life. The last line of the letter expressed Miss George's happiness, so much that she wanted to go up to the roof and shout how much she loved Ruth Peach.

Just as I was returning the letter to the book, Miss Peach walked into the room. She did not appear to be angry with me. She gently took the book out of my trembling hands, smiled at me, and then sat down at the foot of Miss George's bed. Miss Peach proceeded to read the remaining letters in the lovely leather casing.

With Miss George now dead, Miss Peach spent most of her time working around her front and back-yards. It was to be a while before she was herself again.

Anne did not adjust to Miss George's death too well. After all, Miss George stood by her when Anne was in need of someone to hear her tales of woe.

Jerome had come home and was attending summer school at the local college in town. He was such an industrious young man. Rumors began to circulate about the new pastor not wanting Jerome to sing in the church's choir any more. Mr. and Mrs. Goals stopped attending African Baptist Church during that period. Members of the church asked the new pastor why he didn't want Jerome to sing in the church's choir.

"Ask Jerome, he knows why I refuse to have his kind singing in the Lord's Choir!"

Although Jerome spent the whole summer not singing in the church's choir, many church clubs and other groups did have Jerome sing solos at their gatherings.

The Gospel Choir, opted to ignore the new pastor, and had Jerome re-join them. Miss Peach and a number of other members of the church had frequent encounters with the new pastor about his questionable decision makings around the church. After all, he was

pastor of the church at the behest of the members and
not the reverse. Now!

*Child, some of these new young pastors are just too
full of themselves. They are egotistical, irrational, in too
much of a hurry, flashy dressers, and selfish. Oh, did I
mention, HYPOCRITES! And why are these "young bucks"
so rotund? Plus, they never bring up the subject of racism
in church, what's with that?*

Miss Peach and I were especially concerned about
his not wanting Jerome to sing in the choir. After all,
the congregation and the Lord had the last word in this
church!

Anne did not like the new reverend attempting to
keep her best friend from singing in the choir. She
stopped attending church. She did however allow me
to take Roger to church with me.

As Christmas approached, we noticed that the new
pastor's sermons were mostly focused on the subject of
sex. If he wasn't preaching about "sissies in church," he
was preaching about "hoe-mongers" and "hoe-hopping."
Near Christmas Eve, the deacons and trustees of the
church called a special meeting to discuss their many
concerns about the new pastor and his strange
behavior.

One Tuesday evening, the new pastor, the deacons,
and the trustees held a five hour meeting in order to
thrash-out their many issues. Believe you me the

meeting only highlighted the many differences held between the new pastor and the congregation. Now, this is what was told to me!

On a clear sunny afternoon, Sara Mae phoned me and said that the new Pastor had walked by her house. She said Anne and she were cleaning snow off the porch. As the new reverend was about to rush by her house, she said that Anne caught sight of him and spoke to him.

"Good afternoon Pastor, nice day isn't it?"

Sara said the new pastor took one look at Anne Marie, turned his head, increased his pace, and then walked past the house toward the church.

Anne came to visit Henry and me two days after that incident. She informed us that she was not returning to school. She felt she was too old to attend school. She also said that the new pastor had invited Jerome to his office recently. He informed Jerome he did not want Jerome to sing in the choir, because the reverend felt Jerome was a sissy and going to HELL! Anne said Jerome stood his ground on the matter.

"Good Pastor, until God tells me not to sing in the choir, I will not honor YOUR hate-filled request."

Anne said Jerome was not passive about declaring his life-style. She said that following their brief talk, Jerome invited "the pastor" to read, John 3: 16, John 8:

7, and Romans 3: 22. Jerome then excused himself and quietly walked out into the fresh air heading to the library.

"A sissy," I said, "Why, who is he to call someone a sissy? Jerome is a sissy, so what? "Why I've not known Jerome to play with dolls. He was always so active in sports, Have you ever known Jerome to play with dolls Henry?"

Henry smiled at me.

"Billie," he asked, "is dinner ready yet? I'm hungry, Jerome can take care of himself."

"Okay, okay, Henry," I answered. "I can take a hint. Dinner will be ready in a minute. Lord today!"

Around Easter time I observed Anne socializing with her peers more. I saw her walking her children around the block or walking downtown to do some shopping. She would stop by my husband's tailor / cleaners to say hello to him. I also took time to teach Anne how to sew. She quickly became so good at sewing that she was getting more customers than Miss Peach and I put together.

SURPRISE, SURPRISE, AND SURPRISE

My mother always told me that people who live in glass houses should not throw stones, and Lord how true those words have come to be in this town. At my age, I thought I couldn't be surprised, but Spring Oaks could blind side me on any given day.

It was a blistering hot early evening in June and Miss Peach and I were sitting on her front porch. As we sat there two teenagers happened to pass the house. They were driving a red convertible automobile. As they passed by, we heard Miss Etta James's, new song blasting from the car.

"Something Got a Hold on me…"

Miss Peach patted her foot to the beat, stood up, and shouted, "My girl Etta, sing Etta! Sing!"

"Miss Peach, what has gotten into you?," I asked.

We were so caught up in our laughter and chatter, that we didn't see Deacon Jones approach the house.

"Good after-noon Sisters. Fine day ain't it," Deacon Jones said. He then asked if were going to attend the important call meeting that evening.

"What y'all doing up there deacon?" Miss Peach asked, still smiling after our earlier conversation.

"Oh, you'll see," Deacon Jones said sternly, as he walked past the house.

Later that evening when Henry, Miss Peach, and I walked into the church, we noticed that the church had more people in attendance than on any given Sunday Morning. The good pastor was seated in the pulpit. He was surrounded by his few supporters.

Since the new pastor's arrival, a huge chasm had formed between the members of the church. For the most part, this was due to the new pastor's archaic stance on many church issues. Most of the members at the church felt he was the wrong choice to pastor our church, but the few influential ones would not listen to us.

Now at least three-fourths of the church was willing to vote him out of the church.

Sitting quietly in church, Miss Peach and I noticed Anne and Jerome sitting together near the front of the sanctuary. There appeared to be a flurry of activity among the deacons and trustees who opposed the reverend.

As Miss Peach, me and others were sitting in the pews waiting for the meeting to begin, Sara Mae came into the church. She squeezed into the pew with us and quietly sat, fanning herself.

"Where are the children?," I asked.

"Oh Ant Boo, Minnie is watching them," Sara said rather smugly.

Trustee Miles and Deacon Williams, with a tone of defiance, requested Jerome lead a congregational hymn.

Jerome, now a second year law student at an Ivy League university, lead the song with as much gusto as I have ever heard. After a while, Anne slowly walked to the front of the church. With that famous smile of hers, she began to read a resolution drawn up by the deacons and trustees regarding the new pastor.

Among other things, the resolution charged the new pastor with being a hypocrite, a liar, an adulterer and "perverse in his ways."

Child, it was so quiet, you could hear a rat urinate on cotton. Everyone in the church was leaning forward, listening, and looking at Anne as she read the charges against the new pastor.

Anne ended the resolution by saying, "therefore, we the members of African Baptist Church demand your immediate resignation." A loud cheer filled the church. While the new pastor did have some supporters in attendance, they remained silent.

After Anne returned to her seat, Trustee Miles and Deacon Jones again stood in front of the membership. They handed the new pastor a large envelope. The two men demanded the new pastor read the material immediately. Seeing the new pastor was hesitant to open the package, Trustee Miles walked over to three large brown boxes and began to open them. Deacon Jones explained to the pastor that unless he immediately read the materials, he and trustee Miles would start distributing copies of those documents to the congregation.

With a sly smile on his face, the new pastor slowly opened the envelope. As he thumbed through the pages, his smile faded into a grimace. He began to slowly write something on a piece of paper. He slowly got out of his seat and with measured steps walked to the side of the pulpit. Standing at the pulpit and looking around the church, he handed Deacon Jones the paper he had signed. As he turned to sit, his eyes met Jerome's. The new pastor took his seat.

Trustee Miles then stood and made a most surprising announcement. "As of today, Pastor Natas Lived is no longer pastor of this church."

Child, we sat there just flabbergasted. What did those documents contain? What caused this man to resign?

We filed out of the church hardly saying a word to each other. For the most part, any and everything we wanted to say was no doubt best said at home anyway.

Stepping outside some members attempted to question the trustees and deacons, as well as Anne and Jerome, about what was contained in those large brown boxes. The only response we received was, "we will leave that up to God."

"Leave it up to God!?," Miss Peach said to Deacon Jones. "Man if you don't spill that tea, I'll…well I will."

Child, the Peach wanted the dirt dished!

Deacon Jones smiled at us, turned, and strode confidently toward the parking lot of the church.

Dear Anne said her goodbyes to Jerome and quickened her pace to catch up with Sara Mae, Miss Peach, and me. I was tempted to ask Anne what she knew or might have heard about the documents given to the fired pastor, but we all decided not to continue the subject any further.

Sara Mae followed Anne into Anne's house. Miss Peach and I stood in front of the house and continued our conversation about the events at the church.

As I was about to walk away from Miss Peach, she said to me, "you know Billie, the more Anne's children grow, the more they begin to look like their uncle Ish. Now ain't that a thought for the evening?"

"Good night Miss Peach, I'll see you in the morning!," I said.

The next day Henry and I drove around to Miss Peach's house. As we approached her house, we saw Sister "I pay big money to this church" Boca. Before Henry could park the car, Miss Peach was at the curb waving her hands as though something was wrong with her.

"Park the car! Park the car and come in the house," Miss Peach told Henry.

As we entered the house, Miss Peach handed Henry some faded newspaper articles. As Henry began to read through the first article, he slowly began sit down.

"Here, Billie read this," Henry said.

Henry handed me the old newspaper articles. You could barely read the date. The article told of Ishbosheth Pitts, who resides at 426 South Church Street, Spring Oaks, who was arrested for having sex with a girl whose age was listed as six years. If enough evidence was found against him, his trial was to begin in October of that year. Another article said that there was no proof that Ish had committed the crime and that Ish was cleared of all charges and released.

The third article stated that Ish was arrested in Georgia. This time he was being charged with having sodomized a twelve-year old child. The article went on to say that Ish's whole family was praying for him and that they were staying at a relative's home in Georgia awaiting Ish's release from jail.

Not only were the Pitts aware of Ish's improper behavior toward children, but Sara Mae as well was aware of that boy's sickness. Lord, have mercy! Poor Anne Marie!

"Where did you get these articles?," I asked.

"Sister Boca brought them to me," Miss Peach said. As you know, the Pitts left their house to the church." Well, yesterday, the mothers of the church were cleaning out the basement when they come across this old trunk filled with things. They found these articles among the many things in that trunk. I told you I did not like that Ish for some reason, but I just could not put my fingers on it." Miss Peach said as she began to pace the dining-room floor.

"Wait, that's not all," Miss Peach added. Mother Miller told me she and Mother Tellit were visiting the sick at the home for the displaced mothers and children yesterday. They saw Ish. They found out Ish has been employed there every since Roger was..., Billie, you don't think..." His parents said that boy had left the area, but he never left. Why would anyone let him work with our young children?"

73

"Well Miss Peach," I said, "as my mother use to say to us, 'For those that like that sort of thing, that's the sort of thing they like, d—well like…' May the Lord touch his troubled soul."

With that we all gathered our clothing and prepared to drive downtown. Needless to say, we were most surprised by the recent events in the last few days.

Two weeks later, Anne was passing by my house. She had just gotten out of Ish's car. While Ish was no longer allowed to visit Sara Mae, this did not stop him from sniffing around Anne like some dog in the street …sniff, sniff, and sniff! Ish was well aware that he was taking advantage of poor Anne's lack of insight in men like him.

"Good evening Anne how was your day at work?" I asked.

"Oh, I had a great day Ant Boo. Ish keeps me very busy at the home for the displaced, but I really don't mind it though. It kind of gets me out of the house and enables me to meet people."

"Miss Peach said that when one goes out, folk will call you a hoe and when you stay inside, they call you a sneaky hoe. So, you might as well do what you want to do. Besides, they are going to talk about you any way- right?" Anne said, as if she was looking for some sort of justification for what she had just said.

"Well, I guess so Anne," I said hesitantly. God only knows I wanted Anne to live her young life the way she felt she should and not the way others dictated it to her.

No sooner did I get the words out of my mouth that Miss Peach walked up on us.

"Hey Billie, how are you? Hey Anne, how yo mama 'n 'm?"

"Oh, they're all doing well Miss Peach. How are you doing?" Anne asked with that ever-present broad smile on her face."

"Oh, just fair to middling, but I'll make it on these old legs of mine, the All willing," Miss Peach answered.

"Well, I must be getting on home. Sara Mae will raise the roof if I am too late coming home to eat," Anne said.

"Go in peace baby, go in peace," I said as I stood watching Anne's somewhat portly body walk past us toward her house.

"Wasn't that Ish I saw in the car with Anne?"

Not wanting to sound too disgusted, I said, "Yes Miss Peach that was Ish you saw letting Anne out of his car. Miss Peach, you know you be on it, don't you?"

"Lord have mercy on poor Anne Marie, What does it take to keep her away from that fool? What does he have on his…?"

"Miss Peach," I interrupted quickly with a smile, "You know what Reverend Newbreed has told you about your nasty mouth!"

"Well baby think about it, that man has treated that girl like a piece of dirt and yet she runs to him as though he were some type of god or something," Miss Peach said. I still say the man has sugar on his…"

"Hey Miss Peach, how are you today?" Henry said as he came out on to the porch and prevented Miss Peach from being – well, Miss Peach!

"I'm doing fine, Henry, how you doing these days?" Well, I must be heading on home it looks like it is going to rain. Come on dog; let's get you something to eat! By the way, Mrs. Goals tells me Jerome will be home next week. He is going to work with that colored law firm downtown. I'm told he graduated at the top of his class. I've always known he had a good head on his shoulders!" Miss Peach said as she turned and walked towards her home.

NEW EVENTS IN THE LIFE OF ANNE MARIE

Nothing stays the same in the life of those who truly live and so it goes in the life of Anne Marie. She began to grow-up fast. She shared that growth with me, which in turn made me develop just as rapidly as she did.

"Good evening, Anne, how are you this fine October day?" "Are you ready for dinner?"

"Yes sir, I'm ready even if I don't get to go."

"Where are you two going to eat," Minnie said as she was sitting at the dining room table feeding Roger and Rochelle. I sure wish I could go to a fancy restaurant, the only time I get to eat out these days is at church."

"Tell mama I won't be out late," Anne said as she and Jerome turned and walked out the door. They were having dinner at one of the new restaurants owned by the African Baptist Church.

"Anne, order anything you like, besides I have a lot to talk with you about this evening," Jerome said. He had the most serious look on his handsome brown face as he sat across from Anne Marie.

"Okay Jerome, but as late as three days ago, I have started a new slim-down diet. I must watch my girlish figure these days."

"Late last week Sara Mae and I came across some pictures of us when we were children. I looked like a stallion then, but now I look like a Clydesdale horse!"

Both Jerome and Anne began to laugh to the point of tears at that remark. After all, they were the best of friends.

"Jerome," Anne said as she began looking at Jerome with a note of seriousness, "What is this important matter you have to share with me?"

"Anne, you are my best friend in the whole-wide world. I really need you to listen to me, and not say a word until I have completely said what I have to say."

"Okay, you have my full attention. I cross my heart and hope to die," Anne said, attempting to prepare herself for whatever Jerome was about to say to her.

"Anne, you remember when I use to visit my uncle and aunt in Detroit in the summer months?"

"Why yes, Jerome, I…"

"OP, op, op, remember, I asked that you not say a word, you promised," Jerome prompted, with a slight smile.

Anne took her left hand and pretended she had zipped her lips and then sat back.

"May I take your order, sir, madam?" The waiter said.

"Anne, are you ready to order?" Jerome said.

Both Anne and Jerome placed their orders and Jerome resumed his conversation.

"Now where was I, oh yes, I remember now. Anne do you remember when I use to visit my uncle and aunt in Detroit? Well, first of all they are some of the best kin-folk in the whole wide-world. They'd do anything for me. I mean there is not one thing that they would not do for me…Anne, to make a long story short, they both had sex with me when I was a child."

"Jerome, no…, not sex with you!" Anne blurted, as she resisted a strong urge to leap from her seat and hug Jerome.

"Anne, remember your promise," Jerome said with a stern, but pleasant look on his face.

"Continue, Jerome Goals, continue," Anne said as she sat on the edge of her seat.

"First it was my uncle who had sex with me. I must have been seven years old when he performed oral sex on me. Why didn't I say something about it until now, you ask? Well I did not- know- what- to-do- or- say at the time. Besides, my uncle asked me to keep the matter "a secret" between the two of us. He said the act was between two men. After a fashion, I adjusted to the situation and didn't feel so guilty about what he was doing to me. Uncle said that his brother, my father, would kill both of us if I disclosed our little secret."

Anne was sitting with her face looking down at table. Her eyes were swelling with tears. She was feeling a pain of unearned guilt at the moment.

"When I became a teen-ager, my aunt began to have sex with me. Again, I was reluctant to tell any one about this for fear that I would be blamed for initiating these sex acts. What did I know? Again, I recovered from the feelings of guilt and shame. I learned to deal and cope with the matter. I began to find myself looking forward to the summer visits with my Michigan relatives." I prayed, forgave, and "forgot!"

The waiter returned with Anne and Jerome's orders. Jerome, realizing what an impact his story had on his Anne at this point, lovingly coaxed her to eat her Caesar Salad. Anne began to slowly eat with a degree of reluctance. With the same deliberate pace, Jerome also began to eat.

"When I entered my twenties, I stopped having sex with them. I even stopped communicating with them all together. No, I was not angry with them, I just began to lose interest in having sex with them and turned my sexual appetite towards...well other people instead."

The whole time Jerome was talking, he continued his protective gaze at Anne. He was hoping she would and could understand what he was saying.

"Anne, what I'm trying to say? Well Anne..., I AM GAY," Jerome said, his eyes still fixed on Anne.

Slowly Jerome held out his hand, placed it on top of Anne's, and then invited her to say something-anything!

"Anne," now, you may speak!"

"I want to lose at least fifty pounds by this coming spring so that I can wear those short dresses I see the young girls wearing downtown," "Anne boasted with a big smile on her face.

"Oh come on Anne, what do you think of what I just shared with you?"

Poor Anne Marie was searching for an answer to a situation she hadn't been prepared.

"Jerome, I do not know anything about gay this or gay that, all I know is that I worship the ground you walk on- okay?" What you do and who you do it with is between you and God.

By the way, are you all right, did your uncle and aunt hurt you in any way? Because if they did…well I will go to Detroit and…"

"Anne Marie Palermo, I love you. Of course I am alright, what they did to or for me happened a long time ago. After all, you can't hurt a six foot five, two-hundred and twenty pound, muscular, brother like me," Jerome said with a more relaxed smile on his handsome face.

"Besides, I don't wear a size fourteen shoe for kicks!"

"Jerome is that all you have to share with me at the moment? What you just shared is just a little too much information for now," Anne said with a loving smile on her face.

At that point she and Jerome began to laugh. They could finally relax now.

"Yes, oh there is one more item I want to share with you."

"Oh no, what is it now?" Anne asked, jokingly.

"Pastor Newbreed, the trustees, and the deacons asked if I would chair the newly formed Legal and

Community Action Ministry at Africa Baptist Church this year. I told them I would. They also want me to join the trustee board," Jerome said, as he stuck out his chest.

"That's wonderful, now may we eat our meals kind sir, I'm hungry?"

Completing their dinner, Jerome drove Anne home.

As they approached the steps leading to the house, Jerome asked, "Anne, what's this I hear about you and Ish being seen around town together? Anne, everyone in town is aware that Ish is nothing more than a philandering jerk!"

"Get you some business Attorney, get you some business Sir. None of you know Ish the way I do," Anne said with a half smile on her full-size face.

"Good night Anne Marie, enjoy the rest of your evening. Please give my regards to your family for me!" Jerome bent down and planted a kiss on her forehead. For the moment, he saw how useless it was to change Anne Marie's mind about her "dear uncle's" behavior.

By spring of the next year Anne had lost fifty-five pounds. While she did not look sickly, she did act and look differently. She had more of a bounce to her walk.

She was always singing and had even joined the church's Health and Fitness Ministry. She was attending church regularly. Anne even made sure Roger and Rochelle attended Sunday school and Baptist Training Union each Sunday. Just last week as Henry and I were walking past her house we heard Anne invite Sara Mae and Minnie to church. Sara Mae said she was too tired to attend church. What she should have said was that she was too busy courting to attend church. Minnie made a promise to attend church the following Sunday with Anne.

Jerome had convinced the church to convert Miss George's old home into space for the Legal and Community Ministry's permanent home. He also had them set up the Pitts Home to be used for unwed mothers with children.

That Jerome is really a mover and shaker. His contributions to our community made us proud to know him. Why he even found time to continue singing in the choir. Though Anne did not have the best voice in the world, Jerome had talked her into becoming a part of the church's newly formed united choir. That Jerome is some fireball!

By the end of summer, Anne surprised everyone, except Jerome, by announcing she had passed the entrance examination and was now enrolled college.

One day in late September, I saw Anne jump out of Ish's car. "Miss Anne" slammed his car door and walk rapidly toward her house.

"Hey there Anne Marie, what you doing, where are you going in such a hurry?" I yelled.

Anne was crying. She was ignoring Ish's plea to return to the car. The closer she got to her house; the faster she rushed down the street. Ish spotted me, tipped his hat, smiled, and drove off down Scott Street. *The no good rascal!*

Two months later, Miss Peach told me Anne had quit working with Ish. She said Anne and Ish had a fight. Miss Peach saw Anne chasing Ish out of a down-town building with a butcher's knife. Ruth said Ish appeared to be bleeding. He did not press charges against Anne. Miss Peach seems to think Anne has started drinking alcohol; and not in moderation either. Child, please, what'll happen next to Anne Marie?

By the first of the year, Anne had regained the weight she had lost. She stopped attending church and was seen purchasing cheap wine from the downtown liquor store.

With Jerome's help, Anne did make it through two semesters of college. For some unknown reason she did not want to return to college to complete the graduation requirements, though! This caused Jerome and her to have, shall we say, a very spirited conversation about her refusal to return to school.

On the second Saturday in early June, the church held its annual church outing. Reverend Newbreed suggested we no longer refer to the outing as a picnic. It seems that during the time Negroes were held as slaves in America, the slave masters would travel from town to town "picking niggers" to work on their plantations. Pastor said out-door meals were being served while these "pickings" were taken place. Hence the word picnic came into being. From that day on, the church referred to such outings as just that, "church outings."

We were all enjoying ourselves on the forest preserve grounds, when from out of nowhere, Miss Peach and Icky Boo appeared. She originally chose to stay home because she was not feeling well. She rushed over to Pastor Newbreed, Jerome, and Sara Mae. The four of them and the dog then rushed off to Anne and Sara Mae's house.

That evening Miss Peach called and asked if she could visit me. When she arrived, she explained the reason she did not want to talk over the phone.

Miss Peach did not trust the phones. She and I had over-heard too many of our neighbor's conversation in the past, hence "the Peach decided to deliver her *news* to me in person.

Miss Peach got to the house in a matter of a few minutes. As usual, she was panting from the near run she had placed on herself in order to share the *news* she had for me.

"Billie, I was sitting in my bedroom when I heard this loud music outside," Miss Peach said. "Icky Boo was barking something fierce! I raised my window so I could hear where all the noise was coming from. I stuck my head out the window and determined that the music was coming from Anne's bedroom. The music was blasting so loudly I could not hear myself think! As I was about to close my window, I noticed two men going into Sara Mae's house. Girl, I just had a strange feeling that something was not right in that house! I ran out to the sidewalk, flagged some teenager down and asked that he take me to the pastor for help."

"When Pastor Newbreed, Sara Mae, and Jerome, arrived at Sara Mae's, they noticed that the front door had been left open. Sara Mae entered the house first. The loud music coming from Anne Marie's room prevented poor Sara Mae from being heard by Anne Marie. As they we about to file up the stairs to Anne's room, five men opened Anne's bedroom door. As they were coming down the stairs past Sara Mae, Pastor Newbreed, and Jerome, they were adjusting their clothing; two were pulling up their pants, one of them was buttoning his shirt, and the other two were putting on their shoes."

"When they arrived at the top of the stairs," Miss Peach said, "The three of them walked into Anne's dimly lit room and were met with an awful smell. Jerome rushed in to open some windows and to cut the music off. Sara Mae stood at the bed-room door hurling all kinds of curse words at Anne and the men who had just rushed past them. Jerome quietly walked over to Anne. The poor child must have thought he was another one of her partners, because she grabbed him and…"

"Just as Jerome was about to hand Anne a bathrobe, a man suddenly appeared from behind the bedroom door. He tried to run out of the room, but was tackled by Pastor Newbreed. As the pastor and Jerome kept the man's arms from covering his face, we could see that the culprit was Deacon Jones. He was completely undressed. The good Deacon still had a semi erection going…the dog!"

Miss Peach continued. "Pastor Newbreed shoved him out of the room past Sara Mae. He told the deacon that he would deal with him later. In the mean time Jerome and Pastor Newbreed stepped out of the room while Sara Mae, yet cursing, attended to poor, drunk Anne Marie."

"Where's Anne now?" I asked.

"Billie, when I left the house Sara Mae was bathing her. Jerome volunteered to clean Anne's room," Miss

Peach explained, nervously rocking back and forth nervously on my sofa.

"Child, you know Deacon Jones has torn his drawers with the good pastor and Jerome," Miss Peach said. "A deacon of the church, what is this world becoming?" If Anne does not watch herself she is going to get hurt, and I say that without fear of contradiction!"

The next Sunday pastor Newbreed's text was entitled *"There are no little or big sins in God's eyes!"* Pastor Newbreed said sin was a sickness and the church was likened unto a hospital where the sick could receive help. Pastor said God had the capacity to forgive a sin and Adultery, he said, is a sin. He talked about lying tongues being an abomination in the sight of God. When he got to the part about men having sex with men, there were several members who stood up and shouted a hardy AMEN! Child, that's when pastor smiled and said that some white men, for their own selfish reasons, wrote much of the Bible to meet their own selfish needs. He told us that due to many mistranslations, a lot of the original meanings of what God intended to share with us is missing from the Holy Bible.

You could have heard a pin drop at this point in his sermon. Pastor Newbreed continued by saying that around 1400 B.C., the word homosexuality was not a concept at the time Leviticus was written. The word abomination at that time meant idolatrous and unclean. He cited some of the abominations and unclean acts named in that book of laws—not touching pigskin (like footballs), not eating that which crawled on the bottom of the sea (like shrimp, crabs and many river and sea animals like lobsters), certain fowl of the air, and not mixing one kind of apparel clothing with another.

Child, the man continued by saying that at one time in the eyes of the Hebrews for a man to lie down with another man as with a woman was considered a violation of a man's dignity-an act of idolatry. He spoke of this being a Hebrew custom, a means of survival *for that nation!* Yes he did go there! Yes he did!

Pastor Newbreed went on to quote John 3:16, *"For God so loved the world that He gave his only begotten Son, that whosoever believeth in Him should not perish, but have everlasting life."*

You should have seen folk's eyes darting all around the room at each other. But at that moment they dared not do anything.

Then he read from Romans 3:23: *"for all have sinned, and come short of the glory of God!"*

The good pastor ended his sermon by asking us to stop gossiping about two certain members of the church. We were invited to take a look at our lives from that day forward.

"He who is without guilt come cast this stone," he said!

He held a stone up for what seemed like forever. Child, folk were squirming in their seats and fanning like they were burning up in that newly air-conditioned building.

By the time Pastor Newbreed completed his rather lengthy sermon, the room was dead silent. No one said a word. Not one of those "brown baggers" said or moved in their seats!

At the end of the service, Pastor Newbreed shook as many hands as possible as the people exited the sanctuary. I had never seen the pastor look as confident before that day. His broad shoulders and bright smile only added to his look of assurance. While there were those still digesting the full meaning of his sermon, all those passing by the pastor were most cordial to him.

As Anne, Miss. Peach, and I approached the pastor, we overheard one of the members inquire about the whereabouts of Deacon Jones.

"Deacon Jones will return to his duties somewhere in the near future," Pastor Newbreed, said rather hesitantly.

"Good morning Sister Anne, I'm glad to see you this fine morning. May God bless you. We hope to see you next Sunday-okay?" The Pastor said with a broad sweet smile on his face.

"Pastor Newbreed, that sermon really helped me today, you are a good, good man of God," Anne said as she walked past pastor Newbreed. She then walked down the street singing with her head held high.

Just as Miss Peach and I were about to leave the church grounds, we passed Sister Rose and Sister Hightower, both of whom were prime supporters of Pastor Newbreed. They were members of that "brown bag group" at the church. You know the ones who are forever mentioning how their grandfathers helped found the church. These folks always strutted around as though they were "the cream of the crop." They could be found bragging about how light-skinned they were. They never failed to mention how they were mixed with anything but African-blood and something about their "good hair" was thrown in there for extra measure.

Both were arguing about Pastor Newbreed's sermon. In short, Sister Rose liked the sermon and Sister Hightower thought it "too controversial."

Miss. Peach, forever the tease, walked up to the two of them and asked what they were arguing about. She ended their argument by saying, "Ladies, please, please, don't fuss so, you are both pretty!" They looked at Miss Peach, raised their heads, turned, and then walked their separate ways down the street.

I walked Miss Peach to her house. I then approached Sara Mae and Anne's home. Stopping on the Southside of her residence, I could hear the loud music of Aretha Franklin playing. Anne Marie loved to hear Aretha's new single, "*Respect.*"

Several weeks passed, only a few of us saw much of Anne Marie. Only Miss Peach got a chance to see Anne Marie entering and leaving the house on a daily basis. Miss Peach kept Roger and Rochelle while Anne was away at work these days.

One day as I was looking out my window, I happened to see Anne coming past the house. I walked onto my porch to speak with Anne.

"Good afternoon Anne. How are you today?"

Anne looked at me with a blank look on her face. She did not say a word and continued her walk home. She looked as though she had gained more pounds back on her short frame. Her hair was not well attended and her over-all appearance was shabby at best.

Leaving the porch, I immediately phoned Miss Peach. Sister Peach said that Anne barely spoke to her when she brought her children to Miss Peach's house. She said Anne had the "sugar blues," meaning Anne was in love with Ish and could not get him to return the love. Miss Peach expressed great concern over the

way Anne had been acting-out as of late. She feared
something bad was going to happen if Anne persisted
in brooding over that "no good uncle" of hers.

Later that year, Sara Mae told me that one of the
senior mothers of the church had suggested Anne take
some kind of herbal tea to rid her of "that low down
feeling." Sara Mae also said that Anne's doctor had
placed her on some special diet in order to assist her in
losing weight-again!

"I'm telling you, that b—is something to live with.
Putting Anne's name in mother's will as part owner of
the house was not a good idea. Sharing the house with
Anne Marie is a living hell these days. I can't get her to
do anything I tell her," Sara Mae protested, with a look
of utter bewilderment on her face.

"Why before she got on this new diet, she was
always crying. I could not get her to stop eating candy
and sweets. At first, I thought she was pregnant again-
oh Lord, that would be all we needed in this life," Sara
said.

"I just do not know what to do with Anne Marie,
after all she is my oldest daughter," Sara Mae said with
tears streaming down her round silky face.

"I have just given up trying to help her. What did I
do wrong?"

Until Anne recovered from her "illness," she opted to quit her job.

After a few months, Anne began to look and act like herself old self. She could be seen playing with her children in the yard on many days. She would even venture out to the downtown area for a night out on the town.

While she seldom ventured out too far, she did appear to be regaining some degree of the Anne we all knew and loved so much.

One cool spring day, when Henry and I were taking a leisurely walk around the block, we stopped to talk with Mrs. Goals.

"Good evening Mrs. Goals," Henry and I said. "How are you and your family doing these days?"

"Good evening to the both of you," Mrs. Goals replied, bending over to place something in a beautiful multicolored hanging flowerpot.

"Isn't this a wonderful spring day to get out and be among God's children?"

"Why yes it is. How is Jerome doing these days? We hear that he is being offered a partnership at the law firm downtown. Wow, he is really moving up in the world."

"Yes and he's been kept rather busy these days. He now contacts Anne Marie by telephone calls, that being the only way he and she have been able to keep in contact with each other," said Mrs. Goals as she stood from a kneeling position to place the water container on the top-step of her porch.

"That Jerome just has to be in contact with Anne Marie, no matter what or where he is in this life. Why they act more like brother and sister than friends. By the way, how is Anne Marie doing these day, I heard she was not doing so well a while or so ago?"

"Oh, she is doing well," I said.

At that moment, I heard Roger calling me, "Ant Boo, Ant Boo!"

We heard what seemed like some familiar sounds coming towards us. We all looked around. Anne, Roger and Rochelle were walking in our direction. They were out for an early evening stroll. Roger had on a red and black checked coat with a matching hat. He wore a pair of black corduroy pant and a pair of black cowboy boots. Rochelle had on a blue coat, a blue print dress, and some black shoes. Anne was wearing a tan trench short coat, a pair of white boots; that came just below her knees, and some kind of animal print wrapped around her head. It looked like she was wearing one of those "short, short-skirts" that are now in fashion. Child, I thought those skirts were suppose to be worn by women twice as small as Anne-a short skirt- indeed!

Still, I love me some Anne Marie. Though!

"Good evening all," Anne said as she and her children walked slowly past the three of us. "How are all of you doing on this fine spring evening?"

"Quite well," we all answered to Anne as she continued her walk down the street and made a right-turn around the corner.

A SHORT-SKIRT, WHAT WILL THAT GIRL THINK OF NEXT?

Henry took a quick look at me, and said, "Well, Billie, we best be moving, I have some work to do before I retire to bed."

"Okay Henry," I said, as we held hands and walked toward our house.

Walking away from Mrs. Goal's yard, she quickly stepped toward us and said in a whispered tone, "are you sure Anne is doing well?"

"Didn't you see her just then, now you tell us how she looked!"

Mrs. Goals aware of Henry's wit, returned Henry's smile, excused herself, and returned to her gardening tasks.

I was walking toward the church a couple of months later. As I approached Anne's home, I heard Jerome and Anne talking about some sewing Anne had completed for him. He was asking Anne if she would like to sew for some of the lawyers' wives at Black, Moore, Black, and Goals' Law Firm. Anne appeared to be hesitant, but Jerome, ever persistent in what he set out to do, was about to convince Anne to accept the job, when I walked by the house.

"Good evening Ant Boo, how are you doing?" Anne asked looking as though I were her only hope out of a bad situation.

"Don't change the subject," Jerome said, his eyes firmly fixed on Anne. "Why this small task will make a lot of money for you Anne!"

"Alright Jerome, but if one of those uppity women says one thing out of the way to me about anything, I'll, I'll, just..." Anne said as she sat looking at me.

"Good, then you'll do it," Jerome said looking at me with a smile as he walked away towards his new black sports car.

"I'll speak with you about the details later Anne." Oh, good evening Ant Boo, where are my manners this fine day?" Jerome asked as he drove his car off toward the law firm.

"Ant Boo, I'm scared to take on that sewing job for those women. What if I don't meet their expectations when it comes to making their clothing?" Anne asked with a childish look on her face.

"Baby, those women will appreciate the skilled work you do. Why you can out sew any woman in this town. You can even beat me sewing and here I am the one who taught you how to sew!" Besides, those gals are human just like you and me. They have the same needs as you and I. And God knows their behinds point to the ground just like yours and mine," I said to Anne, hoping to calm her unfounded fears.

"Ant Boo, I just don't know what I'd do without you and Miss Peach. While I know Sara Mae loves me deep down in her heart, her love is not quite the same as yours. You know, I think I'll take that job, what the heck-any way!"

With that, Anne smiled and gave me a hug, turned and entered the house humming some old religious hymn.

Walking past the front of Miss Peach's house, I saw her sitting on the L-Shaped porch in her rocking-chair. Icky Boo as seated next to Miss Peach. He stood up wagging his tail. You would have thought I was talking to him instead of the Peach.

"Hey there Miss Peach," I yelled across the gate. "Aren't you going to the business meeting tonight? Don't you want to hear the results of the Farmland Project?" I just know we made a huge profit off those eight thousand acres of vegetables the church owns. I hear the money we made will allowing us to build an addition to the church. Child, baby child, we all know how much we need to enlarge that sanctuary. Henry said that at the joint deacon/trustee meeting last month, Mr. Care reported that some five-hundred new members joined African Baptist this year!"

Before I could complete my thought, Miss Peach interrupted me.

"No baby, you go on to church without me. I've been feeling kind of poorly as of late. And besides, I have to do some paper work. These three buildings I own are requiring more and more of my time. Next week I think I'll do as Jerome suggested and let his law firm handle the management of those buildings for me. Besides, I'm getting too old to deal with the day-to-day running of those properties. Child, I'm telling you the truth, dealing with your own is more than a notion. Do you know that?"

"No," Miss Peach said. "You go on and tell me what went on after you return from the meeting. Besides, I overheard Anne tell you she will return to work soon. If I know Anne Marie, she'll be calling me tonight asking me if I won't mind keeping Roger and

Rochelle while she begins her sewing for those uppity colored women downtown. God knows I want the best for Anne Marie and it looks like she is slowly coming around. I hear she's not been seen in Ish's company for quite some while. HALLELUJAH!" Miss Peach said, as she continued to look over her paperwork.

"Child I know what you mean," I said. "For too long poor Anne Marie had what my mama use to call "the hot stove effect." She hung on to Ish like he was a hot stove, knowing full-well he was too hot to handle! She just burned her fingers trying to win over that hot NEGRO! She got burned every time she came near him. I hear Ish is dating some younger woman now! What is wrong with that brother? Why won't he find some women his age to date? Goodness knows a fellow as tall and good looking as he is should be able to find one of these grown women. I'm sure they'll gladly take him in and turn his sinful ways around," I said.

"No, Billie, let him go about his way. He has already hurt our precious Anne. And besides, with what is said about him, what woman around here would want to keep company with someone like that any way? Well, I take that back, there is that old Miss…"

"Miss Peach…! I'll see you later, you have gone to meddling now. Have a God filled evening. I'll bring you a copy of the "farm land report" tomorrow," I said as I pushed myself off Miss Peach's fence and turned and walked toward the church.

That Miss Peach is a PEACH INDEED!

As I was about to enter the church, out of the corner of my eyes I happened to see Anne coming out of her house. She had stopped at Miss Peach's fence. No doubt she was asking Miss Peach to watch Roger and Rochelle while she worked downtown. That Miss Peach sure knew how to call them!

The next morning, I saw Anne walking towards downtown to her new job. She had a bounce in her step, a look of confidence on her face and a tailor made blue suit that fell below her knees!

ANNE'S DOWNTOWN EXPERIENCE

My mother used to say "sometimes the fear is worst than the actual happening. Our Anne Marie was a success story in downtown Spring Oaks. Her experience there was quite the story.

Anne began her new job bright and early that Monday. Jerome had talked Henry into providing some space for Anne in his shop. Henry wasn't a greedy man. After all, Anne was his god-child!

"Good morning Mr. Henry, how are you doing?"

Anne was dressed in a navy blue skirt, a black knee length jacket, and some three-quarter inch high-heels adorned her tiny feet.

"Oh I'm doing okay for an old man, how about you?" Are you prepared to conquer down-town Spring Oaks with your work?"

Henry was grateful to see Anne sounding and looking so much better these days.

"Well, Mr. Henry, it feels good to be downtown hobnobbing with all you "high on the hog folk," Anne said with that sweet grin on face. Anne knew Henry would respond to her joking about him living the rich life with an uproarious amount of laughter.

"No, baby, I'm, just making ends meet from day to day. I'm down here trying to make a living just like every body else. Trying to make that dollar stretch from one pay day till the next," Henry responded, as he moved about the tailor shop preparing for his workers to come and start the day.

"Don't be nervous, these folk are made of flesh and blood just like you and me. Don't worry Anne Marie. If they start giving you any trouble, just put the word of God on them! That will set them straight!"

It was not until two hours before closing that Anne received her first customer. Mrs. Hightower came into the store lavishly dressed and with an air of self-importance that would choke a mule.

"Good afternoon Henry, I'm here to see Annie Marie, Jerome referred me to her. I need her to mend some of my suits. It seems they have gotten a little too tight for me or something," Mrs. Hightower said as she began patting her well coifed hair.

Before Henry could say a word, Anne stood and addressed Mrs. Hightower.

"Good afternoon Mrs. Hightower, I'm Anne Marie Palermo, how may I assist you?" Anne asked, looking straight into Mrs. Hightower's eyes. "How are you today?"

"Oh, you are that Annie Marie I've heard so much about! I think I have seen you a couple of times at African Baptist Church," Mrs. Hightower said, standing back as if she wanted to get a better look at Anne. "Attorney Goals sent me to you, he said you could do magic with garments, is that true?"

"I have always been told to let God guide my work and the customers will always return," Anne said with an irresistible smile on her face. "What would you like me to do for you today Mrs. Hightower?" Anne asked, continuing to keep a smile on her round face.

"Well these suits some how have become too small for me, I want them adjusted so that I can wear them again without choking to death," Mrs. Hightower said, in a rather straight forward manner.

"Won't you step this way and I will begin to take your measurement Mrs. Hightower, Anne said as she guided Mrs. Hightower to the fitting-room.

Anne began to measure Mrs. Hightower. Each time Anne measured Mrs. Hightower's five foot ten inch frame, she would recite the measurement to Mrs. Hightower and write them on a note pad. Each time Anne shared the results, Mrs. Hightower would feign a degree of great surprise.

"Oh my, are you sure those are my measurements, dear heart?"

"Yes indeed, I'm sure. See for yourself where the tape-measure stops."

"I wonder how that could have happened, not that I would refute your word or anything. I'm sure you know what you are doing-though," Mrs. Hightower said, attempting not to anger Anne Marie. Mrs. Hightower as well as everyone in the church had heard the rumors of how Anne could put on a terrible display of unmatched rage when pushed to that point.

"Yes, I'm as sure of these numbers as I am sure of you're standing before me."

The mirror and the math would not lie to a good Christian such as you, Mrs. Hightower! Anne thought.

"Well, I guess if you say so Annie," Mrs. Hightower replied, with a note of resignation in her voice.

"Oh please call me Anne?"

"Very well Anne, my dear, when may I expect these suits to be completed for wear.

"Does a week from today meet with your approval?"

"Why sure my dear, that will be fine with me," Mrs. Hightower said, as Anne placed a customer's reminder slip in her hand. "Thank you and you have a nice day Anne, you hear me," Mrs. Hightower said as she turned and left the shop.

As Mrs. Hightower, was walking out of the store, another customer entered. They too had been referred to Anne. This second customer made my Anne feel a lot better about her pending success downtown.

In just a short time, Anne became busier than a beaver. She was so busy that she often found herself remaining after work at least three times a week.

Had she not the cooperation of Miss Peach and me in caring for her two children during these times, I do not know how Anne could have survived. Sara Mae was so busy courting the men around town; she hardly had time for anything else. Minnie was so active at school that she did not have nor did she allow time to help Anne with Roger and Rochelle. Oh, don't get me wrong. It wasn't that Sara Mae or Minnie did not love Anne's children, they were just too absorbed in their own lives to assist anyone else, let alone Anne.

That summer found Anne with a new reputation for being the best seamstress in Spring Oaks. Not only did the "top drawer women" like her work, but other people from neighboring towns liked her work as well.

All too often Anne was seen walking past Ish and one of his newer girl friends. Ish would go out of his way to show off his new girl friends to Anne. Anne on the other hand would not appear perturbed by such childish behavior. It was said that whenever Ish introduced one of his girl friends to Anne, Anne would smile, greet the two of them and with a pleasant smile, move on past to the store.

"Greetings Mr. Henry, is Anne in?"

"Here I am Jerome," Anne said, as she was walking from the back room toward the front counter where Jerome was standing.

"I'm ready for lunch. I'm so hungry I could eat a cow." "Don't you dare, say a word, Jerome Goals? Starting tomorrow, I will begin that new fangled diet you told me about, but right now-well, let's go eat.

Anne and Jerome entered the newly remodeled restaurant that had become so popular with the downtown folk. Jerome had talked Pastor Newbreed into purchasing the restaurant from the previous owners. With the church folk's patronage, the restaurant had expanded and became well known beyond Spring Oaks as well. The majority of the fruit and vegetables served at the eatery were grown on the land owned by Africa Baptist Church.

The church owned credit union did all of the financing in order to build the restaurant. All the employees were members of the church.

Not only did the *June Rose Café* serve: fried chicken, greens, candied yams, home made pies, cakes and biscuits, homemade lemonade, butter beans, fried pork chops, meatloaf, "sweet-water," hot-water cornbread, and banana pudding. It was becoming well-known for its serving of: baked chicken, steamed vegetables, freshly made fruit salads, green salads, and home-made ice-cream sweetened with honey or molasses, freshly made orange, apple, carrot, watermelon, and vegetable juices were also popular items on the menu.

Notables from all around the surrounding area could be seen eating at the cafe. Child, on some days, there were just as many non-African-Americans eating there as there were black folk *getting down on that" off the bone food."* The place was kept so clean; you could eat off the floors. The service was most professional. The manager did not tolerate any one being kept waiting in line for a long time. Unprofessional behavior by employees was a no, no!

After Anne and Jerome were seated, Anne began to look over the menu. A couple of minutes later, she did manage to take her eyes off the list of goodies offered. When she did, she caught sight of Jerome looking very preoccupied about God only knew what!

"Jerome do you see anything you would be interested in eating?"

"No, Anne, I don't see anything yet," Jerome said. He did not appear to be really looking at the menu, but was staring off into space.

"Jerome, is there something you want to talk about?" Anne said, as she began anticipating the worst news possible.

"Anne, what would you say if I were to move to Detroit?"

"Jerome, I think I'll have something from the salad bar, how about you?" Anne said, opting to ignore Jerome's unsettling question.

"Aw come on Anne, I know you heard me!" Jerome said, leaning across the handsome walnut table in order to get Anne's attention.

"Jerome, if this is a joke, I'm really not in the mood to hear of your wanting to leave me here. Even if it is to further your career," Anne said, sitting back in her seat and looking at Jerome hoping to see some glimmer of playfulness in his beautiful brown eyes.

"Anne, I am not thinking of moving right away, but shortly I will have an excellent chance to move into the political arena in the Detroit Area," Jerome said. He was still staring at Anne Marie. Jerome did not want to hurt her, but he did want her to be among the first to know of his opportunity to advance beyond Spring Oaks.

"I thought you were going to become our next state representative from this district." Anne said, returning her attention to the menu. Anne of course was aware that whatever Jerome set his mind to do, he was going to do it-no matter what others thought!

"No, there has been a change. George Prime is being slated for that position. "The powers that be" feel that George can beat the current state rep rather handily," Jerome said sensing Anne would support him no matter what he wanted to do in life.

"Well, all I have to say is, no matter which one of you runs, I will vote for either one of you. Besides, it has been my experience that too many blacks do not vote much for a cause as much as we vote "against" something or "someone." Do whatever you want Jerome Goals, you know that a good woman like me is watching your back," Anne said, with a wink of her eye and the surrender of her famous smile. "If you do not have anything else to share with me, may we please eat now?"

"Oh before we start to order, I spoke with Mr. Henry today, I have outgrown that spot in his shop, I need more space. I need your help in securing a space of my own in the downtown area. Jerome will you help me open a shop?" Anne asked with a childish pout on her face.

"Of course I will, let's talk about it tomorrow evening at my house around six thirty?"

Charles and I will fix dinner for you. "By the way, how are you feeling today, Miss Anne?"

"Fit as a fiddle, Mr. Goals, fit as a fiddle!" Anne retorted, never taking her eyes off the menu.

"Good morning, Sister Newbreed; how are you this Thanksgiving weekend?" Anne asked as Pastor Newbreed's wife entered Anne's couture shop.

"May I help you with anything this morning?"

"Good morning to you, too, Sister Palermo, have you recovered from Thanksgiving yet?"

"Just barely Sister Newbreed," Anne said as she began to tug at her skirt from the hips down. She was proud of having lost some much needed weight. She was again wearing a smaller size these days.

"Anne have you lost weight, I can see it in your face?" I always used to say to Daniel, you know that Anne has such a cute face and such well mannered children."

"Why I thank God and you sister Newbreed for those kind words of encouragement."

"Anne, will you, please make this dress for me. I saw in this coming spring fashion magazine and I just had to have it." I want it exactly as it is shown on this page-minus the giant split up the side of the dress. You may close the split. We must not have the good pastor coming up with a hissy-fit over such matters." Sister

Newbreed said, with a note of mischief in her voice and in her smile.

"Oh no, we must not have that," Anne said, with the same degree of playfulness in her voice.

They immediately began to laugh and talk over the design of Sister Newbreed's gown.

As Sister Newbreed was walking around the store selecting fabric, Anne quickly discussed a business issue with the two new staff persons in her shop. Since Anne had become such a well-known seamstress/designer in town, she advertised for additional help around the shop. She was able to find help from two individuals who were members of the church. One was Stanley Wear and the other was in the person of Mrs. Taylor, a middle aged woman, recently moved from Texas. Anne would hire two part-time high school students to handle non-sewing matters soon there after. She allowed Jerome's partner Charles, to manage the business end of her shop.

"Good afternoon, Sister Newbreed, we just stopped in to say hello to Sister Anne. How are you?" I announced.

"Good afternoon to you Sister Forman, how are you doing this fine Saturday afternoon? And who do you have with you? Why its little Roger and Rochelle. How are you two doing?" Sister Newbreed asked.

"Good afternoon," Roger and Rochelle said in unison as they walked over to Mrs. Newbreed and shook her hand.

"Aren't you just the cutest two in this town," Sister Newbreed said, as she pulled two pieces of candy out of her purse.

"Thank you, but we can't eat sweets before we have dinner. Thank you though!" Roger politely said.

Mrs. Newbreed, smiled at Anne, handed her the fabric she had chosen for her gown, kissed the two children on their foreheads, and walked out of the store.

"Anne, the children and I are eating out this evening, do you want to come with us?"

"No, Ant Boo, I have tons of work to do, I'll have a bite to eat with the three of you some other time. In the mean time, go and have a good time on me," Anne said as she walked us to the shop's door.

Anne was obviously in her element these days. She was making a great deal of money, and she had many new customers. She appeared to be happier than I've seen her in a while.

Folk did not mind it when Anne increased her prices for services rendered at the shop. They all knew

Anne was the best at what she did and so they were willing to *"pay the cost for Anne to be the boss."*

By the spring of the year, Anne had hired two additional employees. One was a part-time seamstress and the other was a full-time office person. Anne decided she needed time to create and plan.

The next summer Anne moved into a much larger shop. She started making plans to return to college and somehow spend more time with her children. Anne Marie also wanted to keep her promise to pastor Newbreed; to attend church more than she had been doing in the past. Child, Anne's plate was going to be full, full, full!

One September evening as Anne and her children were entering the house she heard Sara Mae's loud laughter. As usual, Sara Mae had a male guest visiting her. Near the dining room, Anne, Roger, and Rochelle heard a familiar male voice. Each step they took toward that great gathering place brought her to a place she thought she had buried in her psyche years ago. It was a voice she hadn't heard in years.

"Oh, hi there "Annie," come in and say hello to your father. Sam is visiting his good friend, on the northwest-side of town. He thought of us and decided to come over and say hello," Sara Mae said, as she turned a cup of tea to her freshly painted generous lips.

"Hello Sam," Anne muttered, as she gave Sara Mae that "what *the h—is he doing here look.*"

Sara Mae dare not look at Anne, but chose instead to offer Sam another glass of orange juice.

"Sam, do you want some more juice, I have plenty in the kitchen?" Sara Mae asked rushing to the kitchen. The poor thing was hoping Anne would not follow.

"No, Sara Mae, I best be getting along, I was just stopping by," Sam said as he noticed Anne glaring at him.

"Anne, Sara Mae informs me that you are quite the business woman these days and you have returned to school. Are you are coming from school now?" Sam inquired, as he was putting on his hat and coat and walking briskly toward the door.

Sara Mae, returning from the kitchen, saw Sam walking toward the door and said, "Sam, don't rush off, I was preparing dinner. I made a plenty for ALL of us."

"No thank you again, Sara Mae, I best be going. Besides, I think I have over-stayed my welcome already. Have a nice day, everyone, Sara Mae, Miss Anne, children." Sam said as he was walking out the door to his car.

Sara Mae rushed past Anne and the children and followed Sam to his car.

Roger, looking ever so puzzled, said to Anne, "Mother who was that man?"

"Oh just some "*chicken hawk,*" now you two go wash your hands and prepare for dinner."

"Chicken hawk, he did not look like a chicken hawk to me, did he to you Roger?" Rochelle asked as she and Roger disappeared into the washroom.

Sara Mae returned from saying her good-byes to Sam. As she entered the house she handed Anne a package.

Sara Mae mustered forth her best smile for this tense occasion.

"Here, this is from Sam. He said it is for you and the children. He brought a present for Minnie and me also."

Anne walked the package upstairs to her bedroom. At first she placed the package in the trash can. Thinking better of her move, she placed the box on her bed and began opening it. The first thing Anne spotted was a purple box containing two sweaters. One was for Roger and the other was for Rochelle. Then she noticed an envelope. Opening it, she began to read where Sam was apologizing for not being the father he should have been to her. He also mentioned that he loved her in spite of what she thought of him. He then referred her to a travel coupon, which allowed her family to fly to Hawaii and stay in a hotel for one week. The letter went on to say that Sara Mae and Minnie were invited to travel there also. Sam ended by telling Anne he would do anything to make-up for the wrong he did her and requested she phone him so they could *iron out* their differences. Sam Turner ended the letter with *"Your loving father, Sam Turner.*

"I forgive you Sam, but I will not forget what you did to me," Anne thought as a large tear fell from her expressive brown eyes.

With that she took a pair of her largest scissors and cut both the card and coupon into many pieces. She decided to give the sweaters to the church as a part of their clothes give away. She went to the adjoining washroom and washed her hands. Anne took another deep breath and returned downstairs for dinner.

"Anne, Sam gave Minnie and me a sweater, what did he give you?" Sara Mae asked, with a note of caution in her voice.

"Well- good- for- you!," Anne said, with each word sounding more sarcastic than the other.

"What's for dinner Sara Mae, I am so hungry, I could eat a goat. Besides, I'm sure that the children have loads of home-work to finish, "Let's eat-please!"

Sara Mae, not wishing to start a fight with Anne sucked her teeth and began to serve dinner. For the remainder of the evening, she directed all of her conversation to Roger and Rochelle.

Anne could be found in her shop the day before Christmas Eve doing "last minute chores." She had tasted success and it was all too sweet to her. God was blessing her indeed. Anne felt she was on top of the world. Her shop was a financial success. She had customers from all walks of life.

Anne Marie and my husband were negotiating the merger of their businesses. Some-how Anne Marie found the time to take classes at the local college and yet remain in the church's choir. *SHE HAD ARRIVED!*

While she was in the shop and at the front counter, Anne happened to see Ish standing outside her shop. He looked as if he were going to knock on the shop's door, when suddenly he turned and quickly rushed away.

Just as he was out of Anne's sight, Miss Peach and her dog were seen at the door. Anne ran from around the counter to the door before Miss Peach could even touch the door-knob.

"Good, evening Miss Peach, what brings you this way, are the children alright?"

"That darn Ish, he just keeps hanging around. He's just like some buzzard, he can't kill anything, and won't anything die," Miss Peach said as she and Anne began to laugh. Anne escorted Miss Peach into the shop and gave her a cup of red clover tea sweetened with raw honey.

"Thanks Anne, you know I just love my hot teas. Child, just relax, the children are with Billie. I decided to do some last minute shopping. The shopping led to my having lunch at the *June Rose Café* and..."

"Come on Miss Peach, you didn't just happen to stop in and see me. What's really on your mind, I'm on to you!" Anne said leaning forward with great anticipation.

"Well child, I never could tell a lie, so why did I think I could start now, especially with the likes of you." Anne, I have been noticing how hard you have been working. Child, don't you fool around and have one of those", well you know what I mean." Miss Peach said, as she raised the cup of tea to her small mouth.

"Come to think of it Miss Peach, I have been a little irritable lately. I was just saying to myself that I should take a trip somewhere. What with Sara Mae and Minnie gone to Hawaii this holiday, I need to travel somewhere and see what the rest of the world is like. Why do you know in my entire life I have not been beyond Spring Oaks?," Anne said, as she gently clasped her beautiful tan colored fingers around her neck. "God knows I can afford to travel, but what about Roger and Rochelle? What would I do with them? Take them along?"

"Taking Roger and Rochelle with you is the least of your worries. They can stay home or you can take them with you," Miss Peach said.

"I know what," Anne said. "Jerome and Charles have been asking me to take a trip with them to their property in Michigan. I'll call Jerome and ask him if his offer is still good. Of course I will take the train there. I don't know if I'm ready to fly anywhere just yet," Anne said, looking as excited as a child seeing a tree decorated for Christmas.

"Anne, I came to this town all the way from the south by train. I swore never to take a train anywhere when it is just as easy to fly where I want to go," Miss Peach said. "Child, live a little. If I can fly as old as I am, you can do the same and those children will thank you forever. Besides, you need to show the world your new fine brown frame. Who knows, you just might meet MR. RIGHT while you are out of town!"

Miss Peach was convinced she had hooked Anne on the idea of flying at this point.

"Miss Peach, what about my classes, I have a scholarship?" Anne Asked. "You know we black folk must take advantage of this free schooling while these white folk are in the mood to be nice. Today is the African-American's turn in America to get ahead. Tomorrow it will be the Latinos' turn and then the Asians in the near future."

"When will I have time to go on a trip?" Anne continued, beginning to show some interest in what Miss Peach had suggested about traveling.

"Well," Miss Peach said, "all I got to say is there are those black folk who do what we want to do with or without the consent of anyone's blessings. Take time off for yourself. It will do you a world of good. Have the trip be a part of some class project or something. Anne, that's what wrong with black folk today. We are always worrying about what *they* say or think about us. We are always talking about racism. Child, racial prejudice is nothing we should be concerned about. That kind of stuff should be left up to the folk who invented that mess. We have too many other issues to worry about. That is the reason I come up north. Too many black folk down there were always talking about what "*they*" say. Now I'm discovering northern coloreds are much like our southern brothers, always worrying about "*they.*" I bet if we began to deal and cope with our own community issues, we wouldn't be in the crap we are in today."

"Oh Miss Peach, you are always talking about black people. Why are you so hard on our folk?" Anne asked.

"Baby," Miss Peach replied, "because we are always talking about each other. Some of us are just like crabs in a bucket, always pulling each other down. If we're not talking about gay people in the community, we are cutting down people because they belong to one political party or the other. Or we are putting down the drug addict living next door, or the women on welfare who have no husbands and a house full of children. Then there are those who talk about the person who *thinks* she is better than we are. Baby, we fight over the small things and that is what keeps us too busy to fight the real enemy. Now notice, I did not give the enemy a color. My mother always said some black folk will stab you in the back faster than anyone else will. She had a saying that I will never forget. She would say, "They may be the same color, but they are not necessarily your kind." Miss Peach said, with a slight smirk on her small face.

"At any rate, Anne," Miss Peach said "you are too young to always be stuck in this town. How old are you now, Anne?"

"Old enough not to tell my age Miss Peach," Anne said, laughing loudly.

"Okay, okay! When a woman gets to hiding her age, she is too old to be telling anyone how long the Lord has blessed her to be on this here earth," Miss Peach said as she began to laugh also.

"Miss Peach, I'll contact Jerome and see if he is still willing to have the children and me visit him at his summer home near Detroit." Anne said.

"My girl," Miss Peach said, as she slapped her small hands on her lap. Why not travel there or anywhere during Thanksgiving? That way you will have time to tend to all the things you need to before you leave." Miss Peach said, sounding more excited with each word spoken.

"Well even if Jerome says we can't come and visit him, I'll travel somewhere with Roger and Rochelle. You are right Miss Peach; I should get out and see the world." Anne said, looking more confident about traveling. "Well, Miss Peach, I'll have to get back to this project. I'll see you at Jerome's parents' home this Christmas. He and Charles invited Sara Mae, Minnie, Mr. and Mrs. Freeman, and us over. I can't wait to eat some of Charles' great cooking," Anne said.

Charles and Jerome were "lovers." There, I finally said it. Child, you don't know how long it has taken me to say those few words. We loved us some Charles and Jerome, though.

"Well, child, you tend to your business here and I'll continue my shopping and visiting folk while I'm downtown. You know, most of the stores now are run by black folk. I hardly recognize any of the places I use to patronize when I first came to Spring Oaks. These black folk are really thriving. Hallelujah! Come on dog, let's get out of here." Miss Peach said as she exited the store and disappeared down the street.

Christmas Day found the usual suspects at Mr. and Mrs. Goals' home. Many presents where exchanged on that snowy day. It was my turn to be Santa Clause. She read the names of each gift giver and handed the presents to the recipients. At the end of the exchange she stopped to rest.

"Ant Boo are you alright," Anne asked, as she walked over to Ant Boo, concerned about labored breathing.

"Child I'm alright, you know I'm not this morning's milk anymore, I just have to rest more than I use to," I said with as sincere a smile and could muster up. Jerome and Anne discussed Anne Marie's plans to travel to Detroit the week leading up to Easter instead of waiting until Thanksgiving. Jerome had even convinced Anne to travel by airplane.

Mrs. Goals pulled Anne to the side and commented on how much food Rochelle was consuming.

"Anne, if I were you, I would watch how much cute little Rochelle eats. Right now she has a wonderful lady-like shape. Now we wouldn't want her to get fat and out of shape, would we? Just think of what getting fat would do to her self-esteem. Letting her eat all that junk food is akin to fattening frogs for snakes. You know how some of these men feel about "Well, just keep an eye on her diet. She'll thank you for doing so in the end."

"Thank you Mrs. Goals, I will do just that," Anne said.

"Well, just a note of concern dear."

"Does anyone know how Mr. Burden's son is doing," Mrs. Goals asked. "You know the one who recently came home from the war. He was such a nice young man. Now, please don't quote me, but I hear he is still dealing with the residue of having been "shell shocked." Mrs. Burden told me that he has nightmares and that she is the only one able to wake him in the mornings without being nearly karate chopped to death."

"The poor brother! I thought the war was supposed to make MEN BETTER MEN, not make men animals," Anne retorted, as she looked around the room for an answer.

"Yes and I hear some more of our boys are suffering from the same problem as the Burden's boy," Deacon Henry said as he began looking around the room for his house shoes.

"Pumpkin, between this war and African-Americans rebelling in some of these cities, I just don't know what to think any more," Miss Peach said as she walked toward the dining room table. "It is as though the world has gone crazy or something."

"All I know is the Bible does say that in the last days God will allow Satan to run to and fro, having his evil way," Mr. Goals said, directing his stare at Miss Peach as she and Charles were bringing the food to the table.

"Do you need help with anything," Mr. Goals asked.

"No, you just sit there and enjoy yourself Mr. Goals. Jerome and I have everything under control. Dinner will be ready in a few minutes," Charles said, as he raised a plate of mixed greens over Miss Peach's head to keep from hitting her.

"By the way, wasn't that a very spiritual service held at Better Days Church of God in Christ this morning. That new pastor really can preach. Did you notice that the women are wearing makeup now? This sister sitting next to me had on just as much eye-shadow as I did," Sara Mae said.

Everyone in the room opted not to comment on Sara Mae's observation. We all knew that no one on this green earth could wear as much make-up as Sara Mae could. She wore so much make-up one would think she was going on stage somewhere. *I mean!*

Child the silence in that room after that comment was so thick you could have cut it with a knife. Women with more make-up than Sara Mae. Ha!

CARELESS, CARELESS WHISPERS

The way the people gossiped in Spring Oaks was often too much even for an ole soldier like me. The effects of such idol talk often seared the life of individuals.

After Anne and the children returned from their visit to Charles and Jerome's, Anne would constantly complain of not having enough energy. She was always tired. She never left the house other than to complete a homework assignment. We advised her to visit her doctor as soon as possible. Her doctor advised her to take time off from school immediately. Anne promised that she would submit to a thorough physical examination during the Easter break. During the break, Anne was admitted to the hospital because of excessive vaginal bleeding and dehydration.

The summer came and Anne didn't return to school. She had lost more weight and was too pale for her own good.

Miss Peach and I took care of her hand and foot. We were waiting for her to get a wee bit better before we fussed at her for not letting us know about her health problems. We were especially concerned about her excessive bleeding. Miss Peach, forever the healer, mixed up her special brew and began to administer it to Anne Marie. While Anne always fussed about how nasty the brew tasted, she was well aware of how much Miss Peach knew about the healing powers of her herbs.

Near the end of the summer, we saw a vast improvement in Anne's appearance. Her voice was stronger, she began to get her color back and her appetite was returning. Oh the powers of wheat germ and ginger.

One day in late August, Miss Peach and Icky Boo came rushing down the street to my house. She rang the bell about six times before she let herself into the house. I escorted her to the kitchen table where she shared with me what made her appear so anxious and angry.

"Baby, you know what Sister Boca told me just now on the phone?" She said folk at the church are whispering about Anne becoming pregnant by Jerome again! theycometalkingabout our Anne Marie entered the hospital to get an abortion over the Easter break." Miss Peach said, her little chest heaving as though it were going to burst.

"What did you say? Having a what? For who?" I demanded, slowly sinking into the chair in order to absorb this foolishness. "These folk need to quit their lying. They know Anne and Jerome's relationship is that of a sister and brother—don't they?" I continued, this time placing a cup of hot peppermint tea in Miss Peach's hand, hoping to calm her down.

"Vicious, just vicious, that's what they are," Miss Peach gasped, gulping the tea down as though it wasn't hot at all. "Why, if this gets back to Sara Mae or Anne, all "HELEN" will break out. You know how Sara Mae is about those folk at church. And poor Anne...why she will just...well I shutter to think what she will do!"

"Well don't forget about my Henry and God forbid Jerome's reaction to those *careless whispers,*" I said. "Jerome and Henry will set those people on fire for telling such lies. Not to mention the good pastor. You know how much he and his wife respect Jerome and Anne Marie. Child, please! I can just hear a sermon on this issue right now," Miss Peach declared as she began to twist her soft silver ponytail between her small fingers. "I bet you that Sister Hightower is...Shit fire and save matches, those cows are really too much for words!"

"Miss Peach, may we join hands and pray to our God about this situation, He'll settle this in His time."

"Okay," Miss Peach said. "Should He not do so, I'm going to kick me some..." Miss Peach said as she interrupted me.

"Miss Peach, please, let us pray? Right now, please!" I pleaded.

For the next two Sundays, Pastor Newbreed didn't mention one thing about what Miss Peach had shared with me. His First Sunday Sermon dealt with "Keeping the Lord's Temple Clean and Prepared." He preached from Proverbs 23:21; "For the drunkard and the glutton shall come to poverty: and drowsiness shall clothe a man with rags."

Now that's a topic you just do not hear too many pastors preach about...gluttony- I wonder why not? Child, you should have seen the folk in that church squirm in their pews. They were grunting as if they had some kind of bug in their throats. Child, most of them looked down-right ill at ease about the subject. The pastor even invited us to the church's fitness program. He implored us to keep evil thoughts out of our minds. Why, he even said that cleanliness was next to Godliness!

The following Sunday, Pastor Newbreed preached about Noah not placing a curse on Ham. Hence, Blacks not having any cause to feel cursed by our Lord and Savior, God. He said that some of his African brothers in the pulpits needed to step into the arena of "independent" thinking regarding this subject.

No child, the shoe did not drop on those two Sundays as we had expected. Maybe, the good pastor was leaving it up to God to handle that aspect of his sermons. At any rate, no one ever approached me in church about Anne being sick and being involved with Jerome in an intimate manner. Praise the Lord!

"Hey Anne Marie, how are you doing?" Baby, you look like you could stand a good back rub and some lies told to you," Peter Burden said, as he was walking across the street, heading to his house.

"Oh, I'm alright Peter; I just need to regroup before I return to the store. I have a lot on my mind these days. How are you doing since you've come home from the war?" Ann asked, looking up from her sitting position only to see Peter crossing the street to her front porch.

Peter Burden was six foot two, a buck ninety-five pounds, and coal black. He had a short fade haircut with lots of Murray induced waves adorning his well shaped head. The brother had long, come-hither dark-brown eyelashes. His lips were full, and the top one was shaped like the letter M. He had a thick neck, a broad chest, bulging arms and large hands. His waistline was just too small for a man that size, and Pete's behind and legs were as solid as they could be. Young Burden had a very LARGE foot.

Peter Albert Burden was a sight to see!

"Peter, don't you come across those streets messing with me. You know we black women are weak for brothers with those aero-dynamic builds like yours. Lord have mercy boy, you sho look good. What you been doing for yourself?" Anne asked, attempting to sound confident and without giving Peter the wrong idea about the randy comment she just made. "We heard you'd come home. What are you going to do now that you're a man?"

"Hell Anne, I'm home to find the man I am supposed to be! Although it doesn't look like I'm having too much success at finding him." Peter said, scratching his body and slurring his words. "The question is, how are you doing, Mom told me you were sick. Are you alright?"

Before Anne could comment, Miss Peach came walking down the street.

"Good afternoon Miss Peach," Peter said, what's that you munching on so?"

"Cherries," Miss Peach said, as she stopped in front of Anne's house.

"Cherries? You mean to tell me that you still have some cherries to…"

"Look son," Miss Peach interrupted. "Before I put you in your place, yes I still have cherries. I have enough to make a cherry pie," Miss Peach said as she gave Peter that sly smile of hers; indicating she was in a very cheerful mood.

"Peter, you really do look good." Miss Peach said.

"Yea, but he's still got those skinny legs," Anne said, smiling at both Peter and Miss Peach.

"Child, no black woman worth her weight in gold cares about how skinny a black man's legs are. The only thing she cares about is what those skinny legs are carrying!" Miss Peach said, placing her small hands to her mouth, nearly choking on a cherry pit.

After a friendly exchange of neighborhood news, both Peter and Miss Peach separated and slowly walked to their individual homes. Peter continued his walk across the street to his parents' home on the north end of the block. Miss Peach walked to her house next door to Anne's.

ANNE'S RECOVERY

Jerome and Charles invited Anne to shop with them in the city. After shopping they decided to eat at one of the fancy restaurants there.

Charles informed Anne that he and Jerome would drive to her house and pick her up. Anne convinced them she would rather walk to their house. She felt the added exercise would be good for her.

Jerome and Charles lived close to the downtown area of Spring Oaks. Their home was a good eight blocks away from Anne's home.

As Anne walked up to the front of Jerome and Charles' home, she noticed that the storm- door was unlocked. She walked up the steps to the front porch and rang the doorbell several times. She even knocked on the inner door a couple of times. Anne started to feel a little bit uncomfortable at this point. She turned the door knob to see if the door was locked. It wasn't, Anne opened the front doors and entered.

"Jerome! Charles! where are you?" She called.

Again Anne Marie loudly called their names before entering the large foyer. She walked up the stairs leading to the second floor of this fashionable home. As she got to the top of the stairs, she softly called out their names again.

"Jerome, where in the blazes are you?" Don't play with me boy!"

Standing in the hall, she heard sounds coming from the front bedroom. Anne walked in the direction of the sounds. When she reached the bedroom, she cautiously opened the bed-room door and yelled out.

"Now I know you two grown brothers..."

At that very second, Anne stopped mid-sentence at the entrance of her two best friends' sleeping quarters. With the door now ajar, Anne was embarrassingly made aware of why she received no response from the two men.

They didn't notice Anne standing at the door with her eyes transfixed on the two *giant* "love-birds." After standing at the door for what seemed like too long a time, even for an on-looker, Anne tore her eyes from the men. She attempted to walk backwards into the hallway.

"Oh my God, Anne, what the," Jerome said, as he looked up and saw Anne standing at the bedroom door. He pushed off of Charles and the bed. He then attempted to run and catch-up with Anne Marie.

Anne was in a near trance. She slowly backed away from the bedroom where Charles and Jerome were making love. With her face burnt red at this point, Anne did a quick about face and took the stairs two and three at a time heading for the first floor living room. Jerome, without realizing it, followed her without any clothes on his towering frame.

"Anne where, "How did..., Are you all right?" Jerome asked, searching for something to say to Anne that could possibly explain, explain, explain...!

"In the words of that immortal song, *"don't explain!"* Anne said, looking somewhat embarrassed. "I didn't mean to interrupt you two, Jerome. I knocked several times. I even rang the doorbell a couple of times. When that failed, I got concerned and entered the house only to find...Jerome, is Charles alright?" I mean look at you, that thing is huge. Jerome, that's a double digit..." Anne said, not able to complete a full sentence.

"Jerome, are you aware that you are standing before me naked?" Anne Marie jokingly managed to say.

Jerome finally seemed to break-through his mental fog; and realized he was standing before Anne Marie in his birthday suit!

Poor Jerome slowly sat on a couch opposite Anne. He placed *the smallest pillow* in the room between his well-developed thighs.

"Anne, is that you down there?" Charles yelled from the up-stair's landing.

"Yes, it is I, how are you doing Charles?" Anne said; glad that someone had said something to break the silence between her and Jerome.

"Just scrumptious, Anne. Just scrumptious!" Charles said. "Jerome, why don't you excuse yourself. We need to get ready for the trip downtown!"

Jerome slowly stood. He was looking at Anne as though he wanted to make sure she was okay. With the small pillow still placed over his crotch, Jerome slowly backed out to the bottom of the stairs. He peered up the stair-case and ran to his love nest.

"Lord, Jerome, how in the world can Charles...," Anne thought "Oh my...! Oh dear...!"

Forty minutes later the three of them were driving to the city. Anne enjoyed being with Charles and Jerome. She always felt safe in their company. What would she do should and if the two of them moved to Detroit? For the moment though, the three of them were in a world of their own and no one could break the solid bond between them.

Anne did not return to school that semester. She decided to attend classes the following term. Pastor Newbreed spoke to her about applying for one of the many scholarships offered by the church. He said that the church had some one hundred thousand dollars set aside for church members who attended college. Pastor

Newbreed felt Anne's high academic standing would earn her one of those full-time scholars' awards.

The following semester, Anne, again, decided not to re-enter college. Instead she found herself returning to the hospital for a one-week stay. Doctor Dear wanted her to go through a series of exams in order see what if anything could be done to address her long history of health problems.

After getting out of the hospital, Anne immersed herself in her work and her children. She even went to New York for a combined business and pleasure trip. Of Course Jerome and Charles accompanied her. Roger was attending an all black college in the south. Rochelle was attending a small college in Wisconsin. Sara Mae was exclusively dating men who were from the Westside of the city. Sara Mae said that there was something about those Westside men that set them a part from all the rest of the men in the city- or anywhere else for that matter. Hum!

"Good morning sisters." Pastor Newbreed said as he walked past Miss Peach and me. "Have either of you seen Peter. I wanted to talk to him. He promised to be in church today. I want to introduce him to our Career Center. He said he didn't know what kind employment he wanted!"

"Tell him to become a preacher, everyone else is becoming one. Just yesterday Councilwoman Ward said she had received twenty-four applications from

NEGROES wanting to open storefront churches downtown. She felt the Spring Oaks' City Council would refuse all twenty-four of them. There are already three storefront churches located in or too close to the business district. Someone should tell those folk to get a real job somewhere and stop taking advantage of folk. And I say that without any fear of contradiction!" Miss Peach interjected with her head held high and shoulders arched back.

"Well sisters, if you see Brother Peter, please tell him I'm looking for him," Pastor Newbreed said as he briskly walked to his office with a smile.

"Miss Peach, you know better than...," I said.

"Oh child, the good pastor knows I didn't mean him any harm. It's just that I get sick and tired of these good for nothing folk always looking for a game in order to take folks' hard earned money." Miss Peach replied, as she and I prepared to walk to church.

"Besides, *who called* all these folk to preach anyway? Every time you look up, some young buck is blaming God for his having *found* some new church. If you ask me, some of these cats are chewing on something," Miss Peach said.

After church services, I walked Miss Peach home. We chanced to see Anne in her back yard. She had just taken the trash out. Her hair was in rollers and she had on a bathrobe. As she was about to climb the backstairs of the house, she noticed Miss Peach and me. She smiled and waved at us, then entered the house.

"Child, these young people have just forgotten about how good God is to us. They sleep all weekend and skip Sunday Worship Service. Billie, God has been too good to Anne for her to flounce around the house all day on Sunday!"

"I know, I know," I said. "You just get ready, I'll see you in a couple of hours. Dinner will be served on time. You know how Henry is about his victuals!"

I then walked past Sara Mae and Anne's house and headed home singing *"what a mighty God we serve, what a mighty God, we serve…"*

That summer, word reached us that some students at Jackson State University in Mississippi had been killed by National Guardsmen. Several members of the church had children attending that school and were concerned about their children's safety. Jerome organized a bus ride to Jackson for a fact-finding tour. While there, Anne Marie also took the opportunity to visit Roger who was attending a school in a neighboring state.

Anne returned to Spring Oaks reassured that Roger was safe and well. Child, Anne worried so much over Roger that she had to be given medication in order to settle down. Even with Jerome and Charles making frequent visits to see Roger, Anne appeared to worry about her son's safety. It was weeks before Anne began to show signs of calmness regarding Roger's safety. She threatened several times to transfer him to an in-state school to complete his training. Child, folk don't know what we black women go through when it comes rearing our sons in the land of the brave and the free!

That Fall Semester, Anne finally returned to school. She waded into her work with the force of a tornado. She even took on added hours to make-up for the time she'd lost.

When she was not attending school, she was working. And when she was not working, my Anne was doing something around the house. When she was not doing something around the house, she was visiting Charles and Jerome or attending church.

Soon, Anne Marie's health status again became the focus of our concerns. She kept us all in a state of high alert.

One cool October day, a handsome man walked into the store. Anne was in the shop preparing to close for the evening. She described the man as being five foot-ten inches tall and one-hundred and sixty-pounds. The stranger had a smooth brown complexion and was well groomed. The brother had an Afro haircut and a tapered beard that extended from his chin past his ears. His blue suit fit him perfectly. The smile on this young man was enough to light up the sky. His baritone voice could send any gal into flight. All this caused Anne to stop what she was doing and address his immediate needs.

"Good evening sister, I realize you are about to close, but may I trouble you a moment. I'd like these pants altered," The gentleman said, looking at Anne with his warm warm-brown eyes.

"Well we are closing now, but I can help you if it is not too much work," Anne said with a smile. She was unable to keep her eyes off the new brother in town.

"What may I do for you this balmly evening?"

"Well, somehow these pants have gotten too small for me; I need to have them let out some," The stranger said as he smiled at Anne Marie and exhibited a full set of straight, pearly, gleaming white teeth.

"Oh yea..., sure. Somehow they got too small for you! Please step in that room and try these pants on for me," Anne said attempting to keep her remarks as witty as she possibly could without appearing flirty.

As the stranger stepped out of the dressing room, Anne could see how well built he was. His shoulders were very broad. His arms appeared equally developed, even under his crisp white shirt. He was sporting a thirty-two inch waist. The brother's butt was so round and tight you could bounce a quarter off it. His stomach was as flat as an ironing board. The man was built for speed and comfort!

After Anne completed the "measuring project," she discovered that the brother was a visiting biology professor at one of the universities in the city. His Name was Hori Brown. Professor Brown was reared in Savannah, Georgia. He received his Ph.D. in Biology, from an Ivy League University. He was thirty-two years old. Both mother and father were medical doctors in Savannah. He had an older sister and younger brother who were graduates of a university in England. His family was among the elite in Savannah.

Hori Brown began attending African Baptist Church this past summer.

"So Miss Palermo, how long have you been attending African Baptist Church?" Hori asked, still staring into Anne's eyes.

"All of my life and by the way please call me Anne," Anne said as she placed his pants in the clothes hamper.

"Why didn't you ask your wife or girlfriend to repair these pants for you?" Anne continued, attempting not to sound too nosy or desperate.

"I'm not married, nor do I have a girlfriend at the moment." Hori answered, again smiling at Anne as she switched from one standing leg to the other.

They continued their conversation in the store one hour past closing time.

"Oh man, look at the time. I've kept you here well past your closing time. Please forgive me, but you are such an interesting sister. I just lost track of the time, gee…!" Hori said as sincerely as he had ever done in his life.

"Miss Palermo, I mean, Anne, if you are not busy this weekend, would you accompany me to "Jazz Among the Stars" in the city? I can't think of anyone I'd rather attend that gathering with than a sister such as you!"

"This brother is hot," Anne thought. "just wait until I tell Jerome and Charles that I have a date this weekend and with a man such as Hori."

"Anne, are you still thinking about your answer? If this is bad timing, I'll understand."

"Oh, oh, why yes. I mean allow me to check my appointment book to see if I'm available…"

"And even if I'm not, I'll rearrange my schedule so that I can attend the affair with you Hori," Anne finally said as she regained enough composure to respond to Hori's invitation.

"Good. By the way, I am wearing some jeans and a white shirt to the concert. It's one of those dress-down gatherings," Hori said, smiling as he offered to help Anne close the shop and go home. I'm sure you will enjoy the music, Anne."

When Hori went to meet Anne at her house, he was introduced to Sara Mae, Jerome, and Charles, who just happened to have stopped by the house that evening! Also just happening by the house were Miss Peach, Henry, and me. Child, we were without any shame that day!

Anne wore an African print dress that draped just below her ankles. She also wore a matching head-wrap. She was the picture of loveliness that night. Hori was a perfect gentleman. As they walked out the door into the evening air, Hori led Anne Marie down the stairs to his automobile. He then opened the door, seated Anne on the passenger side of the car, walked to the driver's side, and got in and drove east toward the city. We stood on the front porch watching our Anne Marie being driven off and wishing nothing but the best for the two of them.

We began to re-enter the house and close the front door, when Henry yelled out, "Hallelujah, thank you God, our Anne has got herself a beau!"

"Not so fast, Mr. Henry," Sara Mae said. "This is just the first date. Tomorrow is another day! You know how fickle you men can be after a first date."

"Well who said that he will drop her…she might just not care for him." On this mild October evening *under the stars!*" I said.

"Let us lift our girl Anne up to God in prayer this fine evening. Didn't she look beautiful?" Miss Peach asked.

"The brother better have good intentions while he sits under the stars with our Anne Marie," Charles said.

"Well folks, the show is over! I have to get home. I have a couple of briefs to prepare before I get to bed." Oh by the way, I did hear from the firm in Detroit. They are interested in talking with me very soon," Jerome said as he and Charles got out of their seats and walked to the door.

"Jerome, have you spoken with Anne about this move lately? You know she has to have some input into this matter before you make any kind of move," Deacon Henry inquired, looking as if he had heard of Jerome's wish to move for the first time. "I thought you were happy at the law firm downtown?"

"I am…, but I've gone as far as I can with the firm. This firm in Detroit is among the most visible in the country. Besides, no one there can match my track record for winning cases in my area and they are offering me three times more money than I am currently making. Don't worry Deacon Henry…we'll still see each other more often than not. After all,

Detroit is just a few minutes away!" Jerome said, realizing how his words must have impacted those in the room.

Now he was wondering how he could sell his move to Miss Anne Marie.

Hori and Anne were home by eleven o'clock that evening. They sat in Hori's car expressing how much they had enjoyed being in each other's company. The jazz concert was but a fleeting thought in the minds of these two young people.

Hori asked Anne for another date, to which Anne gave a rapid response affirming her desire to be with Hori again. At the end of their conversation, Hori Brown gave Anne's arm a gentle squeeze, and then he began to get out of the car.

Anne's whole body was in a state of total bliss. Before Hori could reach the passenger side of the car to assist Anne out, she gave a sigh signifying total satisfaction, and then waited for the car door to open. Hori opened the car door for Anne. He extended his hand toward Anne. She placed her right-hand in his and they walked toward the house.

"Good evening y'all, did you enjoy the concert?" Sit down dog, sit!" Miss Peach said, as she sat on her porch.

"Did you have a good time?" I asked, as I got out of the lawn chair on Miss Peach's porch.

"Oh, good evening Miss Peach and Ant Boo! What are you two doing up so late? Shouldn't you be getting ready for your morning chores?" Anne asked, teasingly.

"Good evening Mother Peach and Sister Forman," Hori said. "How are you doing this wonderful evening? We had a wonderful time at the concert. Anne Marie was the most beautiful sister at the concert."

"You don't say!" I could not help but say a loud.

"Oh Hori, I bet you say that to all the sisters," Anne said, bowing her head, cupping her hands, and pointing her left foot out as though she were some school-girl.

"Well, Anne Marie, I want to thank you for making this evening one of the best I've had in my entire life. So, I will see you tomorrow around six o'clock? I'm sure that concert will be just as enjoyable as this evening's concert," Hori said, as he gave Anne's hand a light squeeze and began walking toward his car. "Oh, before I forget, here's the phone number to my home and office. I'll call you when I get home."

Hori drove off leaving Anne standing on her porch. She didn't want to enter the house at the moment. Anne just sat on the stairs leading to her house and gazed into the starry heavens!

"Well, good night Miss Peach, I'll be talking with you," Anne said.

"Good night, Anne." I said, as I began to walk down Miss Peach's steps.

"Good night Anne, have a blessed evening," I said as I got almost past her house.

Anne did not hear me. She was still staring at the shiny blue, starry sky!

"Oh Anne…, Earth to Anne Marie! Look toward the light baby…, all will be okay!" I jokingly said.

"Oh…, oh…, good night Ant Boo, have to starry night, I mean…"

"That's alright, child, I understand. At one time in my life I only saw stars every night too! Have a good God-blessed evening Anne, see you in church Sunday."

"Night Ant Boo. See you in church," Anne Marie said, as she continued looking towards the indigo sky dotted with millions of shiny stars.

ANNE'S MAN-HORI

There's an old, old saying, "All Negroes ain't black, all that shines ain't gold, and all fish stuff ain't water proof."

Henry and I were sitting on the porch. Henry had just come from a Deacons' meeting at the church. He got up and went into the house to get something out of the refrigerator to eat. Child, Henry was always eating, but he only weighed five pounds more than when we first met. His five foot ten inch frame was still most imposing to me. And his brown skin had turned just a little bit darker these days. That mingled gray hair, salt and pepper goatee plus that mustache, made him look so distinguished. His once first tenor voice was now that of a second tenor. Oh he did have "ARTHUR" come and visit him once and a while, but for the most part, he was free of any illnesses.

My thick gray hair was getting longer. Mother always encouraged me to let my hair grow, so I never put a hot comb to it and kept it in one or two braids wrapped around my head. Henry swears that I was one of the first women in the church to wear an Afro. My five-foot-seven-inch frame has become just a little bit heavier. Child, I no longer wear a size eight, but a size twelve. My Henry always calls me his "fine, brown-framed friend." That Henry is a mess…, really, he is a real tease! Anne said she just loved my soft, clear, honey brown skin-Henry always tells me that I have the skin of a fashion model.

"Hey dare, y'all. I guess you thought I was not going to ever get hur," Miss Peach said as she climbed the six steps leading to our porch. When she got to the landing, she sat down and placed two shopping bags of garden vegetables on either side of her.

"Child have mercy, I'm doing too much these days. What with the fitness group, the food pantry ministry, the sewing group, the Children's Mid-Week Prayer Ministry, that house, and the yard- well...," Miss Peach said, as she sat slightly out of breath. She then took her right hand and pushed the gray hairs off her tanned, face.

"Move dog," she said. "Go sit down. That dog is going to drive be deaf and crazy one of these days."

Henry came out of the house and sat next to me on the porch-swing.

"Hey there Sister Peach, how are you doing these days? You look like some one has been chasing you. I told you to leave these young men alone." Henry said, as he broke into loud laughter.

"Child, these young bucks can't handle me. I'll tell you like my sister Nancy used to tell the men when she was out there in the world..., I can look up longer than you can look down!" Miss Peach said, as she laughed and slapped her hands on her knees.

"Henry and Miss Peach, the both of you should stop that kind of talk, what if Pastor Newbreed should happen by here? Why, he would not know what to think of such talk. Miss Peach, no wonder the Mothers' Board is always discussing you in their meetings," I said, knowing how this comment would get Miss. Peach started.

"Baby..., those old hens better not say one thing to Miss Peach. I'll tell them where they can go and jump! I just got Sister Boca told off last week. She come talk'n bout, I should come join the Mother's Board. She said the Lord told her I was getting too old not to be a member of the Board. She then had the nerve to ask me what was preventing me from becoming a member of that group. "Well child I lit into her like a wind storm. I told her that first of all, I too am a God-fearing Christian and that the Lord speaks to me too! I then told her that as of this date and time God has not said anything to me about joining that Mothers' board any time soon. I also informed that smug cow not to forget that once upon a time she was not the *saint* she is now! I let her know, that when the Lord calls me for anything, it will be my business and nobody else's. I asked the K-legged cow what she meant by saying, *I was getting too old not to be a member*." Miss Peach said, now more animated than I've ever seen her.

"Miss Peach..., Miss Peach..., Miss Peach...," I calmly stated, attempting to calm her down a bit.

"I wish she or any other of those good mothers would say one more word to me about what they think about me." Miss Peach said, as she took her right leg and placed it across her left leg at the knee, sat back, then stood up and uncrossed her thin shapeless legs and walked over to the rocker and sat down.

"Good morning everyone," Anne called, as she passed the house.

"Hey there baby." Miss Peach said. "Where you coming from this early in the morning?"

"Oh Hori and I went fishing. I told him he didn't have to let me off in front of the house. I wanted to share my catch with the three of you. Please, take some; there's plenty for all of us." Anne said, as she pulled the fish out of a large bucket and held them up.

"I'll take some." Let me get something so I can put them in refrigerator." Henry offered.

"Get something for me too, Henry, while you are in there." Miss Peach yelled as she stepped to the edge of the porch. "Anne Marie, just who are Hori's folks?" Come here child and talk to your old Miss Peach. Here, sit in this chair. Now dish the dirt baby!" Miss Peach said escorting Anne to a chair situated close to Miss Peach's rocker.

"Well, Hori's parents are both medical doctors. His father is a surgeon. His mother is an anatomist at one of the colleges in Savannah. His family comes from a long line of educated folk from that region. His parents own a great deal of property in that town. Hori is very close to his family and often commutes from Spring Oaks to his hometown."

"Hori is a tenured assistant professor in the Natural Science Department at an institution in Atlanta. He is currently on leave from that school. Let's see, what else, oh, he was engaged, but the sister called the wedding off due to some strange reason. He tried to explain it to me, but it didn't make a lot of sense," Anne mumbled, as she looked into my eyes, trying to gauging my thoughts concerning Hori.

"Ugh." Miss Peach muttered, returning to her rocker and slowly sitting down looking in the direction of the church. The next thing we knew, she began to hum a song.

Henry returned with the wax paper. He wrapped Miss Peach's and our fish and then took them into the house so that they could remain fresh.

"What y'all talking about?" Henry inquired as he returned from the kitchen and taking a seat next to me on the swing.

"Oh, Anne was telling us about her friend Hori and his folk." Miss Peach said with that blank expression on her wise face.

Anne gave Henry a brief account of what she had told Miss Peach and me about Hori. Henry's only response to the tale was, "God be blessed!"

Anne, sensing something was not as it should be, but reluctant to ask any questions, bid us good-by and strode down the street to her house.

"Well Miss Peach, what thoughts do you get from what Anne Marie just shared with us about this Hori boy?" Henry asked, looking first at me then Miss Peach.

"There's a dead cat on the line somewhere in what she just told us, but I will reserve any further comments until later on in this game," Miss Peach said as she continued to rock and stare into space.

"Oh Miss Peach, you are too much sugar for a nickel!" Henry said jokingly, and then he got up and walked in the house.

Hori met Anne after work for dinner the next day. He brought Anne flowers. Anne brought Hori *a thinking of you card,* that was designed by Charles. Hori showered Anne with many thoughtful gifts. People at many of the surrounding places of entertainment, saw them as the perfect couple. Hori had become a Sunday

School Teacher at the church. He and Charles were co-teaching a Bible Class for the children whose age ranged from nine to twelve. He could often be seen walking Anne home after choir rehearsal, a task previously enjoyed by Jerome and Charles.

"Anne, these last few weeks have really been a dream come true. I've always envisioned a beautiful woman like you in my life. One who is witty, loves to share, and is well read. It's because of you that I enjoy my life more and more each day. You are a real boon to my tired spirits," Hori confided in Anne as they sat in the café holding hands and gazing into each other's love soaked eyes.

"Hori, the fact that you have shown me love, has been almost more than I can bear. I find myself thinking of you more than I really care to. Hori, if this is a dream, let me know now, so I can wake up and come into a global reality-please?"

"Anne, God, time, and I will show you how much I love you. Don't you worry your pretty little nose about me not being sincere about my love for you?" You are the type of woman that smoothes my jagged edges," Hori said, as he leaned across the table in order to emphasize what he had just confessed to Anne.

After the waiter took their orders, Anne said to Hori, "Hori, tell me if you will, how is it that your engagement did not pan out? Just what did happen?" Anne said.

Hori looked at Anne and realized that if this matter were not dealt with at that moment; it would serve as an impediment in their relationship. He leaned back in his chair and took a deep breath.

"Anne, my parents and I are very close. We keep little from each other. They are also my best friends and really want the best for me. I rely on their judgment in most of what happens to me. Well, lets see, Annett, that's my former fiancée, well, she was a most independent sister. She was candid in what she felt and freely expressed her world-views, which by the way, were the opposite of my parents...to make a long story short, my parents and she did not get along. To make matters worse, her parents did not care for me either...etc, etc, etc." Hori said, looking at Anne with much relief in having shared that story with her- again!

Anne, kept direct eye contact with Hori, and thoughtfully inquired, "Hori, you mean to tell me that both your parents dictated your relationship and now you two are separated because of their opinions?" Anne could feel her face beginning to get warm.

"Well..., like I said, these are my parents and we are extremely close! Dear Anne, please know this, I have learned from that experience and will not let that scenario enter our lives-*trust me!* Believe me, I do love you. I will not to allow anyone to come between us. "Annie," please believe me." Hori declared, with a tone of desperation in his voice.

Annie!?

"Well, Hori, let's look at it this way, please let me be the first to know when you fall out of love with me?" Anne responded with a wry face.

Hori reached across the table and held Anne's hand. He wanted to grab and kiss her at that very moment. While holding her hand he assured her that he wanted to get to know her more. He felt sure she was the woman he wanted to eventually marry. While he was aware of Anne's inability to have children, Hori assured her he was amenable to adopting children..., should they mutually agree to do so. Although they had only known each other for a short while, Hori felt he was in love with Anne Marie. Anne's feelings toward Hori were equally unrestrained.

After their meal, Hori drove Anne home. Both of them were extremely happy with life these days.

"Good evening Anne," Pastor Newbreed said, as he walked into Anne's shop. "I have some good news for you and Deacon Forman. The trustees decided to award you and Deacon Forman the money needed in order to open your place of business. Congratulations Anne Marie. May God bless your place of business! Well, I'll see you in church on Sunday; I must get to the Deacon's cleaners before he closes. Have a great day!"

Anne called her two children about the good news. Both Roger and Rochelle were as excited as their mother about this event. Anne then called me about her good fortune. She then called and shared the news with anyone who would listen to her. Anne was ecstatic about opening a larger store. She began jumping up and down, pacing back and forth. She had to make plans to move, and buy new equipment. The sister was pregnant with plans of what the new shop could do in order to be a thriving business. After calming down a little she called Deacon Forman to congratulate him.

Hori took Anne to an expensive supper-club to celebrate her good fortune. Anne retained Jerome's business/legal expertise to setup her expanding business. Anne, Jerome, and Henry agreed that before they moved into the adjoining shops, the new site had to have a touch of Anne and Henry's signatures on it. Anne met with Jerome and Charles regularly in order to personalize everything associated with her shop.

When it came time to move into the restored building, Anne and Henry had Pastor Newbreed come and bless the edifice. The building would house three businesses. Both Henry and Anne's shops would be on the first floor. The second and third floors would house the Midwest African-American Legal Defense League. The league was founded and organized by Jerome and Charles. Both served as President and Vice-President respectively. The building had parking space located on the north, west, and south-sides of the building. The fact that it was set in the middle of the downtown area

P. Nelson Byrd

was an added blessing. Its presence became beneficial to the down-town area and attracted many customers.

"Why hello Jerome and Anne, how are the two of you doing?" Congressman George Prime asked, as he walked into Anne's shop with a yellow pickup receipt in his hand.

"Good morning Congressman, how are you this day, did you come to pickup your wife's gowns?" Anne asked in a very cheerful manner.

"Yes I did, are they ready?" Congressman Prime said, as he attempted to get Jerome's attention.

Jerome did not bother to look at or speak to the Congressman, but continued doing some paper work at Anne's desk.

"What are you doing young Goals?" The Congressman asked to Jerome.

"*Work…!*" Jerome said in a very perfunctory manner. "Work, I'm looking out for the people, trying to keep the snakes from biting them."

Anne, over-hearing the "conversation," rapidly returned to the counter and handed Congressman Prime his wife's clothes.

"Here you go sir, three lovely gowns, all taken out to a size twelve," Anne said, extending her left hand to give the Congressman the garments and receiving payment for her work with the right hand.

"There's a tip in there for you Anne Marie, keep the three dollars in change." Congressman Prime said as he turned to exit the shop.

"You know Jerome, when I was your age, I had all kinds of energy and ideas going for me, but…, well, have a great day folks, don't forget to vote for me next week!"

"Jerome, what's gotten into you? Why were you so rude to Congressman Prime?" Anne asked, anticipating the reply Jerome was about to give her.

"Anne, you know good and well why I was so "*rude*" to George Prime. We put that pond scum in office to serve our needs and what has he done? Anne the brother is a sycophant at best and a pusillanimous fossil at the very least. He has done very little to right the many wrongs that have been done to us."

"He's voted against everything that could possibly better African-Americans in this state. When I met with him last month, I warned him that the black folk in this district would no longer support him. We are fielding Attorney Salle Wright to run against him this time around. He, like so many others of his ilk, kisses the b—of the enemy a lot. And when they miss that one spot, well, that's when the enemy will get rid of them. I just don't understand some of us black folk."

"Four years ago, eighty per cent of the votes supporting him, were African-American. Why then did he become such a coward and betray his own? Well, he'll not get another chance to become a "sell-out" and neglect the needs of our people. Why who in the blazes does he think he is?"

"Here Jerome, here, have a glass of water and cool yourself down! Now, just settle down, there is no need for violence, brother."

Anne rubbed Jerome's arm, hoping, this would calm him down!

"While it is true we made a mistake putting him in office, all we have to do now is replace him with another person. Let's pray that Salle Wright will do the job we expect of her while she is in office," Anne said, as she prepared to serve another customer.

"By the way, how is Hori doing, has he returned from Savannah? Have you spoken to or met his folk yet?"

Anne pretended not to hear him. She briskly walked toward the customer service counter.

Reaching the counter, Anne turned toward Jerome, winked her left eye at him, and began to wait on her next two customers. Anne knew others were asking the same question Jerome had just put forth. She had asked Hori the same question two days ago. Hori's only reply was, "it was not the right time for Anne to visit or meet his family." Hori's response was enough for Anne. She trusted him. She loved him. After all, *he was her first true love!*

Anne kept busy around the store hoping Jerome would not revisit that issue. Anne knew Jerome would not intentionally embarrass her by pressing the matter-at least not now!

At the end of the day Hori called Anne from Savannah. He expressed his love for her and looked forward to arriving home by airplane tomorrow. Whenever he attended an engagement out of town, he made it a point to contact Anne everyday. The women at African Baptist were jealous of Anne. However, they knew that any obvious display of rudeness toward Anne would not be considered lady-like or tolerated. Why child, you could just see the envy in their eyes as Anne and Hori paraded around town. Miss Peach said that some of the young sisters acted as though they were a bunch of buzzards circling over some fallen prey. Miss Peach called them "clean-up women!"

When Hori returned home, he and Anne often took long walks around the neighborhood park. They would walk for a while, then sit and talk for long periods at a time. The cool autumn weather did not douse their "love fire."

Sara Mae did not come home much these days. She was exclusively dating a fellow on the Westside of the city. What is there about those Westside men that make all these gals go wild?

As much as Anne and Hori were in love, neither one broached the idea of staying over night at the other one's home. Anne, "forever the dutiful mother, did not want her children thinking she was *"that type of loose woman."* Anne Marie was determined to set a fine example of motherhood before her children.

Speaking of which, the last time she had to give Rochelle a whipping was when she spotted her standing on the edge of the street curb. She was bent over talking to one of her classmates. Her b—was protruding out and her head was in the car. Anne walked up to the vehicle, shook her finger in Rochelle face, and began to lay those braided Weeping Willow Branches on poor Rochelle's b—.

From that moment on, Anne never had to explain to Rochelle "the finer points of what a lady did and did not do in public." *Anne was determined to live the words she taught to her children!*

SARA MAE AND ANNE

Nothing is more rewarding than a mother and daughter having a solid relationship. The phrase; "like mother, like daughter," could never be applied to Anne and Sara Mae.

From a child onward, Anne never felt Sara Mae loved her. Anne extended all her love and interest toward Miss Peach, Jerome, Henry and Me.

Mr. and Mrs. Pitts reared Sara Mae to become the best at whatever she wanted in life. They attempted to do the same for Ish. With both Sara Mae and Ish failing to become what the Pitts had hoped, the birth of Anne was a God-send. They lavished all kinds of gifts and attention on Anne Marie. It appeared to some of us that they indulged Anne too much, even to the point of ignoring their own children. As a result of the Pitts' affection toward Anne, many of us felt Sara Mae was beginning to build some resentment toward Anne Marie.

Initially, Sara Mae did love Anne Marie, though she quickly decided that having a child was not all it was cut out to be. Sara Mae did not count on what effect the gossip surrounding her having a baby out of wedlock would do to her. She could not have foretold the anger and embarrassment displayed by Mrs. Pitts regarding the rumors of Sara having a baby by a white-man. Mrs.

Pitts never let a day go by, without reminding Sara Mae of how she brought shame on the family by getting pregnant at such a young age. Mr. and Mrs. Pitts found themselves at odds over what they thought was "the proper care of Anne." Mr. Pitts felt his wife was meddling in the affairs of their daughter too much. He argued that Sara Mae should be left in total charge of Anne Marie. At one point in their marriage, Mr. Pitts threatened to separate from Mrs. Pitts over this matter. In the end, Mr. Pitts convinced his wife that Sara Mae was to have sole care of Anne.

It was around that time that Sara Mae had become totally estranged from Anne Marie. In order to spite Mrs. Pitts, Sara Mae, would mostly let Miss Peach and me baby-sit for her while she went to work or went for a night on the town. This caused more friction between Mrs. Pitts and Sara Mae.

Many people believed that Mrs. Pitts never gave Ish as much attention as she gave Sara Mae and Anne Marie. Though Sara Mae always treated Ish fairly, that is until the birth of Anne.

One day while in third grade, Anne's teacher asked the class to write about their parents. The teacher contacted Sara Mae and informed her that Anne was the only child in class who wrote that her "parents" didn't show any form of love to her. Instead of righting her many wrongs, Sara Mae lashed out at Anne and made Anne feel badly for telling that truth. Had it not been for Jerome, Miss Peach, Henry, and me, Anne would have sunk into an emotional abyss well before the fourth grade. In spite of the dysfunctional relationship between Anne and Sara Mae, Anne did well in school.

Sara Mae, as a young adult, spent little time with Anne. She often dated several men in the town of Spring Oaks. Whenever Sara Mae invited her male friends to the house, she would expect Anne to remain in her bedroom. Anne was only allowed to come downstairs to eat, then, immediately return to her room. There were times when Anne would hear Sara and her male company coming up the stairs to Sara Mae's bedroom. It was during those few times that Anne felt the loneliest. These visits by her mother's friends left Anne Marie very sad. Anne would often appeared confused because of the loud laughter, moans, screams, shouts, and other sounds of pleasure emanating from her mother's *pleasure place.* On one such morning, after Sara Mae had entertained her guest in her "private area of the house," Anne confronted Sara Mae about the noise.

"Sara Mae, I can't do my home-work when I hear those noises coming from your room!"

"Well, then you might want to take your little tail over to Jerome's house or elsewhere and do your home-work! Remember, I live here too Missy Anne," Sara Mae responded as she placed both her hands on her generous hips. "Besides, how often do I have company anyway? Do I say that s—to you when

Jerome comes to visit you and you two make noise in your room?"

On many such occasions Sara Mae would rethink her mean comments to her oldest child? While Sara would never apologize to Anne, she would attempt to address the issues Anne brought to her. Sara Mae did not want her parents to become aware of what was happening "in her home."

Almost, from the very beginning, Sara treated Anne's arrival into this world as one of a rivalry between two women! Of which unfortunately, the Pitts did very little to smooth over this tattered relationship between Anne and Sara Mae.

Anne's birth marked a new beginning in the lives of Mr. and Mrs. Pitts. They absolutely adored cute little Anne Marie. Of course it didn't help matters, when Sara Mae would gladly allow her parents to keep her child while she GOT HER LIFE and frequently went on dates.

The Pitts could be seen with Anne Marie at church, downtown, on outings, around their house-everywhere!

They never encouraged Anne to refer to Sara Mae as her mother. One day, when Sara Mae returned home from teaching twenty-one middle school students, Sara Mae entered the Pitts' house to collect Anne and take her home. For some reason, Sara Mae, though looking extremely tired, wanted to be a mother to Anne Marie.

"Come here Anne Marie and give mommy a kiss!"

Anne slowly walked over to Sara Mae and stood in front of her as though Sara was a complete stranger. Sara Mae feeling embarrassed about Anne's passive yet aggressive behavior, grabbed Anne by the right arm, and began to dress her for the short walk home. As Sara Mae was about to gather Anne's home-work and clothing, Mr. Pitts yelled across the living-room to Sara Mae.

"Sara, don't you hurt that sweet child, you could break her arm handling her that way!"

Without saying a word to her father and not wanting her mother to chide her too, Sara Mae rolled her eyes at both her parents, said her good byes, and left the house, slamming the door behind her.

Sara Mae could be seen and heard by all the neighbors on the south end of the street admonishing Anne about her "meddling grand-parents" and how she expected Anne to refer to her as mother from that day onward. Sara continued grabbing Anne by her arms. Sara Mae could be seen lifting Anne's whole body a fraction off the ground as she continued to- "get one thing straight around this house." Anne never did refer to Sara as "mother!" At one time, Miss Peach and I thought to coax Anne into calling Sara Mae "mother," but quickly decided against getting involved in that aspect of Sara Mae's life.

Anne loved to play with Jerome. They would play jump rope together. Although Jerome was never encouraged to jump rope with Anne, no one bothered to stop him from doing so. I guess this was because he was such a talented boy. Anne could be seen playing baseball, soccer, football, basket ball, dancing, and other assorted activities with her best friend Jerome.

Anne Marie didn't have many girl-friends. Most of the parents in the surrounding area didn't want to associate with Sara and so, they did not allow their girls to play with Anne Marie. Whenever some of the girls in Anne's class had parties, Anne was only allowed to attend if she was accompanied by Jerome-which was always the case. Most of the girls in the class thought well of Jerome, but did not care for his close relationship with "Miss Annie Fannie!" While the girls did not talk about Anne to her face, they vilified her behind her back.

One day while in the second grade, one of Sister Hightower's daughters encountered Anne Marie about always playing with boys.

"Anne Marie, why do you always play with the boys in the class and not us girls?"

"Because...you won't play with me!"

While Sara Mae did have the good sense to know that Anne should have been playing with girls as well as boys, her pride did not allow her motherly instinct to come to the surface. Had she not been so narrowly focused on her life, she could have been a great asset in Anne's life.

Most of the parents who knew Sara Mae were not pleased with her having an "illegitimate child." They also didn't care for Pastor Starter breaking the age old policy of the church-which was; demanding "un-wed mothers" stand before the congregation of Africa Baptist and confess their wrong doings! Pastor Starter felt the practice was antiquated and sexist. Besides that, his wife said that the father of the child should be brought before the church also.

The Deacons and Trustee Boards were sold on this change coming to a stop well before now. Quite a number of people didn't agree with this new change, but they were not bold enough to come forward and voice their feelings about the matter-cowards, all of them! Many of them hated Sara Mae for being the focal point for this new change. Miss Peach felt they were angry because they now had little to gossip about in the privacy of their homes.

Although Sara Mae was no longer the svelte person she was prior to Anne coming into her life, she was still a very attractive black woman. While she was still very appealing to the men in town, she did not appear to like her twenty pound weight gain. As a result of this gain, Sara Mae's clothes were worn just a little too tight in the minds and hearts of those who loved her.

She never felt the need to become part of the church's fitness group or any other church function at that time.

With her self-esteem now being very low, Sara Mae became bitter with herself, Anne, and those with whom she came in contact. Since Anne was always around Sara Mae, it appeared that poor Anne caught the brunt of Sara Mae's daily anger. Sara Mae began to ignore Anne and focus her attention on dating. She gladly allowed Anne Marie to frequently visit our home. Sara Mae would do anything to get little Anne Marie out of her sight.

Though none of us objected to Anne staying with us, we did notice how much little Anne Marie needed the love and care of her "mother."

One day Miss Peach asked Sara Mae why she spent so much time away from little Anne Marie? Miss Peach did not think it was a good idea for Anne to be "passed from one house-hold to another" at her tender age.

"Well, she can stay in the house until I come home if any of you are too busy! If she is bothering any one, Anne does have a home, she can be safe at her own home," Sara Mae said, rather sarcastically.

"No, that's alright Sara Mae, Anne is welcomed to stay with any one of us, it's a poor rat that only has one hole to hide," Miss Peach replied as she stared at Sara Mae and watched her rapidly brush past her towards her home. While she knew Sara Mae did not like the analogy, she was confident Sara Mae did grasp the point being made.

Becoming more isolated from her mother, Anne Marie's weight-gain became excessive.

"Look at you Anne Marie; *you look like a little pig.* From now on I'm not going let you eat any more sweets. Don't ask me for any more money to buy ice cream. Do you want to be as fat as your dear mother?"

"I'm spending all my hard earned money on buying you pretty pants, shoes, or some such foolishness, when I'm walking around here with holes in my panties!"

Naturally, Anne was left speechless on such occasions, especially when Sara Mae's intimidating frame was only inches from her face.

At no time did Sara Mae ever refuse Anne "something sweet." Basically, Anne would eat sweets at the same time Sara Mae was ingesting her fair share of home-made sugar filled taste treats- home-made ice cream, lime pie, double layered chocolate cake, in short- anything that mirrored Sara Mae's own need for sugary things.

When Anne failed the fourth grade, Sara Mae became enraged at Anne. I became angry with Sara Mae. Miss Peach and Henry began to put pressure on Sara Mae to soften her approach at getting Anne to focus on her academic work. For the most part Sara Mae's pride was bruised; after all she was a grade school teacher in the district. And having her child held back a grade did not suite her "standing in the community." Sara Mae never accepted blame for Anne's poor performance in school at that time. That summer Sara Mae even allowed Anne to stay at either Miss Peach's or my home. When Anne was allowed to enter her rightful grade, it was Sara Mae who bragged to the neighbors about "how smart her child was!"

When Minnie was born, Sara Mae became "the ideal mother." It was as if she was attempting to make-up for the lost mother/daughter relationship she didn't have with Anne Marie.

On those occasions when Anne was home, she mostly stayed in her bedroom. Anne's room had a west and south view. Her room was the largest of the five large bedrooms. From her window she could see the Goals' back-yard. Her room was painted a soft pink. Anne did her homework in the northeast corner of her "home away from home." There she could create her own world; a world of peace, love, admiration, praise, and pleasure. Sara Mae never entered Anne's "sanctuary," she left Anne Marie to care for it solely. The only other people allowed in Anne Marie's room were Jerome, Miss Peach and me. Anne filled the room with books, toys, a radio, a television, pens, blah, blah, blah! That room was truly a haven for Anne Marie. It was her bedroom, a place where she found peace from a world seemingly gone mad. It was her SAFE PLACE.

Anne was an avid reader. She read almost anything that was either given to her or that could be checked out at the library. Both she and Jerome would often exchange reading materials. They challenged each other to read "the most books." Anne's creativity could be attributed to her love for reading. Both her and Jerome's mastery of the French Language was in part due to their ability to read and understand the English Language so well. They were always sharing what they learned with Miss Peach, Henry and me. Through their reading, they took us to places we had never been.

Although Anne could never be viewed as a jealous child, she did appear to be most cautious about Sara Mae's marriage to Sam Turner.

From the beginning of their marriage, Sam had to be told in no uncertain terms, not to enter Anne's bedroom. On a regular basis Sam was engaged in shouting matches with Sara Mae about his unwillingness to "let Anne alone."

One day when Anne was in the bathroom preparing for bed, she opened the door only to find Sam standing at the bathroom entrance, nude and with a smirk on his face.

"Oh, I didn't know you were in here little girl, come on past daddy, daddy won't hurt you. Go on to your room! Do you want daddy to come in and put you to sleep," Sam whispered as he blocked Anne from leaving the washroom.

At that very moment, Sara Mae could be heard calling for Sam to hurry back to bed with her. Sam rushed past Anne into the washroom, stood at the toilet and began urinating – in full view of little Anne Marie.

It was this and other inappropriate deeds that severed Sara Mae and Sam's marriage and in a strange way brought some peace to Anne Marie.

Anne appeared excited about Ish's return to his mother and father's home. She initially saw Ish as another family member who would take interest in her. Although Sara Mae never allowed Ish to visit her house while Anne was home, it was apparent that Ish and Anne did communicate by telephone or some such means. Ish and Anne were seen talking across the fence while each was on their separate porches. Jerome and Anne routinely would walk through the alley to visit each other. One day when Jerome was entering Anne's back-yard, Ish approached Jerome about visiting Anne Marie.

"Hey boy, are you going to visit my niece, Anne Marie?" Ish asked, attempting to sound as manly as he could with the hopes of getting Jerome's full attention.

"Yes sir," Jerome responded, as he increased his pace toward the steps leading to the backdoor of Anne's home.

"Why are you always visiting my Anne Marie? What are you two doing in her room?" Ish asked, sounding like some jealous lover of Anne Marie.

Jerome chose not to reply to Ish, but did take the occasion to roll his eyes at Ish and suck his teeth at Anne's uncle. Jerome knocked on Anne's door and continued to ignore Mr. Ish Pitts.

"Don't you roll your eyes at me, you little smart a—," Ish snapped, suddenly realizing that he was engaging a child with street language.

At that very moment, Ish noticed Miss Peach and Icky Boo.

"Stop that confounded barking dog, you're going to drive me deaf I tell you."

The sight of Ish seemed to make Icky Boo bark louder than usual. He would run in circles and bite the wires in the fence that separated the two yards.

"Oh..., good afternoon Miss. Peach!"

Miss Peach nodded in Ish's direction. She gave him a quick smile and continued to weed her vegetable garden. Icky Boo continued his wild barking at Ish.

P. Nelson Byrd

When Anne became pregnant with Roger, Sara Mae became the most conflicted parent on the planet Earth. On the one hand she told everyone that Anne's pregnancy caused her a world of embarrassment. You would have thought she was *"Miss. All this and all that," the pillar of Spring Oak's society!* Child, when Sara Mae put on her airs, she was just too much for words. On the other hand, she used the event to gain sympathy for herself. She wanted the world to see how much she had sacrificed for Anne.

"Going out and getting pregnant out of wedlock!" Now ain't that some s___!" Sara Mae was once heard to say aloud to herself.

While she really NEVER suspected Jerome of being the father, she also never knew whom else to suspect of being the father of Anne's child.

I was never sure if Sara Mae questions were based on motherly instincts or if she wanted to be just plan mean to our Anne Marie.

After Roger was born, Sara Mae began to focus a great deal of attention on "her grand-child." Doctor Dear said she was compensating for the loss she had in Anne. Sara Mae was often found carrying Roger all around town. She even used the child as an excuse to come to church and brag about her, "only grand-child!" Whenever Anne attempted to care for Roger, Sara Mae would intercede and perform her *grand-motherly duties.*

Anne began to withdraw from others. She became moody and would cry a lot for no apparent reason. After several of us talked to Sara Mae about denying Anne the right to attend to her child's needs, Sara Mae, begrudgingly surrendered, and allowed Anne to love her child – the likes of which we have never seen! Anne was the perfect mother to Roger. She coped and dealt with her daily affairs quite well.

People at the church praised Anne for being "such a great little momma." Sara Mae was being viewed as being jealous of the relationship between Anne and little Roger. Anne and Roger had that "special something" that made them so unique as mother and son.

When Anne became pregnant with Rochelle, Sara Mae didn't repeat her divisive behavior toward Anne Marie and daughter. Though Sara Mae attempted to take advantage of Anne's wishing to graduate from high school, cooler heads prevailed, and she cooperated in the matter.

Between her school work, caring for her children, and dealing with her own personal life, Anne had her hands full. One day when Sara Mae and Minnie were in the dining room feeding Roger and Rochelle, Anne came into the house, slamming the door behind her.

Anne began to shout, "Roger and Rochelle, go upstairs and do not come downstairs until I tell you to do so, do you understand me!"

"But Anne," Roger said, "we were just about to have our dinner."

"Roger, I said go upstairs now! And another thing young man, as long as you are living, do not ever refer to me as Anne. You are to call me mother. Do you hear me?"

"Yes, mother," Roger said as he began to show a look of surprise on his face. "Come on Rochelle; let's go up-stairs."

"Anne, what is this shouting and slamming doors all about?" Sara Mae asked. "What has gotten into you these days?"

"Yea, Anne, we were only doing *what you* should have been doing," Minnie added.

"From now on I am going to *be my children's mother* and I will be doing what I should have been doing-*thank you very much!*" Anne said in a very measured tone of voice. Beginning tomorrow morning, Ant Boo and Miss Peach will care for my children when I am away. If there are any questions, concerns, or thoughts about me and my children, you are to come to me. Do not ever do anything for my children without my consent-is that perfectly clear?"

As Anne ended her commands, she walked over to Sara Mae and Minnie. She stood only a few inches from their faces, stared at them briefly, and mounted the stairs to her bedroom.

Needless to say, both Sara Mae and Minnie were without words. When they were able to regroup, Sara Mae said in a very exasperated voice, "Well sir re bob, what will she think of next? Minnie don't you extend one hand to help that cow, do you hear me? Imagine that, she is one ungrateful piece of work!"

A few hours later heated words were exchange between Anne Marie, Sara Mae, and Minnie. Sara Mae and Minnie came out on the short end of the encounter, if you know what I mean.

When Sara Mae discovered Anne was working with Ish, all her maternal instincts began to kick in place. For one week she rehearsed what she would say to Anne so as not to hurt Anne's feelings or better yet be hurt. Sara Mae visited Miss Peach and me and sat for hours. We could tell she had something heavy on her mind. One late September afternoon, Sara Mae walked down the street to visit me.

"Good evening Ant Boo, how are you, has Deacon Henry come home?"

"Hey Sara Mae, good afternoon to you also, won't you come in and rest your feet a while?"

"Ant Boo, now you know I don't get much into Anne's affairs, especially since she laid down the law about *she being the mother of her two children!*" However..., Ant Boo..., well you know how much I love Ish, right?" Sara Mae cautiously said.

"Yes Sara Mae, I am aware of how close you and Ish are to each other" I said, somewhat guardedly.

"Well, Anne has started working with Ish downtown and I am..."

"Hey y'all, whatyoutwotalkingbout? What's the scoop...?" Miss Peach asked, as she approached my house with a large brown bag filled with something, no doubt from her lush vegetable garden. "Sara Mae, we ain't seen you in a month of Sundays. What you been up to these days?"

"Oh nothing Miss Peach, just trying to make ends meet and keep a little peace in my home," Sara Mae said, attempting to squeeze a little sympathy from the conversation.

"Well, girl, peace is what comes from the Lord, if He ain't given you peace, you won't have it," Miss Peach said, determined not to be suckered into Sara Mae's pity party. "How's the job treating you, have they made you principal yet?"

"Not yet Miss Peach, not yet," Sara Mae said, as she stood up, adjusted her orange plaid skirt and prepared to walk home.

"Oh, I hope I did not interrupt any important conversation between the two of you," Miss Peach said, with a half smile on her face as she winked at me.

"No, Miss Peach, I was about to leave, I have a lot of papers to grade before I prepare myself for bed," Sara Mae said, as she hugged both Miss Peach and me. Sara Mae took a couple of steps, towards her house, turned around towards us and began to sob uncontrollably.

"What is it Sara Mae?" I asked, as I began to walk down the steps to hug her.

"Oh, I'm just so concerned about my Anne Marie. She won't listen to anybody!" Sara said as she began to wipe the tears away from her overly-made-up face. "I'm just afraid, she and", well just forget it, just forget it! Have a nice day the two of you. Thanks for listening to me Ant Boo."

"Any time Sara Mae, any time," I said, as I stood in the middle of the sidewalk wondering what was going on in Sara Mae's head.

"Miss Peach, it must be that time of the month for Sara Mae to be acting this way-right?"

"Must be, cause must ain't don't sound right!" "Now come on in the house and see what I've brought you and Henry. Child, I don't pay any attention to Sara Mae these days. Sara Mae needs a good dose of Jesus, that's what she needs."

When Anne told Sara Mae that Jerome was "a gay," Sara Mae wanted to use the occasion to berate Jerome and justify her beliefs about him. However, she thought better of her reply and chose to take the motherly approach instead.

"Well Anne, how do you feel about Jerome being a gay?" Sara Mae asked.

"Since he loves it, the least I can do is like it," Anne said. I mean, I don't think I know much about his new lifestyle, but I do know I love the ground he walks on," Anne said as she looked into Sara Mae's eyes. "How do you think he got that way, Sara Mae? He said that he was born that way!"

"Born that way? Well maybe he was born that way. Anne, what do I know about anything these days? What I want to know is what do they do in bed?" Sara Mae said, as she began to sit at the dining room table.

"I asked Jerome that same question and he said that they do the same thing as heterosexuals do!" Anne responded.

"Oh dear...!" Sara Mae said.

"Well, all I know is that whoever lands Jerome as a partner, will have a jewel of a mate. Jerome is one F-I-N-E brother," Anne said as she began having her evening meal.

Sara Mae became distrustful of Hori the moment Anne introduced him to her. She told Miss. Peach and me that Hori didn't appear to mix well with Anne's type!? Sara Mae seemed a bit bewildered about Hori. On the one hand she thought Hori was very kind to her daughter. Then, there were times when she was not quite sure what to think of Hori's relationship toward Anne Marie.

One day when Anne and Hori were about to go out on a date and Anne was upstairs dressing, Hori said to Sara Mae.

"Mrs. Turner, I've shared with Anne everything there is to know about my parents, but when I asked her about her father, all she says is ask you."

"Hori, that is a personal matter that best be left alone," Sara Mae said in a matter of fact manner.

That was the last time the issue of Anne's father was ever raised, other than when our poor Anne...

Anne and Sara Mae had a strange mother daughter relationship to say the least. At first Sara Mae thought she could live her life vicariously through Anne. When that did not pan out the way she had planned, Sara Mae began to passively reject her child and attempt to play "catch-up and live the way she dreamed of living. We all knew she wanted her Anne Marie to be successful and *"an up-right citizen in the community, in spite of the mean way she behaved toward her first-born child.*

Anne never had that special mother daughter bonding. As a child, she was determined she would never have children. Having two children out of wedlock, was not only a blow to Anne's self-esteem, but almost brought her whole world spiraling downward. At first we thought she had become withdrawn due to her being embarrassed about having a baby at such a young age. Having her peers make jokes about her didn't help matters either. Some of the parents made matters worse by not allowing their children to associate with Anne Marie. Anne became more depressed each time she became pregnant. Anne's last pregnancy resulted in an attempt to swallow an overdose of sleeping pills in her bedroom. She would have been successful had it not been for Jerome alerting the family of her telephone call to him and Icky Boo's unusual barking sounds.

Had it not been for the added loving and pro-active support of people like: Pastor and Sister Newbreed, Miss Peach, the Goals family, Henry, and me, Anne would have long ago caved into a deep emotional state.

Anne Marie and Sara Mae needed each other's love, but neither was sure how to go about obtaining it. Both viewed the other as being incapable of giving that sustaining love, so many of us seek and a few receive. Sara Mae and Anne, had mothers who initially placed too much attention on what others thought of them. The moment Mrs. Pitts and Sara Mae began to realize that too much of their lives were becoming too public, their relationships with their daughters began to erode to the point of total disrepair.

Anne had determined in her heart not to repeat this shameful act with her children.

During Anne's period of depression, Miss Peach and I never missed a day attending to her needs. We took care of all her daily necessities. We bathed her, dressed her, fed her, and took care of her two children. We protected her from those who would do her harm. Sara Mae tried to be useful during this most critical period. She became prey to her total inability to care for Anne! You see, Sara's deep seated hatred for Anne, prevented her from ever being the mother Sara Mae knew she should have been. She had never forgiven herself for what she had done to Anne Marie. The guilt of those events was over-whelming in her life. So, she blamed her poor "mother-daughter kinship" on everyone but herself. Sara Mae's abuse of liquor became more frequent during those days. Her reputation with the men was that of an *easy woman with a "white liver!"* At any rate Sara Mae and Anne's volatile feelings toward each other negatively impacted all of us. They were often a topic of discussion in the neighborhood.

As Anne slowly came out of her depression and was out of the company of her uncle Ish, she began to be productive. She began to blossom. She exhibited a degree of independence envied by many. The opening of her business appeared to mark the beginning of Anne's re-entrance into a wholesome well-being. She seemed to have a renewed determination to succeed in life. She began to develop a "win-win attitude." Anne was that feminist, without being angry, not too nationalistic, not anti-anyone, and above all she was God's child-again. She had peace that passed all understanding-hallelujah!

ANNE MARIE-THE ME IN ME

Others have told my story, now let me tell it my way, from the eyes of Anne Marie Palermo.

I can remember everything about my childhood in spite of and because of what took place in those early years.

My younger years were so happy. I felt loved by everyone. The hugs and kisses showered on me by my grandparents made my life an endless cycle of happiness. I can remember lying close to Mama Pitts' soft and large arms. The warmth coming from her made me feel safe.

Mama Pitts always smelled of freshly picked roses. She was a tall woman with a very small voice. She never failed to tell me how pretty I looked in just about anything I wore. She always told me I was "just the smartest cookie" on the whole Church Street Block. Her smile made me smile a lot. And while she seldom fussed at me, the few times she did never made me sad for long. Because I was often left in her company, I sincerely felt she was my real mother.

Grand-pa Pitts was always joking and playing some type of made-up game with me. His laughter was infectious and often left me breathless and tired. He also made me feel safe. He was the first man in my life. Our bond made me trust others outside the family quickly. His man-hood gave me the impression that all men were like him-strong, trustworthy, honest, likeable, smart, and smelling of red Lifebuoy Soap with that carbolic fragrance-a man!"

I loved my grand-parents' home. It always smelled of good things, be they home-made dishes, fruits and vegetables or just a clean household smell. For the most part, the house had a faint "just been washed with bleach smell!" I can remember neighbors saying that the house was *as clean as the board of health.*" Ant Boo would say you could eat off the floors of the Pitts home.

I can remember that childhood initially gave me the distinct impression that, Sara Mae was a stranger in my life. She always left me with thoughts of her being a visitor to her own parents' house! When I became old enough to walk and was potty trained by Mama Pitts, I began to see more of Sara Mae. Many people thought Sara Mae was still too young to care for me. I would often hear Sara Mae complain about, "how they needed to mind their own business." She seemed unhappy whenever she and I were alone in the house. I never saw a female guest in the house except Miss Peach, Miss George, Ant Boo, and on rare occasions, Mrs. Goals would come to the front foyer and wait for Jerome.

Sara Mae was always cursing about some women in the neighborhood *thinking they were better than she was.* Whenever she came to school, she would grumble and pretend that she had too much home-work to do. The times my name was placed on the honor-roll at school, Sara Mae could be heard all around the town bragging about me. However, when I was held back in the fourth grade, she laid "my good name to rest," for being so fat and lazy. Though I never needed Sara Mae to help me with my homework, the few times I did ask for assistance from her, she insisted that she had other more pressing matters "on her plate." She would ask me to call Jerome and see if he could tackle the homework issues.

Other mothers and their children could be seen together and I would covet their close relationships. I quite often day-dreamed about Sara Mae and me bonding together and being the envy of all who saw us. I dreamed of us dressing alike, strolling down the street together engaged in a mother daughter conversation such as my classmates enjoyed with their mothers. Instead, all I ever got from Sara Mae was her walking either ahead or behind me when we walked down the street to a destination. I never liked the clothes Sara Mae bought me. It was a joy when Miss Peach, Aunt Boo, and Miss George dressed me. They dressed me in the BEST of clothes.

Except for the adult neighbors who lived near by, my circle of friends' were-ONE! My only escape from this loneliness would come from the books I managed to devour. These books were "food to my soul."

Mr. and Mrs. Goals often extended traveling invitations to places I only read about. Sara Mae would always refuse their offer. When it seemed that the Goals and others were pressing her about me getting out, Sara Mae would take me to down-town Spring Oaks for a dinner and a movie. This was Sara Mae's failed attempt at showing the world only she knew what was best for me.

There were times when it became difficult to tell if Sara Mae hated me or herself. During those periods she could be seen slumped in her favorite chair and ottoman, crying. I quickly learned not to ask what was bothering her. The first time I asked her why she was crying, she denied doing so. The second time she called me a nosy fat b—and threatened to kick me out of the house-head first! The frown on her face prompted my rapid retreat to my bedroom, where I remained until the next morning. Sometimes she would cry after one of her many arguments with her many male friends. Then there were times when such emotional displays came after she was dissatisfied with me for whatever reason. Not knowing when or how to interact with Sara Mae made me anxious, sad, and frustrated. Because of the aforementioned behavior on the part of Sara Mae, I found myself engrossed in the Holy Bible and attending Bible Studies and Sunday school classes. I would do most anything not to be in Sara Mae's presence!

Jerome Goals was a God-send. He made me smile a lot. He was the brother I never had and he was my confidant. He encouraged me to participate in school plays. He was my friendly competition. He was my protector. Jerome would often remind me that God is good, forgiving, watchful, and all knowing.

Other than my grand-father, Jerome Goals was one of the first few men I completed trusted. I could discuss anything with him. We shared personal issues as though we were a married couple. Talking with Jerome was just that, we never talked to each other; we always listened to one other and were never quick to judge. When I had my monthly periods, Jerome was the one person I deemed most sensitive to my concerns. Because of our special bond, many falsely labeled us lovers.

Jerome was so good looking, and because of our relationship, many girls became envious and just plain jealous of me. This reaction on the part of girls and some of the boys caused a chasm so great between my peers and me that I began to withdraw from many of them. Whenever I interacted with them in school, I saw myself engaging in un-friendly competition. There were times when I would cling to Jerome's arm in the midst of my classmates, knowing that this act would incite bad feelings from them towards me. I felt proud to have this brother as my friend, a boy who was the object of so many individual's attention! Whenever Jerome sang in church, he always dedicated the song to God and to his friend Anne!

It's funny; the thought of having sex with Jerome never crossed my mind. I learned, somehow, that having sex with such a special person as Jerome was a line not to be crossed-after all, he was like a brother to me. After I became pregnant with Roger, my worse fear was that of losing Jerome's friendship and hence, becoming a lost soul. Even when Jerome discovered that I was having a baby, he kept his composure and came to my rescue.

He gave me comfort and continued our unwavering friendship until the end. One day when Jerome came to visit me at the house, I told him what folk were saying about him being the father of my baby. Jerome just replied, "Let them say whatever they want to say. As long as you and I know the truth, what do we care what they say. "Anne, if you want me to say that I am the father, I'll do it!"

Jerome was known to be tough. Few, if any of the boys would challenge him to fight. Therefore, many of the nasty things said about me, didn't reach me. Even when Mrs. Goals threatened to stop him from playing with me for the "umpteenth time," Jerome's persuasive manner convinced her that I was not the poor influence some neighbors had portrayed me to be.

Mr. Goals often offered me his assistance. Jerome's parents allowed him to spend many evenings visiting me. When he was not attending classes, participating in extra-curricular activities at the school, or church, Jerome Goals was visiting me or telephoning me to inquire about my well-being. Our friendship didn't have any selfish provisos attached to it.

Jerome and I were baptized on a bright spring Sunday Morning. We were ten years old. I will never forget that day. After service we met at Miss Peach's home to celebrate our wonderful rebirth into the world of Jesus Christ.

When I became pregnant a second time; again, Jerome did not pressure me about who was the father. Well…, kinda, sorta. At one point, Jerome did ask me who the father was, when I refused to tell him, he no longer addressed the issue.

Not only did Jerome take me to the eight-grade prom, I was invited to escort him to the Senior Prom as well.

It was Jerome and oh yes, Icky Boo who sounded the alert about Sam sexually abusing me outside of the house and away from the prying eyes of those he thought would stop his sick pursuit of me.

Thanks Icky Boo. SMILE.

This was done at a time that I was too full of guilt and shame to speak-up for myself and Sara Mae was in denial about the matter. God bless Jerome Goals forever!

When the former pastor threatened to remove Jerome from all church sponsored activities, I gladly took an active part in the Trustee/Deacon led movement to oust that hypocrite. Though a young man, Jerome always conducted himself in an admirable manner. I was never more proud of Jerome than the day he stood up for himself in African Baptist Church. After that day, his "same-sex life-style" was no longer an issue at the church.

Jerome's encouragement enabled me to start my couture shop and survive.

Jerome Goals was one of the few persons who kept me from spiraling downward, when I began to accept Ish back into my life. He made me realize that the love I was giving Ish was just a one-sided affair. Thanks to Jerome, I finally saw Ish as being incapable of loving me. Ish was a shallow person in his own eyes and in the eyes of others as well.

It was Jerome who taught me the true meaning of sharing with others. When Jerome met his partner, Charles, I initially felt that I was going to lose Jerome as a friend. However, Mr. Goals, being ever true to me, convinced me that he could love the two of us at the same time.

Jerome's love for Charles was real, binding, and something I wanted to experience.

Charles had been sexually abused by an adult when he was a child. That experience became our common bond.

Jerome and I spent many days and nights sharing our dreams of becoming", Jerome, a lawyer and I, - a success at whatever I chose to do!

Although, I was in love with Jerome, my love for him far exceeded the love commonly experienced by anyone I had ever known. In him, I found freedom to be who I wanted to be. With him by my side, I could withstand the many hurts in my life without caving into an unending HELL!

By the time Jerome moved to Detroit, I was prepared for our separation. I wanted the best for him. By then, I was full of hope and saw the future being productive for me. Jerome had aided in my developing into a stronger person. He became a blessing to me and caused me to be a blessing to others.

Ant Boo, Henry, and Miss Peach were special people to me. They were the adults every child needed in their lives. After my grand-parents died, these three people were the primary adults I depended on in my daily life. While Sara Mae was the woman who birthed me, she never was the adult I could turn to for those "mother-daughter talks." Ant Boo and Miss Peach and to a lesser degree, Miss George were the ones who walked me through those times when I was in school and my "monthly" coming on me in the classroom.

They were the ones who came to school, walked me out of a classroom where I was the brunt of laughter and smiles. I refused to move out of my desk. I was too terrified to move out of that seat of blood. They were the ones who explained to me on the way home what was happening to my body. These two cleaned me and gave me much needed comfort on that day! Miss. Peach and Ant Boo were the ones who calmed Sara Mae down and told her of my "bloody experience" at school.

Ant Boo and Miss Peach helped mold my appreciation of stylish clothes, even though at times, too many times, I failed to meet their standards of fashionable dress attire.

"Lord, Anne Marie what are you doing, here put this pretty white satin blouse on. Wear it with that dark blue wool skirt. Don't you think those tights will go well with that outfit?"

"Do I have to wear those ugly shoes Sam bought for me Miss Peach? I hate those shoes. They are much too large for me," I would say to Miss Peach.

"Okay, which shoes do you want to wear? Remember, Anne, it is going to snow today, and you'll have to put your boots over whatever shoes you are going to wear!" Miss Peach would often chant to me, as she began looking around the bed-room she had set-up for me in her large home. "How about these suede shoes I bought you last year, will they do?"

"Anne, a lady always sits with their legs together at a function, or they cross their legs like this. See how my legs are crossed young lady?" Ant Boo said to me one summer day as we were sitting on her porch eating home-made ice cream with freshly picked strawberries in it.

"Like this, Ant Boo," I said, attempting to balance the ice cream and cross my legs at the same time. I will never forget that day. As I brought my right leg over my left leg, the bowl of freshly made ice cream fell to my knees and onto the concrete steps. Ant Boo rushed to my aid, by first giving me a hug and then whipping my stained cotton dress with cold water. She then cleaned up the spilled mess on the steps. Whenever she taught me anything, she never was impatient with me or showed any signs of being angry or frustrated with me. She always made me feel good about learning some new kind of "social grace!"

A couple of times I witnessed Mr. Henry and Ant Boo embracing in public. Their love for each other was real. They were the ideal wife and husband. I always wanted to be like them, married and loved by some brother who was as caring as Mr. Forman was to Ant Boo. They were my idea of a happily married couple. Because of how they related to each other, I was always pestering Jerome when we "played house," to be like Mr. Henry. While Jerome did not object to "playing house," he did have an issue with imitating Mr. Henry's behavior. Jerome wanted to be himself- Mr. Jerome Goals!

The Forman Family and Miss Peach were always protecting me. They were the individuals to whom I turned when I didn't think I could make it through this life. They were the ones who insisted on the hospital increasing my stay for one day beyond the four days allowed by the medical plan.

One day while I was in the hospital, Miss Peach and Ant Boo came for a visit.

"Good Morning Anne, how are you feeling on this God blessed day?" They both asked to me at the same time.

Before I could reply, Miss Peach noticed a broom lying against the wall facing me. She and Ant Boo called for the nurse to remove it.

"Baby, don't you know its bad luck to have a broom in the room with a sick person? It can bring death on them quicker than need be," Miss Peach said as she handed the broom to the astonished young Negro nurse. "Here, take that broom and keep it out of this room," Miss Peach said with a stern sound to her voice. "Lord, these folk around here will kill you, wait until I see that Dr. Morgan, he is from the south and should know better!"

A few days later Ant Boo came to visit me at home. She asked Mr. Henry to turn the foot of my bed away from the entrance to my room. It seems that it was bad luck to have your feet facing the door to your bedroom!? Ant Boo said that only dead people were carried out of the house-feet first!"

At times the house seemed to be closing in around me. It was on just such occasions that either Ant Boo or Miss Peach would allow me to spend lengthy times at their homes.

They were concerned about my threats of killing my child. Thanks to their love, I was able to over come whatever it was that was causing me to act in such a foul manner. Had it not been for Miss Peach's herbal remedies and Ant Boo's wonderful food, I just don't know where my family and I would be today!

Sara Mae never objected to my staying away from home, I often got the distinct feeling that she did not care where I stayed as long as I was not around her.

"Miss Peach, I don't want to take that stuff, it tastes nasty!" I said to Miss Peach as she held my head back and poured a large cup of St. John's Wort Tea into my mouth. I was often surprised at the amount of strength she had when she and I were at odds over that which was "good for me." If she was not pouring some herbal liquid down my throat, she was feeding me something raw.

"Here, eat this watercress salad, it will help you get that demon spirit off you," Miss Peach would say to me as she almost forced-fed me something she had gotten from her garden.

I grew to love that garden and everything that was in it. Between Miss Peach's prayers and that garden, I was able to survive an everyday experience that many in my situation could not have tolerated. God bless Miss Peach!

"Anne, now don't you argue with Miss Peach and me, eat that plate of food and that wheat germ will not kill you!" Aunt Boo said, blending her two cents into the matter.

After I gave birth to sweet Rochelle, I went into what the old folk on the block said was a "poor state of affairs." I lost a lot of weight due to my poor appetite. I refused to leave the house. There were times I didn't want to leave my bedroom. I'd just sit with the curtains drawn most of the day. Sara Mae became frightened by my refusal to come out of my room. She sought help from Miss Peach and Ant Boo about my "strange behavior." Both women quickly began to care for Roger, Rochelle, and my needs. These two soldiers had every body in the church praying for me at that time.

"Good morning Sister Turner, how is that sweet Anne Marie," Sister Tellit inquired one day when I was staying with Ant Boo.

"Oh she's doing well Sister Tellit, she is doing well. Keep her in your prayers, you hear!" Ant Boo, said as she quickly walked past the good sister, then mounted the steps and made her way into my house.

Each time I had an encounter with those low feelings of mine, the two warriors would make sure my bedroom was very clean. I felt so refreshed and alive after those changes.

"Ant Boo, look at that sun-set, it looks like the whole sky is ablaze. Have you ever seen such a bright orange in your whole life?" I asked standing in the window watching the sun setting in the Western sky.

"Anne, if you don't get out of that window, get out of that window, and get dressed for dinner," Ant Boo would say to me as she gently pushed me away from the opened window and helped me zip up my dress. "Here, take these babies and get them ready for dinner too! Child…, this generation, what do y'all use for brains these days? Hurry up, I have to get home and prepare Henry's meal also!"

Each time I returned to school, Miss Peach and Mr. and Mrs. Forman would care for my children. They gave them the love I so often heaped on them, that is, whenever I found the time to do so! I was determined that Roger and Rochelle would receive the warm motherly love that I never got from a mother. Because of the care I received from Ant Boo and Miss Peach, I was able to rear my children in a more responsible manner.

"Roger, I'll let you go out on a date if you remember what we talked about last week. Little girls are not to be disrespected and I am not able to care for anyone one but you and Rochelle, you hear me! And for the love of God, watch your manners in the street. If anyone teases you about doing that bad boy and girl stuff, tell them your mother disapproves of such behavior. You have to complete college before you start making a family. Roger, are you listening to me?"

"Yes mother," poor Roger answered. God, Roger was one handsome brother.

"Roger, don't "yes mother me." Do you really understand? Do you want your child to grow-up and be like…You do understand me don't you son?" I said as I gazed at him with an air of pleading and yet at the same time-motherly authority!

"Rochelle, what have I told you about having these boys call you after hours? All calls to you and by you are to be made before 8:30p.m.! The next time I have to tell you this I will place you on punishment and contact your friends' parents about my rules." I would say to Rochelle on several occasions.

"Now if you have that much to say to your friends, you had better say it while you are in school. You are a lady and ladies have to behave as such. Do you hear me young lady?"

"Yes mother," Rochelle would say to me, daring not to pout or display any degree of disrespect to this *fussing hen.*

Over-all, my children never showed any disrespect to any adult. They were both active in the Young Adult Choir, Baptist Training Union, Sunday school, and various other church activities. In addition to being active in church, they held club offices in both the grade and high schools.

Prior to Roger entering grade school, Sara Mae and I had a dormer added to the house in order for him to have his own sleeping quarters *away from the girlie activities!* He was thrilled about being in his *"own bedroom, away from that sweet stuff mother wore."* He was a loving and fiercely independent "brother!" He cared for his room as though it were a prized castle.

Rochelle was very prissy, always in the mirrors around the house. She too was an independent person. When Jerome offered Roger a job at his law firm during the summer months, Rochelle asked to be employed by the firm as well. She was the type who always paid close attention to details, which made her highly valued by the firm. While she was a most attractive girl, she pretty much respected my wish of not dating until she was a senior in high-school. Her good looks and the fact that she was selected homecoming queen did not make her or break her stride at being humble and kind to all she met. Rochelle was a bit of a jokester also.

"Mom, how are you and your fitness program coming a long?" Rochelle asked me one morning as I prepared to go to work.

"I don't know," I said, attempting to struggle into my black dress.

"I know, you have not been to class in a while, here, let me push you into that size twelve dress," Rochelle said with a smile.

"It is not a size twelve, Miss know it all. I'm still wearing a size petite eight thank you very much," I said, in a half joking voice, fully gathering the meaning of my daughter's dig at me. "I'll rejoin the group this Monday, I'm sure they haven't added any more minutes to their power walk since I was last with them."

"Good for you mom…!" Rochelle said with a note of light sarcasm to her voice.

"Watch it Missy, have you forgotten who holds the purse strings around here?"

In talking with Roger and Rochelle, I was often reminded of what I over heard two adults say about me when I first became pregnant…!

"Yea, child, now that poor Anne Marie has gone and gotten herself pregnant, she's like a well that has salt poured in it."

I never forgot those two women and the mean thing they said about me. However, what they said about me was the sum total of what many folk felt about my being pregnant at such a young age. *I HAD BEEN RUINED!*

As far as Ish is concerned, I have forgiven Ish and wish him all the best that God can bestow on him, he will need it!"

BLISSFUL DAYS

Not all of my life was a tragedy! There were those occasions when it appeared I was floating on air EVERY DAY.

Jerome phoned and said he wanted to visit me. It was on a steel gray Saturday morning in April. Funny thing though; he asked if I were alone. I told him I was the only one home at the time.

"Just a minute, I'm coming, what's your hurry, just a minute Jerome, stop ringing that bell," I shouted opening the front door. "Jerome what's gotten into you?" I took two steps back so Jerome could enter the foyer.

"Guess what! You are talking to the newest partner in one of the largest law firms in the United States. I'm moving to Detroit in the next two months. Isn't that great news, Anne?"

"It sure is great news Jerome! Great news indeed! You'll leave us this coming June?" I managed to say as tears began to roll down my cheeks.

"Oh come on Anne, we talked about this move before; this is my big chance to do more for my brothers and sisters in "hood." I'll be handling constitutional issues brought to the law firm. The firm cited me as the foremost authority regarding these matters. Of course my new book on the subject did aid in my getting the job. Then there is the matter of God's favor being factored into the equation," Jerome said, attempting to ease my on-coming pain by giving me a big manly hug. "Come on Anne Marie, just think of it this way, you'll have some place to visit more often."

"Yes, but the conversation seemed so long ago and now here it is upon us-June!" I was barely able to say as I gently pulled myself from Jerome and fell onto the nearest armed chair.

"Well, actually, I will not have to be there until the first week in July, but, by July 5th, I must start work," Jerome said in a somewhat matter of fact voice. "Please get dressed," Charles is coming over, and the three of us are going to dinner."

As I was coming down the stairs, Hori phoned me. I told him I was going out for "fine dining" and would return his call as soon as I returned.

"Oh, I see you and Mr. Man are still going strong. Do I hear wedding bells soon?," Jerome asked as he escorted me out the front door.

"Not yet Jerome. Not yet and don't you go changing the subject on me. Detroit in two months—Lord have mercy!" I said, as the three of us prepared to drive to P.J.'s Restaurant on the West side of the city.

The next morning, for some unknown reason, my emotions were alive with good feelings. I had gotten up early and prepared breakfast for Sara Mae and me. Sara Mae rarely got up early on a weekend. Her partying the night before prevented her from getting up too early and did not allow her to do anything around the house before 11:00 a.m.

As I had just completed cleaning the five rooms downstairs, plus the washroom, the doorbell rang. The man from the downtown florist delivered Mother's Day gifts from Roger and Rochelle. Roger sent a bouquet of red and yellow roses and Rochelle sent a card signed by the both of them. He also brought my Mother's Day gift for Sara Mae.

"Who was that at the door, Anne?" Sara Mae asked, coming down the stairs and heading for the kitchen.

"Oh, just the florist delivering our Mother's Day gifts, don't you want to see the flowers and card I have for you?" I asked, attempting to get Sara Mae's attention.

"I'll see them later; did you prepare breakfast this morning?" Sara Mae asked as she walked past the dining room table laden with Mother's Days gifts. She was walking straight toward the kitchen!

Just as I was about to follow her into the kitchen, the doorbell rang again. This time it was Hori.

"Good morning, Anne, Happy Mother's Day to you and Mrs. Turner," Hori said as he placed his gifts of beautifully arranged flowers on a table next to the coat stand. He then handed me two cards, one for Sara Mae, and one for me. "Are you here alone, Anne?"

"No Sara Mae is in the kitchen, she just got up!" I said.

"What do you want to do today, Anne?" Hori asked, as he held my hand.

"Let's drive into the next county and have dinner at some off the beaten path diner. Not too far, after all this is still the Midwest and the KKK still conducts some of their meetings in neighboring towns. Just the other month, two teen age boys were riding their bikes down Martha Boulevard when just about one mile before they reached Spring Oaks, four persons with white hoods chased them in a car," I quipped, glad to have Hori hugging me at that moment.

"Oh don't worry, I have my anti-KKK zap gun with me. They won't come near us when they see it," Hori cleverly interjected, displaying his "melt-me-down-daddy-I'm-all-yours" smile.

That man, that man, oh that good man.

"Hey there Hori," Sara Mae yelled from the kitchen. How are you?" What you bring me for Mother's Day?"

"Good morning Mrs. Turner, I brought you some beautiful flowers from the church operated florist shop and a card," Hori said, looking toward the kitchen as if he expected Sara Mae to come out and spend a few moments with us.

"That's nice!" Sara said, as if she were expecting something of greater value. "Good boy. Sit them on the table with the rest of the blooming things. Take your coat off and stay a while."

Roger and Rochelle were thrilled that I had met Hori. The three of them shared a mutual respect for each other. Even Sara Mae began to show signs of liking Hori.

The next day Pastor Newbreed asked Hori and me to remain after church. He wanted us to plan for Jerome and Charles' going away party. Hori and I were selected co-chairpersons of this event. The Chairperson of the Trustee Board told us to spare no cost in planning this *bash.*

Hori and I sometimes worked well into the late evening planning for our Jerome and Charles departure. Little was left to chance in the planning. We even invited relatives from out of state to attend. Classmates from grade, high-school, and college were also contacted.

Why, we even located some of Jerome's former teachers and requested they attend this gathering.

The event was held the Fourth Saturday in May. That was the only spare time Jerome and Charles had in order to attend their "going away party."

As the affair drew closer, Hori and I got to know each other better. He made me feel special. He said I made him feel better than he had ever felt in his life.

"Anne, you are the best thing that has ever happened to me. I get up each morning thanking God for you. I feel blessed to have ever known you. I feel blessed just to be in your presence. I pray that I make you feel just as good as you make me feel. Because of you, I see the whole of mornings differently. I even notice rainbows in the sky. Why, I even go out of my way not to step on ants or any other crawling insects. Such peace has come over me and on some days I feel like standing on the roof-top and yelling-I LOVE ANNE MARIE PALERMO!" Hori confessed to me one day as we were finalizing Jerome and Charles' affair at the church.

As he was talking, it was all I could do to continue sealing the hundreds of envelopes. I became so engrossed in what the man was saying; that all at once I found myself on the edge of my chair and then on to the floor.

"Anne? Anne, are you alright? What has gotten into you?" Hori asked as he rushed to collect me off the floor and assisted me on to the chair. Here. Give me your hands. Wrap your arms around me! Let me help you baby!"

"Hori, thanks. I don't know what got into me. We best be getting these invitations in the mail before the postoffice closes. I like you Hori. I like you a whole lot," I said, unable to say the other "L" word.

"I love you Anne Marie, no matter what others may or may not say about you. I love you and that's what counts in my life," Hori said, still looking into my eyes as he gathered the envelopes for mailing.

Hori and I were like two teenagers. We could be seen walking down the streets holding hands on many a day and evening. Folks saw us sitting on the front or back porches of each one's home. Hori was the "great outdoors" type person. He loved our walks along the river bank east of Spring Oaks. Every Sunday morning he and I would sit next to each other in church or we could be seen together at some social event.

In preparation for Jerome's moving to the Motor City, Hori and I frequently met at my house. We were either supervising the making of decorations for the affair or fine tuning some detail. The Chairman of the Trustee Board kept reminding us that the cost of the gathering shouldn't be our chief consideration. Assistant Pastor Ruth Premier volunteered to help us in getting materials to the printers. She had a special fondness for Jerome because he was among the first to promote the idea of Africa Baptist having a sister as one of the associate pastors. After seeing that Ruth was such an outstanding preacher, the boards and others quickly approached Pastor Newbreed about her becoming the assistant pastor of the church.

"Brother Brown, if you and sister Palermo don't mind, I will complete the ordering of the pastries today. You know how late the bakery was in delivering their goods to the church's anniversary last month. I just do not want a repeat of what happened then to take place at Jerome's party," Pastor Premier said as she began to gather her wraps and walk toward the door.

"I'll meet the both of you at church next Tuesday for the final plans," Pastor Premier said. Oh, before I forget, the combined choirs would like to sing three songs instead of two, is that okay?"

"Sure!" I said.

"Well, I'll see you two love birds then. Take care of yourselves and stay with God."

After the pastor left, Hori and I sat for hours talking about life and what part we would play in it. Hori had arranged for the Biology Department at the College to extend his stay at the university. Although a few of his senior colleagues were opposed to his stay; the majority of his colleagues in the department and the chairman were in full support of his staying.

"You know Anne, the department voted to extend my stay in the department for two more years," Hori said. But two senior members said they weren't aware of any contribution that I had made that would justify my stay in the department beyond the end of this term. They felt my extended stay would set a bad precedent and that they would be cast in a bad light in the eyes of the other academic areas," Hori said as he adjusted his chair and sat closer to me. "The chairman had to remind them that I was responsible for the department winning a two million dollar grant. Another colleague mentioned that I had an article published in the prestigious National Biological Standard for each of the past three years. Another member of the department cited my having a text book published this past semester. Do you know what one of the opposing airhead's" response was? He said that maybe because I was a black man teaching at such a nationally recognized institution gave rise to the magazine being so lenient towards printing my work. He also said that although he had never won any amount close to a million dollars for the department, he was sure that if he or anyone of the department members had tried, they too could have landed millions on behalf of the biological warfare experiment. I tell you Anne, some white folk are just too critically Caucasian for words! If they don't have anything to do with a project, the whole thing is called into question. Darn it!"

"Don't let that worry you, lover man. "What matters is that you are staying for two more years," I said, attempting to quiet Hori by rubbing his hands and giving him a hug. God always takes care of His children and you are one of His own-right?"

"Yes, but…," Hori said, as he was about to continue.

"There should be no butts about it, you have the position, so there," I said, rising to my feet and giving him a kiss on his cheek. "Let's straighten this mess and prepare for work tomorrow," I said, as we gathered up the materials from the dining room table.

On the day of Jerome's send-off, Africa Baptist swelled to its maximum seating capacity.

The place was filled with well-wishers. There were guests from all over the country. Jerome knew hundreds of people and insisted we invite all of them to the gathering. Even the folk, who did not especially like Jerome, attended the party. The church was decorated with all kinds of flowers. A large banner was hung across the front of the church (May God Bless You Jerome-Remember God in Whatever You Do).

The combined choirs sang three of Jerome's favorite songs. Jerome was asked to sing *"I'm Happy in Jesus Alone."* Needless to say, the tears flowed, and the shouts went up, even Sister Hightower stood up and waved her hands encouraging Jerome to…"sing baby, sing for Jesus!"

Pastor Newbreed rendered a wonderful sermon expressing the need for Jerome and others to follow the Lord wherever God led us.

The Trustee and Deacon Boards gave Jerome a huge Chinese vase. After their presentation, several other ministries presented Jerome with their gifts of love and admiration.

I was listed last on the program to do a presentation. As I got out of my seat; I could feel a large hush come over the thousands of people in the sanctuary. I slowly walked to the front of the large room. I turned and acknowledged Jerome as the honored guest. I then took a deep breath and began to share my contribution to this "going away gathering."

A Good Man, a Brother to Me/ You had to leave!

A good man,
Lovable, and
Flexible!
Fine as ancient Egyptian wine!
Intelligent,
Responsible,
Brave, and
Always on time and genuine.
                    You had to leave!
A brother to me!
Someone every man should be.
Sweeter than the honey from the beeeeeeeeeeeeeeeeeeeeeeeee!
A good man, a brother to me!
                    You had to leave!

A protector
A detective
A wise man without being condescending
Patient, forever bending to the needs of others!
Seeing others possibilities
You're a good man and a brother to me.
                              You had to leave1
Your smile lights up my heart!
I become anxious when we are apart!
I wince when I think that some day you will depart!
Oh, I've known that you were destined from the start
                              ...But!
I've loved you from the start...
Brother, you are so smart...
While some may just see your big fine brown frame
I, on the other hand know your whole game
                              Your tears!

Your pain!
Why the tears?
Why the fears?
Why the joy?
Why feign?   *...that private side*
                        ...that side, we all may want to hide!
Why do you walk with such pride?
A good man, a brother to me!
                              You had to leave!
You saw me as a seed in the dirty dirt!
You helped me rise up; as a new plant and become beautiful,
beautiful, beautiful!
May the God of Heaven and Earth continue to be with you!
I am so grateful and thankful to Him for you!
A good man, a brother to me!
                        You had to leave, you had to leave,
                        you, had to leave!

When I completed the last line, I took a deep breath, turned around and walked over to Jerome. I kissed him on the cheek and gave him the strongest hug I could.

Jerome and Charles ended the proceedings by expressing their love to all and said they would visit the church as often as possible. They would always keep us in their hearts. The two handsome men then invited us to visit them in Detroit. Jerome and Charles closed the program by assuring us that they loved God and would continue to seek our prayers.

Pastor Newbreed stood and gave the benediction. He then invited us to the church's large dining area for the celebration dinner.

Once in the dining hall, we were given the opportunity to meet and greet people whom we had not seen for a period of time. Roger and Rochelle had come from their respective schools to be with their "Uncles Jerome and Charles."

"Hi there Anne, do you remember me?" a rather tall, slender, pretty, dark brown skinned sister, asked me.

"Of course I do, sister, how are you and your family doing?" Where are you located these days?" I asked, extending my hand to give our former pastor's wife a hand shake. "I am really glad to see you. Did your husband and children come with you?"

"No, my children are with my parents in New York City and the reverend and I are not together. After he was fired from this church, I found out more about his sordid life-style and proceeded to get as far away from him as possible. I understand he is in some kind of court ordered sex-addiction treatment program, somewhere in the south. After we left Spring Oaks, his life took a turn for the worse and I became his "punching bag." Oh, don't get me wrong, he never physically abused me, but he did abuse me emotionally. He'd yell at me for no apparent reason. He suffered from crying spells, and seemed to have lost his appetite for food-strange! He became delusional and began hearing things in the middle of the night. One day I came home and he was dressed in my best...well, he's gone now, may God bless him wherever he is on this Earth!"

I thought so much of Jerome as a young man. And when I got word of the church honoring him, I just had to come and extend my best wishes."

"Well, I'll say" I said, not knowing what to say after that bit of news. *Child, that was too much information for me to do anything with, but smile and invite sister for something to eat!*

Chairman Green and Pastor Newbreed thanked Hori, assistant pastor Ruth Premier, and me for organizing Jerome and Charles' going away party. The pastor told us that all this could not have been possible had it not been for God touching the hearts of the

Trustee Board. He explained that they were the ones who controlled the money at the church. He told us that he was just a small voice in the financial matters of the church. The party was an over-whelming success and it appeared to have brought Hori and me closer than ever.

My favorite song during this period was Marvin Gaye's, *"If I Could Build My Whole World around You!"* I sang that song to Hori around the house so much; I even heard Sara Mae humming a few bars of the song. Whenever I sang the song, Hori would stop whatever he was doing and allow me to complete the entire song. Sometimes I'd sing the song at my shop; whisper it to him at his office, when we were alone, and at our respective homes. In short, child, I sang that song anywhere I got the notion to express my love for Hori Brown, Ph.D.!

One day near dusk, while Hori was walking me to my front door, Hori said, "Anne, my parents are coming to visit me in two weeks, will you please come and meet them?"

"Of course, I would love to meet your parents," I said, curious as to why I had not met Hori's parents before now.

Ant Boo, Miss Peach, and Sara Mae on more than a couple of occasions asked me why I hadn't been introduced to Hori's parents. I didn't take offense to the question, I would just reply, "In due time, in due time!"

Business at the dress shop was becoming a most successful venture for me. I had to hire two more full-time persons and I was advised to consider moving to a larger space.

With regards to my academic work, I finally decided to major in Business Administration, with a minor in Fashion Design. Sara Mae had discouraged me from entering the world of teaching. She said that now-a-days with so much emphasis on testing, *the heart and true soul of teaching* had been taken out of the class-rooms. She said that most of her time is spent on doing "non-teaching activities." She often complains about not being allowed to teach subject, noun, and verb agreements to her students any more. Sara Mae, as only she can, told me that the district is now demanding that students write in groups and employ the use of *"what comes up comes out writing form!"* She continued to tell me that teachers are now afraid to even hug children for fear of being charged or being accused of "sexually abusing the students. Poor Sara Mae is now considering leaving the public school system and working for the church as a grade school teacher. All too often she blames politicians for the gross mishandling of the town's educational system. If there is one thing that could be said about Sara Mae, she does maintain discipline and learning in her class-rooms. Child, why she even talked Minnie out of majoring in elementary education!

My annual health check-up found me at odds with the doctors. They wanted to perform some type of corrective operation on me, but I refused their advice, maybe next year!

On the day Hori's parents came to visit, I decided to wear a simple black dress. I wore a set of small pearl-shaped ear-rings with a matching necklace. My shoes were kind of on the conservative side. I wore my hair in shoulder length locks and proudly displayed the small patch of gray atop my forehead.

Hori wore a simple pair of brown slacks, a white shirt, and some brown loafers.

When I arrived at Hori's home, the first thing that struck me was the beautiful multi-colored evening gown with matching shoes worn by his mother, Dr. Brown. Her matching diamond earrings and necklace were just dazzling. I couldn't help noticing the large VERY EXPENSIVE looking diamond ring on her well manicured right hand. Her husband on the other hand wore a very conservative tailor-made black suit. Both Drs.' outfits looked as if they had come from the best high end store in the nation. Darling, they were "dressed to the nines."

"Hori, you didn't tell me this was a dress-up affair," I admonished Hori, as he attempted to assure me that I was dressed perfectly for tonight's dinner.

"Oh don't concern yourself my pet with these little details, mom and dad are always *"putting on the dog,"* when it comes to a first time meeting of special guests," Hori replied, cautiously.

"Yea, sure," I retorted, as I began to prepare for my first and, little did I know, my last meeting with the Drs. Brown.

Hori had ordered a wonderful meal from the June Rose Café. I sat next to Hori facing the fire place. His mother and father sat facing us with their backs to the fire place.

"My goodness Hori, it sure is cool in here, might you light the fire place for just a few minutes! I mean just enough to knock the chill out of the air," Dr. Brown said with her most "southern of southern drawls." "I mean it never gets this chilly in July in dear Ole Savannah."

"Are you sure you don't want a shawl or something dear?" Dr. Brown inquired as he reached over to sip some more sherry.

Before his wife could reply, Hori had walked to the fire place to prepare a fire, in mid-July!

Dr. Brown removed his jacket and wrapped it around his wife's round narrow shoulders. She thanked him and began to direct her conversation towards me.

"My dear, what do you do for a living? Have you ever been married before? Who are your people and where did they grow-up?" Hori's mother inquired.

Initially, I thought to ask her which questions did she want me to answer first, but thought, what the heck and began to comply with her request. Hori's father by this time was on his fifth shot of sherry, while his dear wife followed closely behind him downing just as many glasses of wine.

"Mother, I told you about Anne Marie when I last came to visit you, did you forget what I told you about her?" Hori interrupted, with his voice sounding overly controlled.

"Well Dr. Brown, I'm the proud couturier of my own designs. My shop is located in Down-town Spring Oaks. No, Dr. Brown I've never been married and I'm the proud mother two wonderful children. My great, great grand-parents were the second Americans of African Decent to settle in Spring Oaks," I said, as I noticed the Browns "downing" more and more of their "thirst quenchers." I thought it best not to ask the same questions posed to me for fear that the trumpets would start to sound and a flood of American History would descend upon the room!

"My dear child does the father of…," Mrs. Brown started to say, when Hori interrupted and announced that dinner was being served.

The whole time we were eating, the Browns directed all their comments to Hori. Hori, in an attempt to include me in the conversations; would direct a comment or two to me. Each time he did, his mother would find some excuse to talk about something only familiar to the three of them.

By the time Hori served dessert, both the Brown's speech had become slurred. Their eyes were now glassy and red, and their dining manners had eroded badly. Hori appeared at his wits end. He began to stutter and sweat. I offered to complete the washing of the dishes while Hori stayed to continue *their dinner time talk.* I collected everything off the dinner table. Walking to the kitchen; laden with dinner plates in my arms, I happened to looked down and saw that both Hori's parents' laps were filled with food crumbs. The floor around them was well covered with the droppings from their evening's dinner. Both by this time were talking loudly. They became fully animated-they were drunk! These people were too much sugar for a nickel!

"Oh here Annie, let me assist you with the dishes," Hori's mother said as she braced her hands on the table in an attempt to rise. When she took one step towards me, she fell to the floor with a loud thud!

"Dear, are you alright, allow me help you?" Hori's father asked extending his left hand out to his inebriated wife.

Dr. Brown took two steps toward her and he too fell to the floor. As he started to grab for one of the chairs, he fell back to the floor. This time, instead of attempting to get up, Drs. Brown began laughing uncontrollably on the floor.

Poor Hori looked at me, shrugged his shoulders, and began to laugh with them.

Wishing to have no part in the "the whatever-it-was game," I turned and walked to the kitchen wondering – what the h—is the matter with these folk? Surely, this was not the fine family from Savannah, Georgia, acting out in such a manner-*surely not!*

About a quarter of the way through the washing of the evening's dinner dishes, Hori entered the kitchen making all sorts of excuses for his parents' poor behavior. The whole while Hori was talking about his family, *I was thinking how my family and friends would react to their behavior had the opportunity resurfaced.*

"Anne, are you listening to me?" Hori asked me, as I began to come out of my thoughts about his family.

"Why yes, Pudding, I'm listening to your every word." I said to him, as I attempted to come out of a near trance over this matter.

After Hori's rather long speech about his parents' drunken behavior and how often he had to endure such conduct from them; I quickly assured him that he was all that mattered to me in the grand design of life.

"Are you sure you are alright with what took place tonight?" Hori asked me as he held me by my shoulder and rubbed his nose against mine.

"I'm sure, I'm okay with what took place Hori, now please, go and be with your parents! I'll put these dishes away and be in there soon," I urged him attempting to make my words sound as even and positive as I could.

Hori returned to the dining room and joined his parents at the table. I over heard Mrs. Brown, loudly whisper to Hori, "That girl is not your kind, why she isn't even our kind Hori. I forbid you to marry her!"

"Mom, I was hoping you would like Anne Marie because I'm going to ask her to marry me. I will NOT allow you to destroy this relationship as you have done the last three. Anne makes my heart sing, why, she has been my other eye, my other arm, and I feel honored to be with her," Hori said.

I turned the kitchen lights off, and loudly cleared my throat and returned to the dining room.

"And besides, what about your...," Dr. Brown said, as she looked up and saw me approaching the table with a tight smile on my face.

"Is everything alright?" I said as I pulled my chair closer to Hori then opted to sit on his lap.

"Oh, we were just telling Hori how tired we are, and how it is nearing our bed time. We southerners are not use to late hours. *We are early to bed and early to rise type of folk.*" Besides, we're sure you and our son have things to talk about," Dr. Brown said, as he placed his right hand on his wife's arm and began to walk her gingerly towards the stairs leading to the second floor.

"Good night, son, good night Miss Palermo, we enjoyed meeting you and I hope to see you again."

As they reached the bottom of the stair-case, they both fell down and began to laugh again. Hori rushed over to aid them up the stairs to their bedroom. After a short while, Hori returned to the table with a look of utter dismay on his face.

"Anne, are you sure that you do not..."

"Hori Anthony Brown, if you don't stop that foolishness, I will just scream. Why those are your parents and you do not have to apologize for their behavior-strange as it may seem to me! While I like them, I am in love with you. Okay?" I said, hearing my voice begin to get louder and noticing my hands slowly shaping into a fist. "Let's not talk about your parents' behavior any more tonight-please, DEAR?!"

"Well, Anne, I've been so busy preparing for my parent's visit, I forgot to do the most mundane of things around here. As a matter of fact, for the past two weeks, I've felt like a one legged man in an a—kicking contest," Hori responded, attempting to add some levity to the night's ending and to unruffled my nerves.

When I returned home and walked into the house, Sara Mae asked me how my evening had gone with the Browns. When I gave her a less than enthusiastic response, she just sucked her teeth, turned and went upstairs to her bedroom.

No sooner had I turned on my bedroom light, than Miss Peach telephoned me inquiring about my evening. When I told her what happened, she assured me that everything was going to be alright and to put my trust in the Lord.

Moments later, Ant Boo called me. She asked me how I felt about the parents' drunken conduct. I told her I was okay with what took place. I said that while I was a bit disappointed, I did feel sorry for Hori having to endure his parent's drunken behavior. Ant Boo wanted me to call her if I needed anything. In the background I could hear Deacon Forman repeating what Ant Boo was saying to me. The last thing I heard him say was how he wasn't surprised at those *"phony just came out of the cotton field black folk." I've seen their type before!"*

For the next two days, Hori and I did not see each other, but we did talk a lot on the telephone. Hori said that between teaching and attending to his parents, it was a pure joy hearing my voice.

Four days after the Browns left, I received a *thinking of you card,* from Dr. Brown saying he was most glad to meet me and that he wished me much success in everything I did. He underlined the word *everything.*

My days and nights became increasingly busy. The Chairman of the Trustee Board at the church and I began to meet on a regular basis in order to help me in with my wish to open another store. We also were looking into the possibility of expanding the current store. The store's reputation had expanded into the surrounding communities. Business had become so brisk, the Chairman and I had to seek the aid of the Mayor in order to secure more parking for my customers. I was never good at handling the affairs of politics. The Chairman was an astute lawyer and the Mayor of Spring Oaks was a member of the Trustee Board and a long-time member of the church. With the help of these two brothers, I was able to make my dreams come true.

I started attending church and participating in the business aspects of Africa Baptist more. Pastor Newbreed approached me about becoming a member of the Women's Mentoring Board, a group of women dedicated to encouraging younger women to start their own businesses.

Between the shop, attending school on a part-time basis, the Women's Mentoring Board, my lover Dr. Hori Brown, and my home life, I had too little time for anything else.

My advisor at the college said that I had twelve more college credit hours to take in order to graduate. Ant Boo and Miss Peach had planned a big party when that event took place. Jerome and Charles expressed an interest in joining the graduation observance also.

"Hey Anne Marie, how are you doing on this fine morning?" Miss Peach asked me as I was about to park my car in the drive-way.

"Good morning Miss Peach, how are you doing? "And a good morning to you Icky Boo!" Isn't that a great sunset? I can't remember when I've seen the sky so beautiful," I said as I walked toward Miss Peach's porch.

"Baby, how are you doing in school these days? You look a little tired, are you losing weight or something?" Miss Peach asked me as she got out of her rocking chair and sat on the top step and began questioning me about a myriad of issues.

"How is your business going? Miss Tellit told me she was in your store and there were so many people in there she had to wait a full twenty minutes before someone assisted her. She said she was most impressed at the degree of professionalism exhibited by your staff. Ann, what is going on with your class-work? Are you graduating soon? Billie and I want to give you a graduation party-okay?"

"The shop keeps me quite busy these days. The Lord has blessed me. If I continue carrying three classes per semester, I should be graduating this coming summer-hallelujah!" I said as I began walking toward my house. The long day at work did not prepare me for the barrage of questions coming from Miss Peach. "Well, Miss Peach, I must be heading home, this has been one heck of a day for me. Tomorrow, the village inspectors come to do their annual inspection tour and I have to complete a five page take-home final exam by tomorrow evening."

"Okay, dear, take good care of yourself. Don't over-work yourself. Life is too short for that sort of stuff. Go with the "All" and be safe! Say hello to Hori for me and let us know more about your graduation plans. Please?" Miss Peach pleaded, as she returned to her rocking chair and began to sew and quietly hum, *"Tis the Ole Ship of Zion!"*

That Miss Peach, I love her to death. She's been one of the many people God has sent to help me deal with this world.

When I entered the house, I discovered that Sara Mae had prepared dinner. Whenever she did this rare deed, I could expect almost anything to come from her. This time she wanted to borrow some money. She wanted to purchase another fur coat. She said that although she could get the money from anyone of her many *friends-meaning her male friends,* she would rather not bother with them this go around.

Whenever Sara Mae borrowed money from me, I'd have to threaten her with bodily harm in order to get her to remember how much money she had borrowed from me.

"Sara Mae, how much money do you want to borrow this time?" I asked sounding as exasperated as I possibly could.

"Oh, come on now, didn't I repay you the five thousand dollars the last time I borrowed from you? Sara Mae purred, displaying her school girl charm and softening her voice. "I only need three thousand dollars, the rest I can get from…well that's neither here, or there. Anne, I must get this coat before the sale ends tomorrow morning. I would go into my account, but the bank and I are in a little dispute about their charging me for some little over-sight on my part. I'll repay you the money out of my pay check at the end of December."

"Okay, okay, but Sara Mae I do not want you to forget this transaction," I said as I made out a check to the furrier where Miss Sara Mae planned to purchase her fifth fur coat. Sara Mae was one of those individuals who did all she could to keep-up with the Joneses. Although when she wanted to save her money, she cared less about getting the money from whomever or for that matter however, for what she wanted! Sara Mae had money saved in two credit unions, two bank accounts, a teacher's retirement account, and monies left her from her parents' U.S. Savings Bonds. *She really thought she was one slick chick!*

"Oh thank you sweetie, I'll repay you as soon as I get my holiday money, you won't have to remind me about it, you just wait and see," Sara Mae said as she snatched the check from my hand and ran up-stairs to her bedroom.

Just as I sat down to eat, the telephone rang, it was Hori. We talked for twenty minutes and shared how much we are in love with each other. We ended our conversation vowing never to allow anything to come between us.

After my conversation with Hori, I telephoned my children. They were doing well in school. Both Roger and Rochelle were maintaining their academic scholarships and were looking forward to the Christmas break. Roger was graduating from college the week before Christmas. He would pursue his law degree at an Eastern university beginning in January. Rochelle would graduate from college next fall semester; with a degree in mathematics. She wanted to receive a graduate degree at some school on the West Coast. We were especially looking forward to Jerome and Charles coming to visit. He and Charles were staying with Jerome's parents. Mr. and Mrs. Goals had resolved their issues of Jerome and Charles living together as partners. They felt that as long as the two of them were not committing any criminal acts and were productive adults, they did not have anything to gripe about. All things considered, they counted themselves blessed to have such sons in their lives.

After I completed my home work assignments, I was just too tired to eat. I slowly climbed the sixteen steps and went to bed. When I awoke the next morning, I was surprised to see that I had on my clothes from yesterday! Child, please!

Arriving to work the next morning, I was greeted at the door by two white males. One of them was about six feet, four inches tall. He was some thirty plus years old, and had a large garment bag folded over his large arms. Standing beside him was an older white man who was somewhat shorter in height. As I approached the shop's door, I could not help but notice a large black sedan parked in front of the building. These two men did not live in Spring Oaks, but a neighboring town.

"Good morning," the older man said to me, as he tipped his hat and displayed a broad smile.

"Good morning to you also," I said, as I walked past them, opening the door to the shop.

When I opened the door, members of my staff began to file into the shop behind us. I asked the two men to please have a seat near the counter. In just a short while, I was able to serve these two men.

"Now, that we have set-up, what may I do for you?" I asked, as I walked in front of the counter and approached the two men.

"We heard that you do the best tailoring work in this area. I need these five suits adjusted. I seemed to have gained too much weight over the years," the older man said, as he took the garment bag from the taller man and placed it on the counter.

The gray haired man opened the bag; I could see that three of the suits had been well worn. The other two were brand new. All of the suits were made of very expensive gabardine material.

"Do you think you can do anything with these suits?" the older man asked, as he ran his hand across each one of the suits. "I'll pay whatever amount you charge me for repairing or altering them."

"Well let's begin by trying on each one of the suits. Do you have time to try on the suits?" I asked, walking over to the men's dressing area and pulling back the curtains so the man could change his clothing.

"I have all the time needed to get this matter addressed. You really don't know what a relief it is just being in this store," the older man said.

I began measuring each one of the suits, I noticed that the taller man kept staring at me and smiling. Each time I looked away from my task, his eyes appeared fixed on me. An eerie chill came over my body at that moment.

"Pops, you have gained a lot of weight, we'll have to put you on a diet or something soon," the taller man said, as he sat near the older silver-haired man.

The older man appeared to have a heavy Italian accent when he talked or laughed with the other accompanying man.

"Sir, just turn this way, I am just about finished with the measuring," I said, as I completed the final markings on the newer suits. "There now, you may take the suit off and come to the counter when you are dressed."

Just as he stepped into the dressing room, the church's floral shop had made their delivery of two bouquets of red roses. When the older man stepped out of the dressing room, he quickly made mention of the flowers.

"Red roses! Do you like red roses?" the older man asked, as he approached the counter with his five suits. Placing the suits on the counter, he sniffed the flowers and ran his hairy, wrinkled short salmon colored hands across one of the roses.

"These flowers really brighten up your place Miss Palermo," the older man said.

"Yes they do," I said. "Ever since I opened my shop, some anonymous person has been sending me roses. On opening day, they sent so many flowers I couldn't find room for them. We think it is the same person who has been sending me flowers since I graduated from grade and high school, and the times I spent in the..." I stopped talking mid-sentence, finding I was becoming too relaxed in sharing information with this complete stranger. "The flowers really make my day around here. God bless whoever is sending them to me. They must have loads of cash, because they have been sending flowers once a week for as long as the shop has been open. I'm certainly not mad at them for being so kind-though!"

"Well, he must love you a lot to be so kind," the older man responded, a tear fell from his right eye, "Oh d—, I must be catching a cold, my eyes are beginning to water, young lady lets figure how much damage you are going to do me so I can go about my way."

"Okay, what is your first name?"

"Alphonso!"

"What is your last name?" I asked, as I noticed the younger man get up, walk over to the counter, and place his left hand on the older man's shoulder.

"Alphonso will do for now," the older man said, as he continued to give me a P.O. Box for an address.

"Okay," I said, as I tore off the yellow sheet and gave it to him. By this time the older man was pulling out a large white handkerchief in order to wipe his sweaty forehead.

"Is it hot in here or is it me?"

"Well, it may be too hot for you, after all, you have been changing in and out of those five suits. Why don't you remove that lovely camel haired over-coat?" I asked, attempting to make him comfortable in his obvious state of discomfort.

"Well Anne Marie, I mean, Miss Palermo, I'll return in about two weeks to collect my suits. Thanks for taking care of me," the older man said, as he began to walk out of the store. Just as he was leaving and about to close the door, the mail-person walked past him and delivered the mail. My air-plane tickets to Atlanta as well as guest tickets to Roger's graduation had arrived. I was beside myself with blissful relief. My oldest child was graduating from college. As I stood there thinking about Roger, tears began to fall down my face. Helen, my assistant, walked over to me and gave me a hug and a kiss. She gathered the older man's suits and began waiting on the next customer. The day had been extra-ordinarily busy. People were getting ready for holidays and they wanted to look their best. I felt honored that they chose my shop as the place to help them look their best. I felt God was smiling on me.

Hori walked into the shop while I was preparing to close-up for the evening. He had a rather faint smile on his face. He slowly walked to my office and sat down.

"Greetings Professor Brown, are you feeling alright today?" I asked as I stopped what I was doing and held his hand.

"I'm feeling just fine Anne. I will feel better when you answer my question," Hori said to me as he took off his coat, got on his knees, and held my hands a little bit tighter than usual.

Before I could say anything Hori asked me to marry him. I was speechless for a about a couple of seconds.

"Yes, I will marry you Hori Brown," I managed to say, as I got out of my seat. Hori placed his hand in his pant pocket and pulled out a blue velvet box. As he slowly opened the box, my head began to swell with the possibilities of the contents in the box. Hori pulled out the most beautiful engagement ring I had ever seen. The platinum ring held three large diamonds. They were dazzling to the senses. My whole body seemed as though it was going to explode. As he placed the ring on my finger, both our hands began to shake uncontrollably. We started laughing, I guess in order to deal with the high emotions. When the ring was finally placed on my finger, we hugged and kissed each other for what appeared to be hours.

Peter Burden's knock on the front door broke our embrace.

"Ms. Palermo, I come to clean," Peter said, as he stuck his head in the door.

"Oh come on in Peter," I said, as I showed him my engagement ring.

Peter looked at the ring and then looked at Hori and me. He was slow to smile, but did eventually congratulate the both of us. "Ms. Palermo, may I speak to you when you have time," Peter asked as he began to mop the floors.

Gee Peter, don't jump up and down so over my pending wedding!

We were so proud of Peter. When he arrived home from the armed services, he showed signs of being shelled shocked. His situation had become so bad that he had to be hospitalized for a couple of months. The folk on the block thought we were going to lose poor Peter. He was the main subject of all the prayer meetings for about a year. Then, on a Monday morning, a year and a half ago, Peter returned from New Jersey professing to be a *"Baptist- Buddhist."* He was managing his own cleaning service. He was attending college on a part-time basis and was majoring in Business Administration. Peter was his old self again! While some folk took issue with his having changed his "religion," the folk on the block were glad he was alive and being productive-*"what a difference a day makes, twenty-four little hours!"* Why do people insist on dealing with the small stuff, instead of looking at the over-all picture...the boy was well, not causing any problems, and worshipping God in a way that worked best for him?

I was too happy for words during this period. I could be found singing, laughing, praying, exercising, and being in a constant state of bliss leading up to the wedding.

Some how Jerome had convinced Roger's college administration to allow Mr. and Mrs. Forman, Miss Peach, Jerome and Charles, Sara Mae, Rochelle, Minnie, and me to attend the graduation service. The college had some silly rule that only five tickets, at most, could be granted to each graduating student! We all stayed with relatives of Miss Peach. After the graduation, we gave Roger a graduation party to end all parties. At the party, I noticed that Mr. Roger had acquired some new skills. He was the best dancer at the party, at least so it appeared. His shy persona had vanished. He now seemed taller, more muscular, more socially out-going, and though he was dancing a lot, most of his attention seemed focused on his male friends.

"Miss Peach, Roger seems to be well liked by all the students, especially the males, what thought do you get from that?" I asked, holding my breath in anticipation of Miss Peach's answer.

"Roger is a male, males like males, Roger is a well-liked male," Miss Peach quipped getting out of her seat and walking over to Roger asking him to dance with her.

When I reach that age, I want to be just as agile as Miss Peach.

Hori did not attend Roger's graduation. He did send a present and telephoned my son from Savannah, Georgia.

The day after graduation we made our way home. Roger remained in Atlanta. He would meet us in Spring Oaks on Christmas Eve.

On Christmas Eve, Jerome and I met Roger at the airport. Roger was so very glad to see us. He was still on an emotional high. We talked about his future plans as we drove from the airport. Roger wanted to be a well-known lawyer like his god-father Jerome.

Jerome was doing very well in Detroit. He was working on a case where a local Child-Welfare Agency was accused of abusing gay and lesbian youth. Jerome felt the agency was unfairly profiling children who had been put out of their parents' house because they were males who professed to be gay or females who were lesbians. Documents indicated that these children were never placed in homes. They were often physically and emotionally abused. Two months ago, three gay teen-agers ran away from the center. Two ended up dead. They were never reported missing from the agency. Another was found in a hospital- he had been raped and beaten by three men who had left him in a ditch for dead. The fourth and fifth youths had been arrested for prostitution. An investigation proved that they had been prostituting for two of the staff-members at the agency. A media expose' on the matter, disclosed wide misuse of the public's money by such agencies. Jerome is representing this issue before a state committee next month. How can parents be so insensitive as to throw their own flesh and blood into the street because that child is obeying the laws of nature, and or wants to be something other than what their parents have *planned*? Don't these parents realize that Satan is just waiting for these young tender ones to be wasted in those mean streets? These folk will have to answer for their hatred.

Christmas Day was one of gift-giving, merriment, lots of great eating, and being thankful.

We all decided to gather at Mr. and Mrs. Goals' home. Mrs. Goals had excellent taste when it came to home decoration ideas. Never one to make a faux pas, she was the perfect hostess. While Mr. Goals mingled with the rest of us, Mrs. Goals was making sure we were well fed and comfortable.

After the presents were opened and exchanged, Rochelle and Jerome blessed us with three songs. Rochelle had a beautiful first alto voice and of course Jerome was the only baritone. Their duets took us through all kinds of holiday emotions. Sara Mae and Mr. Forman wept when Rochelle and Jerome sang *"Away in a Manger."* Ant Boo, Charles, and I did a little dance when *"Go tell it On the Mountain"* was rendered. Miss Peach rocked back and forth when *"Children Go Where I send you"* was done. Roger, Rochelle, Charles, and Jerome all took turns playing the baby grand piano and we all took turns leading other Christmas songs. Mrs. Goals had set-up a seven foot pine tree. Deacon Forman reminded us that in the book of Jeremiah the Tenth Chapter, the children in the Bible were warned against decorating trees. But he did hand the decorations to us as we placed the ornaments on the impressive tree.

Jerome and Charles remained in town to attend "Watch Meeting." Every year on New Years Eve, all the surrounding churches gathered at one site. This year, we gathered at All Saints Church. They had just enlarged their sanctuary to accommodate their fast growing church. Their new pastor had wanted to move the congregation into another town, but that idea was quickly rebuffed by the majority of the membership composed mainly of senior members in the church. The seniors had to remind the new pastor that they were the ones making the greatest financial contribution in the church. The fact that their combined choirs sang *"Santa Clause is coming to Town" and "Jingle Bells,"* did little to calm the concerns of the senior members at All Saints Church. Nor did the two songs sit too well with many of us who were not members of that church.

All the pastors agreed that Miss Peach should give the history of "Watch Meeting." She started her presentation by informing us that the service was not to be taken lightly. She then informed us that President Abraham Lincoln granted Americans of African Descent freedom at twelve midnight in 1863, (The Emancipation Proclamation). Since that time, the black church has been bringing in the New Year with a "Watch Meeting."

While other towns brought in the New Year with loud gun shots, our community quietly filed out of the host church and made our way to our homes; savoring the hallowed moment.

Our entourage decided to gather at my house after "Watch Meeting Service." All was going well, when I began to feel faint about an hour into our celebrating the New Year. Hori seeing me slump in the chair, rushed to my side with a glass of water. The next morning, I discovered I was in the hospital. The doctors advised I get plenty of rest for the next couple of days.

He strongly suggested I have corrective surgery on my cervix.

Slowly opening my eyes to the bright, warm, and the many hues coming from the sun light entering my hospital room, I could see Miss Peach and Sister Tellit at my bedside. Miss Peach, always priding herself on *not participating in any form of gossip,* was bent forward. She was slowly turning the pages in her Bible while Sister Tellit shared the latest town's gossip. I never once saw Miss Peach look down or read one page in that Bible while being engaged by Sister Tellit. They were too involved in "pouring the tea" to notice me.

"What are you two doing?" I murmured, somewhat startling Miss Peach and Sister Tellit as they were engrossed in dishing the dirt on whom or whatever came to mind.

"Oh, hey baby, we didn't mean to disturb you," Sister Tellit said, looking as if she was caught in some misdeed and was up for trial.

"Hey baby, are you sure we did not get you out of your sleep?" Miss Peach asked me as she got off the foot of my bed and held my hand. "How are you feeling Anne Marie?"

"I'm doing fine Miss Peach, I just feel a little weak that's all," I said, as I began to sit up and adjust my pillows.

"Here, let me to do that," Sister Tellit said. "Let a sister do her job around this place once in a while. After all, they pay me quite well to take care of the patients around this joint. Why come this August, I will have been employed at this place for some twenty-five years as a nurse. Can you imagine that, me a colored women? There now, if you need anything, just give me a call. Sister Tellit will take care of you Anne Marie."

"Thank you Sister Tellit," I said, praying that she would leave the room, quick, fast, and in a hurry.

"Well, you two, I must be off to my duties, we must keep everyone happy and well around here. This afternoon, I'm assigned to the Alternative Health Unit. I don't know why they refer to it as that, before there was such a thing as *non-traditional medicine*," all we colored folk ever used was God's herbs out of the ground- this was our tradition!"

"See you Tellit, take care of yourself," Miss Peach said, as she walked Sister Tellit to the door.

"Child, that Sister Tellit knows she can gossip," Miss Peach joked, as she pulled up a chair close to my bedside.

"Miss Peach, I thought I saw you listening to her as she poured the latest tea," I teased, looking at Miss Peach and waiting for one of her classic responses.

"Child, I don't gossip; I was reading my Bible while that woman released those demons out of her mouth. Somebody has to stay in touch with the Lord while she is talking," Miss Peach said, giving me one of those famous "Miss Peach's" winks. "Now Sweetness, you know Peach don't get involved in that devil talk put out by those women at church."

"Yea, sure, Miss Peach, sure, you don't"

Just then Hori walked into the room. The smile on that man's face almost brought tears to my eyes. He always brightened up my day. My being with Professor Brown seemed to make sense out of a world gone mad for me. Yep, Hori was my other eye, my other side, the other-side of my brain, my gift from God.

"Good morning Miss Peach, how are you today?"

"Quite well, Baby, what about you? Have you been eating? You look a little poor. That suit looks a bit too big for you." Miss Peach noted, as she pulled up another chair so Hori could sit next to her.

"Oh, I've been doing entirely too much these days, but I'm doing okay," Hori said, as he sat in the chair, holding my hand, and kissed it with his generous M-shaped lips. I've been helping Representative Salle Wright in her efforts to retain her office. Do you remember that George Prime, the fellow who I am informed was once supported by the community until he stabbed the Black Community in the back? Well, he is now supporting a known white racist against Salle. While it's true that we have the numbers to get her back in Congress, I just can't get over some of us when it comes to selling out for just "thirty pieces of silver!"

"Child, there are those of us who will do it "every teem, every teem!" Why this reminds me of a story my mother use to tell me of a place where three fourths of the town was composed of Negroes. A minority of white people ran the town. Whenever the whites got into trouble, they would run to these five *intelligent brothers and sisters* and request their assistance. The Negroes would meet for a "few hours" and return with a resolve to the white's problem. This scenario went on for many years. One day, the younger Negroes of the town approached the *gifted five*. They informed the five that the Negroes made-up the majority in the town and should be the administrators in the town. They wanted the talented five to help them in their efforts to take the town back from the whites. The five requested *a "couple of days" to think about the matter*. A couple of days mind you, when if the whites had asked for help, these Negroes only took a few hours to solve any type of issue. I tell you, some of us are just not ready for FREEDOM!" Miss Peach said as she began shaking her small head. "Someone told me that when George lost to Sister Salle Wright in the last election, he switched to another political party, divorced his wife and married a white woman, moved into the city, and has even changed to another religious denomination! I'm glad some of us had the good sense not to vote for him.

"Baby, I keep telling y'all, the enemy comes in all shapes, colors, and sizes! Like they always say, they may be your color, but they ain't your kind."

"Really now, Miss Peach, who knew?" I said, unable to complete the rest of my sentence when there was a knock at the door, it was Ant Boo, she stuck her head between the door and the pristine walls of my hospital room.

"Good afternoon folk; how are you "peeps" doing these days?" Ant Boo asked, as she entered the room with a bright smile, some more flowers, and some of her home cooking. "Wow, look at all the pretty flowers in this room, one would think that you were...well, they would! "

"Who sent you all these flowers to Ms. Celebrity Anne?"

"I don't know Ant Boo, my guess is that it's the same person who has been sending them ever since I was in the eight-grade," I said, as my eyes wondered around the room and happened to catch Hori smiling at me.

"I spoke to your doctor; he informs me that you are refusing to go through a life saving operation!" Ant Boo announced, as she pulled another chair to the other side of my bed. "Now, please don't fuss at the doctor for telling me about you. He told me out of a great sense of concern about your health status."

I felt completely surrounded by peering eyes. They were inquisitive, and yet loving stares. I felt that although these three loved me, they could not possibly understand my fear of being cut on. I did not want to be *hurt again!*

"I didn't refuse an operation, I told the doctor I needed more time to think about an operation, "I said, attempting to sound unafraid and in charge.

"Child, in the mean time, please drink that mixture, Miss Peach and I take! It's guaranteed to help fight anything like what you are going through," Ant Boo insisted, as she wiped the sweat from my forehead. "All you have to do is mix, eight cloves of garlic, eight ounces of any of your favorite juice; please, make sure that it is natural and has no processed sugar added, and one banana. Blend it until it is liquefied and drink it twice a week. Oh, and eat an apple immediately after you drink the brew! Also, take an enema of thirty cloves of garlic at least twice a month," Child, I'm sixty-one years old and Miss Peach is as old as the written word…"

"Now, wait a minute, Forman, you are about to go too far with this mess. I am a young ninety-"something" year old sister. I mean!" Miss Peach said as she winked at me, then smiled and began to gather her clothing to leave. "I'll be getting along, Anne, take care of yourself; after all, we want to see you march down the aisle this summer."

"Oh, I almost forgot to tell you, Hori and I have delayed the wedding until the fall," I said, feeling a little bit sleepy and yet hearing the deafening silence in the room when I made my announcement.

Ant Boo and Miss Peach did not say another anything else. They let out a sigh, gave each other a curious look, and then said their goodbyes to Hori and me as they exited the room.

Hori walked them to the door. He thanked "my two right arms" for coming to visit me and then he returned to the room. As he was walking toward me, I too noticed how much smaller his face appeared. He looked as if he hadn't shaved in a day or two. Hori is a person who has to shave every day. His pants was wrinkled and his shirt collar was soiled. I also noticed a faint sour smell coming from him.

"Hori, how have you been doing, you do look a little worn," I said, as I reached for his hand.

"Look, Anne, don't you start that mess too," Hori said, with an angry tone in his voice.

This was the first time I had ever noticed his exhibiting such behavior towards me. Until now, no matter what happened to him, he never displayed any displeasure with what I had to say to him. *What was going on with my honey-bee?*

"I'm sorry Anne, I didn't mean to snap at you, it's just that a lot has been going on and I've been missing you these last several days," Hori quickly said, as he gave me a hard kiss on my lips. "Please don't take what I just said personally, please?"

How else was I to take such a response? H-ll-, I'm the only one in the room who asked him the question! Oh well, I'm too tired to give this matter any energy right now.

"Hori, will you please excuse me, I'm feeling my sleep come down on me just now. I love you, always remember that, okay?" I pleaded. I then turned over to get some much needed sleep.

I heard Hori say good night to me as he closed the door, and whispered that he loved me.

The next morning a team of doctors came into my room examining me from head to toe. My doctor again brought up the issue of my needing corrective surgery.

"Good morning daughter," Sara Mae said, as she rushed into my room as I was peaceably having my breakfast and listening to the radio.

"Morning, Sara Mae, how are you doing?" I asked, anticipating the worst from her after last night's visit from my doctor.

"Your doctor tells me that you are refusing corrective surgery. What in the name of all that is holy do you think you are doing?" Sara Mae asked, displaying her usual lack of tact and sensitivity. "Girl, just who in the world do you think is going to have the time to care for you, should your health become worse?" Sara Mae demanded, her voice beginning to tremble. Tears started to roll down her face like some giant water fall.

"Sara Mae, I did not tell the doctor that I would refuse an operation. I only told him I needed time to think about the matter," I calmly said. I knew that no matter what I said, Sara Mae, would only turn it around to where I was painted as selfish and causing her an inconvenience. "How are things at home?" I continued with the hopes that the tenor of the conversation would change to one more be-fitting "a patient and a mother." Please, God, doesn't Sara Mae realize that I'm too sick to argue with her COLORED BUTT!

"Well, since it appears you don't want to talk about your living or dying, things are fine at home. Hori has been coming over to help around the house. Pastor Newbreed requested the members keep you in their prayers...Anne Marie, are you sure that you want to wait any longer in order to address this potential life threatening matter?" Sara Mae continued to say to me. "Roger and Rochelle are on pins and needles about this hospital stay. Anne, why don't you try that "bio-frequency method" Miss Peach swears the procedure has greatly relieve her arthritis problem. She's always talking about "an ounce of prevention is worth a pound of cure." Do something; don't just lie around here doing nothing!"

"Sara Mae, just for today may we talk about something we can both agree on?" I pleaded, turning my head away from her pitiful stare.

Just then, I noticed Sara Mae had become silent. As I turned to look at her, I saw tears rolling down her heavily made-up cheeks. She began to slowly rise from her chair, put her coat on, and walk toward the door. When she got to the door, she turned, looked at me, and said "good-by b—ch, I hope your butt rots in hell."

Good-by b——, I hope your butt rots in hell! Now that wasn't a nice thing to say to your daughter. My, my, my!

When I arrived home, all my personal belongings had been moved to the seldom used, first floor sun porch. Hori, Ant Boo, and Miss Peach, all agreed with the doctor that I should not climb too many stairs for at least a month. The room was situated just past the dining-room. It wasn't as large as my bed- room, but it served the purpose. This room had been reserved for guests. The space didn't give me the comfort I had been so accustomed to when I was able to look south at Miss Peach digging around in her vegetable garden. Actually, the room did more to dampen my emotional and spiritual juices than anything else. I felt as though I was coming down from some kind of high in this room. I prayed that I was not returning to that period when I was afraid to meet every day life, a period where nothing made any sense or difference to me. There was one measure of comfort the room held, and it was the large bouquet of flowers that adorned the room. *Who could be sending me this many beautiful roses?*

A TIME OF DELAYS AND DISAPPOINTMENTS

Sometimes God puts us in a holding pattern until we are ready to carry out His plans for us.

I thought that delaying the wedding would give me more time to plan for the "wedding of my dreams," my pending graduation, and Rochelle's summer graduation as well. It appears that the most to come out of the slow-down were more disappointments.

My illness caused me to withdraw from college that semester. This meant I would have to "bust my buns" and take more classes than I had planned in the summer term. The thought of doing this did not sit well with me. Although I was sure I could graduate from school by the end of the Fall Term, I did not want to put too much needless stress on myself. The aforementioned made me have to give quite a bit of consideration to my shop as well. Although my assistant was a very capable person, I took on the major tasks of running the shop, which was something only my special touch could provide.

Hori was the perfect gentleman the whole time I was recuperating. He visited me every day. He helped Sara Mae clean the whole house, tend to the yard, and on some occasions, ordered my favorite take out foods. We'd sit for hours together. While visiting, he sometimes graded papers or attended to some college related project. I'd attempt to review one or two of the four classes I had withdrawn from previously. Many times I could be found attending to some aspect of my shop. Very often, Ant Boo and Miss Peach would help with the house cleaning or monitor the daily events at my clothing store. These two sisters were always there for me. Without them- well, where would I be?

Through it all, I did plan on getting married! While she did not say anything to me about it, I sensed Ant Boo was having some misgivings about the wedding. Oh, not that she was opposed to my marrying Hori; she just felt I was crowding too much into my "fragile life." What she and others did not know was that if I did not at least plan for a wedding, a veil of "not accomplishing something," would have tossed me back into that blinding white abyss! Somehow, I felt a great sense of making-up for lost time come over me. I felt that if I did not marry Hori, my chances of any future marriage would be lost! It was now or never. How could I ever explain not marrying to three strong-willed women like Sara Mae, Miss Peach, and Ant Boo? While they fully understood the importance of brothers in some phase of their lives, could they really understand my break neck desire to be with a man who did not make me feel like...? While I do not subscribe to the age old adage "that a good woman has to have a good man," I do feel that it sure helps from time to time to have one around. In the words of Miss Peach and Charles: BLACK MEN! EVERY HOUSE SHOULD HAVE ONE! I was on a very tenuous time-frame. My illness added much to my desire to achieve all that I had planned. Because, if I should not live beyond well, at least Lord allow it to be said that I married a man who finally treated me like a human being. Darn this illness, it makes for such mundane thoughts and fool-hardy behavior. Child, please. *(2 Corinthians 12:10)*.

Besides, Hori and I have had some pretty close calls when it comes to "heavy-cuddling." Ant Boo, told me about a research study which mentioned that having sex on a regular basis improved ones total physical appearance. The study even said the participants looked younger! Sharing this information with me, Ant Boo, for the "umpteenth time," asked me when Hori and I were going to "tie the knot."

"Anne, now you know your Ant Boo does not want to get in your business, but I'm only saying this for your own well-being- Anne, when are you and Hori going to get married? "Baby, what are you waiting for-Christmas?"

"Ant Boo, I want to be sure things are right," would be my reply.

"I'm sure he has asked you to marry him-right...?" Ant Boo would say as she smiled, her head bent down, and looking me square in the face.

"Yes, he asked me to marry him twice, but "well, it just ain't time Ant Boo," I found myself saying rather defensively.

While Ant Boo wanted me to get married, Miss Peach, on the other hand, had a different spin on the matter. She saw something in our getting married that did not sit well with her. Whenever I'd ask her what she thought about us getting married, she'd reply, "Oh I can't put my hand on it just yet," she would say to me with a great big smile.

Sara Mae over-heard Miss Peach sharing her misgivings about the marriage; my wedding plans. She asked me not to pay any attention to what Miss Peach had to say about the issue.

"Take your time baby; it will come to you; it will come to you."

"After all, everyone knows Miss Peach ain't ever been married and just may not know what she is talking about. After all, rumor has it that she is a "well, take it from me, she may not know everything."

My assistant, Clara Mae, and I kept in regular contact with each other. Her husband, James was a supervisor at one of the Post Office branches. Rumor had it that they had the ideal marriage; sharing house hold and child rearing duties. Clara Mae had a great rapport with my shop's staff. Her loyalty to me was unquestionable. Our relationship gave me great satisfaction while I was away from the shop.

With Roger attending summer school in the Detroit area, I was now left to focus some of my attention on getting well, my wedding plans, and Rochelle's graduation.

Rochelle was a very gifted student. She had graduated first in her class completing a four year program in three years. She was unsure of what to pursue in graduate school. Whatever degree she wanted, I wanted her to know I was proud of her accomplishments. I considered her progress to be mine also.

By summer, I had returned to the shop, and was working at my usual "break neck speed." While moving about the store; there was no denying that it felt great returning to my creations-something that was my own!

Two days before Rochelle's graduation, Jerome, Charles, and Roger drove from Detroit. They stayed with Sara Mae and me.

Those two days were filled with great fun and renewed relationships. The last evening was very special for me.

Just before we retired for the evening, Jerome and I took a walk around the block. Mr. and Mrs. Goals were vacationing in Ghana and the Ivory Coast for two weeks. Jerome and I approached his parents' home. Standing there dredged up many old, and held wonderful childhood memories.

"Anne, do you remember when I first met you?" Jerome asked, as he held my hand as we stood in front of the home where he was reared.

"Not quite," I said, guessing that it might have been on this block.

"I was sitting on this very porch with my parents and my rude cousin Harvey. You and Sara Mae were coming from some place west of here. Sara Mae spoke to us and began to take a short cut through our yard. Harvey, being his usual self, stuck his tongue out at you. Your response was to display your radiant and fetching smile. I hit Harvey on the back of his peanut shaped head for being such a smart butt. I returned your smile and hoped I would see you again." Jerome said to me as we continued our stroll around the block, returning to Church Street.

As we made a right turn from Lewis Street onto Church Street, we noticed the porch light at the Forman's had just gone out for the evening. Memories of Ant Boo and Deacon Henry flooded my mind like an on coming ocean-tide. In those few moments it took to walk past their house, in my mind, I had traveled from childhood to now. The experience was exhilarating, to say the least.

"I really miss the peeps on this block," Jerome said, as he took a deep breath while continuing to hold my hand as we walked toward my house.

I was beginning to get tired, but I didn't want Jerome to worry about me. So I asked Jerome if we could stop in front of my grand-parents' former home, which was now a part of the church's property.

"Jerome, lets stop here for a moment, okay? I want to feel the love that always greets me when I sit or stand in front of this building," I huffed, attempting to disguise my growing fatigue.

"Anne what a great looking engagement ring you're wearing. When do you plan to make it a matching set?" Jerome asked, with a slight smile on his brown face. "I mean after all, what are you waiting on-the year 2050?"

"Now Jerome, let's be nice," I said, hoping Jerome would not prolong this conversation to the point where it became an irritant.

"Okay, okay, I'll drop the subject, but you know I only want the very best for you," Jerome said, as he held my chin up with his large well manicured long fingers.

"Have you gotten all the rest you need?" Jerome asked, as he looked at me, with eyes indicating he was on to my attempt to disguise interest in this old building for what was really my challenge-I needed rest from that short walk around the block!

"You know Jerome, there was a time I could walk forever and not get tired, but now I can't do that. I even rejoined the church's "Walker's Club in an effort to build up my strength, but still I tire easily," I said, as I held Jerome's arm for support in getting off the porch steps.

"Well, in due time you'll be stronger and able to resume your daily routine," Jerome said as he placed my left arm inside his right arm and we continued to walk the few yards home.

I was somewhat surprised that Jerome didn't mention my ignoring the doctor's warning about *"corrective surgery!"* I knew he and everyone else had been talking about it. As we approached the steps leading to my house, I almost brought up the subject, but quickly decided against it. I was sure Jerome, would in due time, broach the subject soon.

The next morning we got up at three-thirty a. m. to prepare ourselves for the long ride to Rochelle's graduation. Charles decided to drive, while Jerome and I took on the role of passengers. Jerome sat in the front seat with Charles. I sat in the back seat.

"Would either of you like a turkey sandwich?" I asked as I prepared to eat one of the several sandwiches Sara Mae made for us.

"No thank you, I am still trying to down the big breakfast your mother made for us," Jerome said, sounding as if he were about to say something more.

"Nothing for me Anne, not while I'm driving, maybe later on-okay," Charles said as he continued to drive.

"Anne, what made Sara Mae change her mind about accompanying us to Rochelle's graduation?" Jerome said.

"Oh, she said something about the long ride hurting her back," I replied as I continued eating my sandwich. "You know, people do what they want to do, when they want to do it-right?"

"I guess," said Jerome as he continued looking out the window at the inviting multi-colors Mother Nature provided in the on-coming picture post-card landscape.

"I really think she over indulged herself, when others and she successfully got the state reps to cut down on the number of state mandated student tests. She also worked hard in getting them to increase the amount of pay to the teachers in the state. As a result, they project better prepared teachers will be more willing to teach our young folk. By the way, Sara Mae and her group discovered that the two white accounting firms in charge of administering the state-wide tests to teachers were cheating on behalf of some white folk. They were giving advance copies of the tests to the white folk. Upon testimony from some people, several hundreds of the tests were unaccounted for before the test exams were given. Americans of African Descent, who had graduated first in their classes in college, were now finding themselves barely able to pass these tests! White teachers, who had graduated from lesser prestigious institutions and who maintained lower grades while in college, were now receiving perfect scores on these state-wide written tests! Some folk are going to jail and some contracts aren't going to be renewed as a result of this well-documented injustice. Sara Mae is always going around the house saying-"we are in a war for the souls of our little black children; something has to be done to save them!"

"Good for Sara Mae and others like her" Charles exclaimed, still focusing on his driving us to our destination.

"I'm proud of Sara Mae, may she continue, to stand-up for our young," Jerome said, turning to look at me.

"Charles, are you going to tell Anne now or wait until the return trip?" Jerome asked, looking lovingly at his partner.

"Tell me what? What are you talking about Jerome?" What is he talking about Charles?"

"I am a survivor of child abuse...I was raped by a black detective when I was nine years old. This went on well into my teen years. He threatened to hurt me if I told of his abuse towards me. He said that my parents wouldn't believe what I told them. The dog, also said the authorities might have my parents thrown in jail for child neglect."

"Initially I experienced emotional, spiritual, and physical pain. These feelings began to lessen during my teen years. On my nineteenth birthday, the bottom dropped out of my young, joyful, and impressive life. The detective stopped all contact with me. I began to brood. I fell into a state of depression. My parents were at their wits ends attempting to help me pull out of my "deep funk." Not telling them about my secret rendezvous and *other life,* only added to the mounting guilt building up in my soul."

"One year later, my parents and I traveled to Iowa to visit my Aunt Irene. My aunt had prepared dinner for us one Sunday evening. She told us that my cousin Kirk had befriended a newly arrived detective. It appeared the detective had turned my cousin's long standing maladaptive behavior around to that of an *upstanding citizen.*"

"When the detective entered the house I broke into a cold sweat. I became sick and excused myself from the room. The one year of healing, came tumbling down. I fell into a depressed state again. For some reason-be it envy, rage, hate, rekindled love, or what, I informed my parents, aunt, and uncle about my past relationship with this detective. My father and uncle contacted the police commander about the situation. My aunt notified the juvenile authorities."

"My mother's interaction with me became unstable at best. Some days she hugged me until I thought I would lose my breath. Then, there were those days when she would give me the silent treatment. The days of silence were the worse days. The detective had been fired from his job in Iowa, but for some reason beyond me, he was allowed to leave the state without any consequences. Mother began to suffer frequent crying spells. She withdrew from my father altogether. She even slept in our guest room until she died of a sudden and massive heart attack. Until that time Mom was "*as healthy as she could be!*"

"My mother's sudden death did little to bring my father and me together. We grew very distant as father and son, so much so, that one day, I up and moved out of the house. I never had contact with my father again. My life after that was full of guilt, confusion, rage, and loss, you name it! I spent several years in and out of public run counseling sessions. Then I discovered God, and life began a turn for the better. I received a scholarship and completed college. I met Jerome and now I must meet "the dragon" again!"

"Meet the dragon again? What does that mean Charles?" I asked as I rested my chin on the back of the front seat.

"When Jerome and I moved to Detroit, I discovered that the detective is now a "higher up" on the police force. The detective is still having sex with under-aged boys." Charles said, as tears began to roll down his cheeks.

Jerome asked Charles to pull over so he could drive.

As Jerome continued driving us toward my daughter's graduation, I could hear Charles snoring. I couldn't help but relate to Charles' emotionally riddled life. I began to weep silently.

About five miles from the college, we encountered a detour, which caused us to drive some ten miles out of our way. Well sir, another delay in my already "delayed life!"

Finally arriving on campus, we were greeted by Rochelle and two of her friends.

"Mom what took you so long to get here, I thought you were due here about an hour ago?" Rochelle asked us as we were gathering luggage to take into the house.

"Good evening Uncle Jerome and Charles. How are all three of you doing?" I said to Rochelle in a rather corrective tone. "Girl, please show some kind of proper home rearing."

"Sorry mom, are you three okay? I was beginning to worry about you," Rochelle asked as she and her two male friends began to taking our bags. "Mom, Uncles Charles and Jerome, please meet two of my best friends, Willie and Aaron, we share this house together. It saved us a whole lot of cash and worry," Rochelle said, looking straight at me.

"Oh, I didn't know you had roommates Rochelle, and I certainly did not know they were two males," I said, surprising even myself at how rapidly the words came out of my mouth.

"Yes Mother, but don't worry, both Willie and Aaron are "partners." Besides, we have all been respectful of each other since we've been living here," Rochelle said, in a rather perfunctory manner.

"Good evening Miss Palermo, I'm Willie Brown and this is my partner Aaron Goods, welcome to our home," Willie Brown said to me as he took my bag and led us up the walkway into the spacious house.

"Thank you kind sir, I'm Jerome and this is my partner Charles, thank you for allowing us a stay in your home." Are the two of you graduating tomorrow?"

"Yes sir," said Aaron as he grabbed Willie around the waist, "our parents are in town also, but they decided to stay in a hotel down-town."

Jerome looked at Charles and me. He then smiled and took a seat in the front-room of the spacious Victorian. Charles took a seat beside Jerome.

"Please, don't sit, let us show you to your rooms," Rochelle said, all the time keeping her eyes on me, knowing she and I had to have our "mother-daughter talk about her not telling me of her living arrangement.

After the three of us had settled down, Jerome, Charles and I met in the upstairs hall-way. Jerome asked me to wait until Rochelle and I were alone to have our little chat. I promised I would. After the three of us washed-up, we met our hosts in the dining-room for dinner.

After dinner, the men decided to play a couple of hands of bid-whist. Rochelle and I sat on the front steps.

"Rochelle, I know why you didn't tell me about your living with two men, and just how long did you think this could be hidden from me?"

"Mother, I knew that you'd attempt to talk me out of this move, so I made the decision last year without informing you. I haven't been promiscuous while staying with my two friends. *Don't worry mother, I'm still a virgin!* Willie and Aaron have been respectful since I've been living here. Besides, they have convinced me to enter the field of medicine. I've been accepted at Howard University, provided I take two more science classes and receive at least a B-grade or higher in both of them. Thank goodness I had a strong general education background in the sciences before I got this far in college," Rochelle, said.

"So you are not going to become a…"

"No, mother, I want to become a pediatric specialist. I want to educate the world about the folly of bad eating habits and therefore prevent some of the needless sicknesses in our babies," Rochelle said rather emphatically.

"I see…!"

"Will Willie and Aaron's parents be attending the graduation?" I asked, now feeling more at ease about Rochelle's living arrangement.

"Yes, yes indeed they wouldn't miss it for the world. They are very old-fashioned, but loving parents. Not unlike you, they too love their children, and will not tolerate my two buddies sleeping together," Rochelle said, quickly standing and walking toward the screen-door.

"And I guess I'm not so old-fashioned and am now a member of "the contemporary mothers of the century club"-yes?" I said, maintaining a tight smile and following my precious daughter into the Victorian framed house. *Child please!*

Later on that evening, Willie and Aaron went into the kitchen to wash the dinner dishes. Rochelle tidied up the down-stairs, and said she would see us in the morning at graduation. Charles, Jerome, and I went upstairs to our rooms. When we got to the top of the stairs, Jerome said to me, "I am so proud of your having such a mature understanding of the living arrangements in this house!"

"Jerome, don't press your luck, good night!" I replied entering my bedroom without smiling.

"Good night sweet pea, don't let the bed bugs bite," Jerome and Charles jokingly said to me.

The next morning, I became a mass of fingers. I couldn't get my hair to look the way I wanted them to look. I couldn't fix my face the way I wanted, and last, but not least, I was beginning to feel over-whelmed, as I sat in a chair in the room unable to get it together, Willie happened to pass by the room. Willie was a tall six-foot four, light brown skinned brother weighing in at a buck ninety-five pounds and his hair was locked. The brother had hazel eyes beneath long eye lashes, generous pink lips, framed by a full mustache, and a neat sandy colored goatee. The boy's body looked as though he had been body building his entire young life. His voice was so soothing.

"Having trouble with those locks Miss Palermo, want some help?"

Before I could say a word, Willie was attending to my hair, applying my make-up to my face, and a deep massage to my shoulder area. The brother was good.

"There now, that should do it. Miss Palermo you might want to try some of this for your locks next time," Willie said, handing me a jar of pure coconut oil he had been using on his shoulder length locks. "Aaron and I wouldn't use anything else. It really keep yours locks looking in top shape all day long."

"Thanks Willie, you've been a god-send!"

Just then Aaron's voice could be heard coming down the hall. Willie directed him to my room.

"Righteous, there you are. Good morning, Miss Palermo. Willie we had better get to the ceremony. You and Rochelle know we are due there at least forty-five minutes before everyone else! Let's get going!" Aaron motioned for Willie to come out of my room and prepare to leave the house.

Aaron was somewhat shorter than Willie and was a dark brown-skinned muscular man. One could tell he was the manager of the household.

Like Jerome and Charles, these two brothers didn't fit your stereotypical, media hype of, gay brothers. As a matter of fact, had they not said a word and just gone about their business, nothing would have suggested they were *gay!*

Taking our seats in the large auditorium at the graduation ceremony, we noticed that we were seated next to the only few black folks in the place. We soon discovered that they were the parents, friends, and relatives of Willie and Aaron. We shared our mutual pride in our children's feats while waiting for the program to begin.

After the graduation ceremonies, we all met in the President's Dining Hall for an evening meal. Willie and Aaron, in addition to dancing with each other at the affair, danced with other males and females in the room. Rochelle was having a wonderful time on the dance floor. It appeared that most of the boys in the room were dancing with her. Since the school had a majority white student body, these ten black students were highly visible. While the atmosphere among the people in the room was friendly, both Willie and Aaron's parents were most uncomfortable at seeing their sons *"behave in such an uncommon manner." While I must admit, I too was not used to such in-your-face shenanigans, I decided to follow Jerome and Charles' lead and-cool it.*

The next morning Jerome, Charles, and I drove back to Spring Oaks. Rochelle was scheduled to come home in three days. She had to complete her last days of work-study.

"Anne, how are you holding out?" Charles asked, as he craned his neck over the back of the front seat only to see tears rolling down my cheeks, onto my lips, past my chin, and into my tear soaked lap.

"Yes, I'm alright, I'm just thinking how blessed I am," I said, as I began to wipe my eyes with a napkin.

"Oh heck, I thought you were going to say how blessed you were to have two wonderful friends like Jerome and me," Charles said, attempting to make light of my tearful exhibition.

"Oh boy shut-up, you know how every day I thank God for the love that you and Jerome have shown me. Why what would I do without the two of you in my life?" I joked as I leaned forward to plant a kiss on Charles' and Jerome's cheeks. *What would I have done without the two of them?*

"What strange and new adventure have you been working on lately dear Jerome?" I asked having regained my composure.

"Well let's see, last Friday we met with some state reps in order to discuss giving rubbers to the men in our penal institutions. Some state officials feel that doing so, only encourages "homosexual behavior!" Others and I feel that as a preventive move, prophylactics are the only way to go. We feel that since men are having sex with each other in these institutions, why not at least save their lives while they are housed in these prisons."

"Until we have defeated H.I.V./AIDS, some caring folk must demonstrate good sense and compassion in this matter. Without the measure we are proposing, a lot of brothers and sisters are going to be statistics," Jerome said as he continued to get us to our destination.

"Can you imagine someone being so callous as to allow the spread of such a dreaded disease in and among such a captive group?" I asked.

"A group of black pastors are lending their support in this effort also. They are having their congregations contact their representatives to voice the need for rubbers being passed out in jails," Jerome said.

"You know, I never could understand why this country does not place more emphasis on PREVENTION instead of always being so CRISIS ORIENTATED," Charles said, looking at Jerome.

"The system does not promote prevention because there would be a loss of too many jobs in this country. Just think of the number of people employed due to crime in this country. There'd be fewer: judges, social workers/counselors, criminal justice case-workers prison guards, court reporters, lawyers, criminal court buildings, black men and women placed in jail, and on and on. I was told three days ago that each prison cell costs in the range of some tens of hundreds of thousands of hard earned dollars to build," Jerome said, as his voice began to display more anger with each word he uttered. "PREVENTION" is such a nasty word in the minds of those who would have the need to be greedy. Prevention cuts out the need for the number so many doctors, law-makers, nurses, and other public health people. No, Charles and good lady Anne, prevention is a mountain that only a few wish to climb and conquer."

"Prevention saves lives and that includes you Miss Anne," Jerome said, as he looked into his rear-view mirror catching my eye and my attention.

"Um," I said, knowing full well that his words were aimed at my unwillingness to have an operation. "Well we are almost home. Boy, will I be glad to get home and get out of these clothes," I said, in order to break the silence that was a direct result of my not taking a preventive stance on my health.

Arriving home, we were met by friends and family members. They all wanted us to share with them the news of Rochelle's graduation.

The next morning Hori and I drove Jerome and Charles to the airport. Before they boarded the plan to Detroit, prayers were said in support of Charles' effort to bring the detective to justice. We also prayed with

Jerome in his fight for to litigate the many issues these days!

On our return from the airport Hori renewed his wish to get married. Having no real excuse for further delaying our marriage, we settled on a June date. At that moment a strange feeling came over me when I agreed to become Mrs. Anne Marie Palermo-Brown. On the one hand, I was relieved to finally make some sort of move on the matter. My thoughts appeared to be somewhat clearer as a result of setting a date to get married. It was as though a cloud had been lifted. While I was experiencing these thoughts, that nagging element of doubt could be seen raising its ugly head in the distance. What could be so wrong in my marrying such a fine brother as Hori?

By September, I had returned to work on a part-time basis. Rochelle had moved to Washington D. C. to attend medical school. Roger was doing well at New York City University. I was feeling much stronger, thanks in part to the attention and care giving of friends like Miss Peach, Ant Boo and other folks in the neighborhood. I had returned to the choir, but had to take a leave of absence from other duties at the church. The few classes taken over the summer semester enabled me to register for the last couple of classes I needed to graduate. The only other hurdle now was a written senior project. My advisor and I agreed the project could be accomplished soon.

I had begun to lose weight as a result of my hospitalization. Lately, I began to smile more. The fear that had lodged in my spirit was beginning to disappear. I began to return to a full night's sleep and I was more willing to face the on-coming days, and what used to be dreadful, nights.

"Hey Anne Marie, I hear tell you're getting married, why hasn't Sara Mae or someone told someone about this yet?" Ish asked as he entered the shop.

"Good morning Ish, yes, I am getting married next June and you're invited to the wedding," I said, grabbing the large sack of clothes he had placed on the counter. I tagged them and placed them in a basket on the floor. "The usual, and do you want them starched light or heavy this time?"

"For heavens sake, come on Anne Marie, why so dry with your uncle Ish, don't be so thick, lighten up a little. Let's bury the past. After all, we are kin folk you know?" Ish said with that half snake eating grin on his face.

"Ish, I have too many things to do today and a very short time to do them. Now, I would appreciate you answering my question about your laundry," I said, pulling a pencil and pad from under the counter. As my hand landed on the counter, Ish took one giant-step away from the counter.

"Okay, okay, I can take a hint. I'm sorry I didn't come to see you while you were in the hospital, but you were in my prayers Anne Marie," Ish said, sounding a lot more sincere. "Did you know I joined African Baptist last month? I haven't seen you there in a while, Anne?"

If you were truly there, all you had to do is look up at the choir, SIR!

"Here is your receipt, your clothes will be ready this coming Wednesday, have a blessed day," I said as I lifted the basket filled with Ish's garments and handed them to the folk in the back room.

Immediately after Ish walked out, Mr. Alphonso walked into the shop with his son and another man. For some reason we had established a very close relationship. His son had become less "stand-offish" toward me. He even shared a few clean jokes with me. I thought it strange that he refused to give me his last name-he always insisted that I call him MR. ALPHONSO.

"Well baby, far be it from me to insult a customer, after all, "The customers are always right.""

"My son has some suits he would like you to clean and press for him," Mr. Alphonso said, signaling his son to step closer to the counter.

"Miss Anne, will you clean and press these four suits? However, before you do that, I'd like to have two suits made," Angelo said to me. "I plan to spend time in the sun for about a week. Can you make me two suits like the ones on this page?"

He handed me a men's magazine that had two male models standing on the deck of an ocean liner. The suits were very fashionable and expensive looking. As I stood studying the pages, he handed me some very costly silk material.

After I finished measuring him for the suits, another gentleman stepped closer to the counter and made a similar request for suits to be made. He wanted his suits made from some very fine linen material.

Just as I was completing the other man who had accompanied Mr. Alphonso, Mr. Alphonso began pulling out his wallet. He asked me how much I was charging for the three of them. He always paid in advance and he always left a generous tip. Mr. Alphonso had referred several customers from the surrounding area to my shop. To be more precise, that month, twenty-five new customers were informed of my *"excellent tailoring and dress making skills" by Papa Alphonso*. Money, money, money, and more money I always say! Oh the power of money!

With the exception of attending Morning Service at African Baptist, spending time with Hori was my "safe place" on Sundays. Whether we were found: cuddling in each other's arms, attending to our individual tasks in the presence of each other's company, looking out at the evening sky or watching television, watching the events on the streets from the porch, or enjoying the pleasure and warmth of each. *Hori was my safe place.* He was a harbor away from the impending storms that might come into my life.

One evening while we were sitting on the balcony of Hori's condo, which over-looked the river; he and I began to share newer insights about each other.

"Anne, I always wanted to marry a woman who was even tempered, loving, God-fearing, and had a high degree of independence. Not only do you fit the bill, but you are a good looking sister to boot. I love the kinks in your raven hair. Your lips are as exciting to me as they could ever be. Your voice is as soothing as the flow of water running along a fresh green landscape. Your mothering skills are to be envied by most women. While I love your independence, I yet find you fragile and in need of a strong hand- and I pray that I'm that appendage when you need it," Hori said, as we sat in an over-sized lawn chair together.

"Hori, all my life I wanted someone besides my children to call my own. While, I have a great support system, something is always eluding my basic needs. Yes, God has been that which has kept me from that feeling of being totally alone. However, that physical need yet creeps in and nags at the core of my being. Hori I'm sure glad you're in my life. Before I met you, I felt like a pot full of boiling water about to spill onto a hostile surface. I felt that after I boiled over, all that'd be left of me would be that of a scorched pot," I confessed to Hori, as I snuggled into his muscular body. "Look at the time! I have to get home. It's time for Roger and Rochelle to call. I'd better freshen up and get home. Thanks for the lovely meal; I really enjoyed the home-made pie and ice-cream, may I take some home?"

"Sure, you may," Hori said, kissing me on the cheek and then helping me to my feet.

As I rushed from the balcony to the bathroom I happened to brush against an open door to one of the cabinets in Hori's dining-room. In my attempt not to be a "busy body," I quickly closed the door. *I didn't know Hori had so much liquor in the house-wow!*

"Hi Mom, how are you? I called you earlier, but no one answered," Roger said.

"You called earlier, lets see, yes I know now, I was visiting Hori. I got home a little late, but I am glad you called back Roger. I really enjoy our getting together. Are you eating like you should in New York City?"

"Sure mom, I eat like a pig, you know that," Roger said. "I spoke to Rochelle last night. She seems to be doing well. Willie and Aaron had just walked her home from studying in the library when I spoke with her. Aaron and Willie managed to enroll in a near-by university a few miles away."

"Well, let's not tie the phone up too long. She'll be calling me soon. You know she's not the most patient person in the world. When she makes one attempt to call and you're not home, Rochelle moves on to the next task," I said, as I began pulling off my clothes in order to retire for the evening. Well, dear, Mother loves you and I'll keep you in my prayers. By the way, everyone here sends love your way. Did you receive the money Sara Mae sent you?"

"Yes, I did and I sent her a thank you card this morning."

"Take care of yourself and stay near the arch of safety son!"

"Love you Mom!"

I walked upstairs to my bedroom. As I was about to kneel and say my prayers, the phone rang. It was Rochelle.

"Hi Mother, what's going on there?"

"Fine, everything is just fine baby girl. Rochelle, are you feeling alright, you sound a little tired. I hope you aren't over doing it in D. C?" I asked her as I got off my knees and sat on the bed.

"Yes, I'm feeling quite well mother. So far I have managed to stay on top of my eighteen credit hours. If I sound a little down, it's because I have been working my "well, you know off," Rochelle said, sounding as if she could hardly get another sentence out.

"I won't keep you baby child, I just wanted to hear your voice. Thanks for calling me. I too am a little bushed this evening," I said, trying not to yawn.

"Keep the faith Mother Dear and remember that I love you. Say hello to everyone for me. Oh, I received some money from Sara Mae, I'll send her a thank you card tomorrow," Rochelle said.

"Please do, I don't want to hear her mouth regarding how today's children are so ungrateful. Take care and stay with God daughter."

THE WEDDING DAY/FINAL DAYS

My advisor and I agreed my senior project could be completed by the close of the term. She had approved my outline and given the okay to proceed with the twenty page senior paper. By mid-March I had completed my project, but I decided to wait until the last week of school to give it to Ms. Palmer.

Ant Boo and Miss Peach began attending to the wedding details. This included the design of my gown. At first the big issue was what color should the wedding-gown should be. We agreed I shouldn't wear anything white! Miss Peach suggested I wear an off-white or cream- colored gown. Ant Boo felt whatever the color; the material should be silk and satin. When I brought up the idea of the gown being made of a print with Mother Africa on it, well, you would have thought I had lost my mind and committed a crime. As a matter of fact Miss Peach asked me if I had lost *my ever-loving mind!*

I finally decided to get married in a black off-the-shoulder dress. It was a beautiful form-fitting silk gown, with the bodice to the waist. The dress would have a slight flare just below the waist. My few bride-maids would wear sky blue dresses. Hori will wear a black tuxedo with a rounded lapel. The wedding ceremony would have Hori and me jumping the broom. We were going to recite original wedding vows that we had made-up. Pastor Newbreed would then pronounce us married. Of course Jerome would sing two songs befitting the occasion. My sister Minnie, Sister Newbreed, and Rochelle would serve as brides-maids. One of Hori's colleagues and one close friends as well as Charles would act as groomsmen.

You can imagine how challenging it was to get Ant Boo and the Peach, as we sometimes called Miss Peach, to understand such a "radical form of wedding attire." While these two sisters weren't totally sold on such an idea, they did love me, and as such supported me in my wedding plans. Sara Mae was surprisingly quiet about the whole matter-Praise the Lord! Though she was amazingly reticent about the issue, she was most cooperative in whatever she was asked to perform. At each rehearsal I was tempted to ask Sara Mae what her thoughts were concerning the wedding proceedings, but all thanks be to God for the presence of mind not to tread on such shaky ground. Sara Mae and I didn't pass one negative word between each other since she questioned me in the hospital about my *"need for an operation."*

The whole church was abuzz about the wedding. Folk who never before spoke to me, were talking about "my wedding!" Everyone in the surrounding area now wanted to contribute something to *my grand affair!?*

"Good morning, Anne Marie, how are you this morning? I'm told you are getting married, is this true?" Mrs. Hightower asked, as she entered my shop and placed her expensive hand-bag on the front counter.

"Why, yes, Mrs. Hightower, it is true, I am getting married this coming June."

"Surely, you won't forget to invite George, Crystal and me to your wedding?" Mrs. Hightower said with a surprisingly loving tone to her voice. Most of the time she entered the store, she was all business. She responded the same when we met in church. Miss Peach referred to her behavior as being; "Miss Nice Nasty" to those she considered beneath her socio-economic group.

"Now, Mrs. Hightower, why would I forget to invite your lovely family, Mrs. Hightower! "I said, with a strained smile on my face. *Talk about being nice nasty, I'll show you how to be nice nasty!*

"Good, then that does that, George and I are going to take a nice jaunt to the Motherland just before your wedding. I'll be sure to bring you something elegant from the land of our fore-fathers," Mrs. Hightower said, as she took her receipt, turned, and walked out of the store.

"Miss Palermo, the brother from Ghana called and said he was having trouble reaching the fabric makers. He's doing his best to get that material for your wedding gown before the end of this month," Cherri, one of my employees, said to me as she approached the counter to wait on a customer.

"Dear God, what's next?" I exclaimed, as I began my day at the shop.

At the end of the day Hori came by the store. He said his parents regretfully would not be able to attend the wedding.

"Hori would you hand me that stack of catalogs off that table in the corner?"

"Anne, did you hear me, my parents will not be able to attend the wedding, "Hori said, as he stood facing me waiting for a response to his "groundbreaking news!"

"Hori, what else is new? Now, will you please pass me those three catalogs," I said, as I prepared to close the shop for the evening.

Hori was disappointed and so was I about his parents not attending the wedding, but I was too tired to put any more energy into the matter. After all, there are those issues I can control and then there are those that I can't. Given Hori's parents had only sent one word of greeting to me since our first and last meeting-how could I be surprised at their not attending our wedding? Poor Hori, he looked so dejected.

We drove to the house in dead silence. Hori was most disappointed and did not know how to introduce the subject of his parents' ill-will towards me into our conversation. I decided not to re-introduce the subject as we drove to my house. Besides, I had too much on my plate at the time. Hori would have to deal with his family's dysfunctional behavior himself.

As we parked in front of my house, I noticed a tear fall from Hori's handsome face.

"Hori, what is it, do you want to talk about it?" I finally asked, fearing at that moment, I had allowed this situation to go on too long without saying something.

"Anne, all my life I've attempted to please my parents. However, in return, all they've given me is a lot of grief. They're never satisfied with what I choose to do with my d—life. They have never wanted me to become a biologist, no; they wanted their son to be a great medical surgeon. What's wrong with doing what that little voice inside you says you should be?" Hori sobbed.

"Hori, go ahead and cry. Get it all out of your system, let it all out Sweetie," I said, attempting to give some comfort to my future husband.

"My parents have never told me that they loved me. Why, they've never even so much as spanked me, let alone given me a hug," Hori continued, as he grabbed the steering wheel with both hands. His whole body began to shake un-controllably.

I began to cry also.

"Hori, do you want to come in and eat something? A bite to eat might do you a world of good," I said, as I placed my arms around him and gave him a hug.

"No, Anne, if you don't mind, I'll tough this one out and drive back to the house," Hori said, adjusting himself and getting out of the car to escort me to the front of the house.

After a long kiss and our saying good night to each other several times, Hori returned to his car, he did not drive off immediately. He sat there for a little while, then, he sped off like a race car driver.

"What's the matter with that boy?" Miss Peach whispered from across the yard.

"Oh, Miss Peach, you startled me," I said, as I turned and walked to the edge of her porch. "Hori was just getting rid of some excess baggage; he'll feel better later on this evening."

"Excess baggage? Well sir! Excess baggage indeed!" Miss Peach mocked.

I often wanted to question Miss Peach about her obtuse remarks regarding my relationship with Hori, but something deep within prevented me from treading on such slippery slopes. Why could I not ask her what she really thought about Hori and me marrying? And most importantly, why has *the Peach* not confronted me about what appears to me, her misgivings about me getting married to Hori. Any other time she would not have held back! What did she see in Hori that I could not see – what was it?

"Anne, do you believe the brain can see as well as interpret?" the Peach asked me as she leaned over her porch railing.

"I don't really know Miss peach," I said very cautiously, wondering what if anything the question had to do with anything relating to Hori and me.

"Well, baby, the brain can see and the older I get, the more I'm convinced of this. Sometimes I see stuff that if I were to share it with others, I would be viewed as more of a freak than is often said of me," Miss Peach confided, as I began to notice the rays from the street-light catching the top of her silvery gray head. She then turned around, walked to her front door, and entered her house. "Good night baby, go with the "All" in whatever you do!"

"Get in here dog. Anne Marie wasn't talking to you! Mercy me!"

I hate it when Miss Peach becomes so secretive about concerns that are so close to my heart. Why couldn't I confront her about this thing?

The next day Hori phoned the shop. He wanted to speak with me. He sounded very anxious. He offered to bring lunch for the both of us.

"Greetings, Hori, I'll be with you in a minute," I said, as I hurried to complete the last stitch on a pair of pant.

As I walked out of the backroom, I noticed how Hori's hands were shaking. He appeared to have a rather tight smile on his face.

"Hey there, kind Sir, what brings you to this neck of the woods at twelve noon?" I asked, as I came from behind the counter and gave Hori a kiss on his cheek.

"Anne, you won't believe what happened to me. The Centers for Disease Control has invited me to take on one of their top positions. This is a once in a life time chance for someone in my field. Just think what it will mean to us?" Hori said, as he looked at me somewhat hesitatingly. We won't have to move until a few months after our wedding. This way you will have enough time to close the shop and set-up in Atlanta."

"Wait, wait, wait...!" I said, barely able to catch my breath and comprehend what this would mean in its total resolve.

"Anne, I know I didn't share this plan with you earlier, but my parents and I agreed on it this past February, when I interviewed for the position. Why I didn't let you know about it before now, well…, I thought, just in case I didn't get the job…I didn't want to worry you?" Hori said, as he began to hold my hands.

"But did you want to worry your parents about your securing the position!" I blurted out, sounding angrier as the conversation continued. "Hori Brown, just listen to what you just said, you shared a most personal decision with your parents'…, but not the woman you are going to marry in the next few months!" Now how do you think I feel about such news?" I replied, attempting not to raise my voice any louder than it had already become.

Hori looked at me, pulled me close to him, and we embraced in the middle of the shop.

"Hori let's take a walk," I said, as I grabbed my coat off the rack and headed toward the front door of the shop.

"But Sweetness, it's cool outside," Hori said, walking toward the door in order to allow for my rushed exit.

"That's okay Hori. I need some cool air at this juncture-SWEETNESS!" I said, as I swiftly walked past him and exited outside into the brisk sunny winds of March.

We walked past several people we knew. When we got to the corner, Hori said, "Anne, please don't be angry with me, I didn't mean to be a sneak about this …My singular thought was about making you happy. I thought you would be happy being married to a man with such stature. I meant you no disrespect in this matter. Can you, will you please forgive me if I've caused you any discomfort?"

"Hori, my only observation and hope is that from now on, you realize I will be Mrs. Anne Marie Palermo-Brown. We'll have to be open to each other's goals, thoughts, and dreams-no matter what may come into our lives. As your partner, I expect to come before anyone else in your life-God not withstanding! While I understand your relationship with your parents is important to you, brother, you are your own man and as such, well…" I said, feeling a little bit calmer with each step I took walking down the cold, hard lifeless sidewalk of the business district.

Walking always seemed to clear my head and give me a new outlook on whatever I was dealing with at the time.

"Hori, and as far as my moving to Atlanta, well, I will need some time to gather my thoughts about that. I'll need more time than you might think regarding this issue," I said, dreading to deal with this new chink in our relationship. "Hori, I'll no doubt move to Atlanta, but not as soon as you or I might think I can or should."

"Anne, again, I never meant to cause us any hardship," Hori said. "It's just that I'll be making a lot of money and well…" Hori paused and gave me a hug as we continued our walk.

"Hori, the couture shop is a-dream-come-true for me. I have come too far to just drop it and walk off into the sunset. No Hori, I will have to move to Atlanta after you settle things there!" I said, sounding surer of what I wanted out of this partnership.

"That's what I had in mind Anne. We will get married, and I'll fly back and forth to Spring Oaks until we secure a space in Atlanta for your shop. I'm sure you'll take Atlanta by storm with your designs and craftsmanship," Hori said, sounding more relieved that he had convinced me of his desire to marry me and that I was sold on his idea.

"Atlanta? Who do I know in Atlanta other than Hori?" I thought. All that I know and love will not be in Atlanta, Georgia!"

The news of my impending move south spread quickly and was greeted with mixed emotions from those I love so dearly.

"Gal, why can't Hori find a job in this area after you marry? Why do you have to close your shop and follow him?" Ant Boo said to me as she was preparing a fourth fruit pie for the church's bake sale.

"And guess what, the brother didn't let her know he was interviewing for the job!" I over-heard Miss Peach defiantly state as she was helping Ant Boo finish up the last touches on the double chocolate frosted cake. Sometimes I think these brothers feel they are back in the Cavemen Days in Europe where they can just drag a sister around by her braids and make them do their bidding at will. C-H-I-L-D, please!" Miss Peach said.

"Well, I thank you and Ant Boo for that great meal. I must be getting home now," I said, not wanting to get into a pissing match with these two sisters about my private life.

Jerome and Charles, though cautious about the move, did extend their very best to me in whatever I decided to do.

Roger and Rochelle were also in full support of my move to Georgia.

Sara Mae, on the other hand, pointed to "Hori's sneakiness!" She told me to duly notify the Negro that I was not going to tolerate any such future acts. Ms. Turner advised me to nip this kind of behavior in the bud-pronto! Sara Mae asked if I wanted her to have a talk with Hori and set him straight! Of course I declined her kind offer.

For the few weeks left in April, I was as nervous as a bad woman attending a fortune teller's convention. I began to tire easily. My visit to the doctor only confirmed the immediate need for an operation. I agreed to have corrective surgery as soon as Hori and I returned from our honeymoon.

In the meantime life for me was filled with the usual high speed daily tasks. My customer load was such that I was strongly considering taking an immediate break. Decisions, decisions, decisions!

The church always held a memorial service for those who transcended this earth. The event was held on either the third or fourth Sunday in May. The Holocaust Memorial Service had been a tradition of the church for some one-hundred sixty years. In that service we honored our fore-parents, especially those who left Mother Africa via the international slave-trade's "Middle Passage Era!" The service was a new experience for pastor Newbreed and his family. Beginning another year at the church, he convinced the Trustee and Deacon Boards to have a two-day program with most of the speakers coming from the various countries in Mother Africa. Attendance at these occasions had become so large, the boards decided to hold next year's affair at our twenty-thousand seat church operated, community center in Down-town Spring Oaks.

"Good-evening sisters," Mother Times said to Miss Peach and me as we walked into the Holocaust Service. "Sister Peach, God told me to ask you again to join us on the Mother's Board!"

"Well Sister Times, until the Great All tells me the same thing, you will just have to wait a w-e-e bit longer," Miss Peach said, as she directed her famous "go on about your business and leave mine alone smile" towards Mother Times.

As Mother Times walked ahead of us, Miss Peach turned to me and said "Child…, I know too much to become a member of such a slow set of sisters. Now what would a sister with my knowledge and skills be doing with a group like that?"

Miss Peach and I took our seats next to Ant Boo.

After a two hour service of emotional highs, the four of us walked out of the church. We were drained and yet filled with a renewed insight into the beauty of Mother Africa.

"Billie, what are you and Henry going to do tomorrow evening? Anne and I are going to attend a movie in the city. Come join us," Miss Peach asked Ant Boo and Deacon Henry.

"No, we can't Peach. The Trustee and Deacon Boards are in charge of tomorrow's Holocaust Memorial Service, and I volunteered to help serve the meal. I really think we should have used a catering service for the two days instead of the one day," Ant Boo said as she and Deacon Henry excused themselves and walked towards their house. They were holding hands like two newlyweds.

"Miss Peach, do you want to come in and have some ice-cream with me?" I asked.

"No baby, I ate too much at church, I think I'll take it on in and prepare for tomorrow. You know a girl has to get her beauty rest these days," Miss Peach said as she began to climb the steps to her home.

As I was about to enter the house, I heard a strange sound coming from the end of the porch. As I quickly turned in the direction of the noise, I caught sight of Sara Mae sitting alone in the swing.

"Good evening Anne. How was the Holocaust Memorial Service?" Sara Mae asked, placing a plate of food on the porch floor.

"Oh it was most moving and inspiring. I wish you could have been there," I said, taking a seat beside Sara Mae in the swing.

Sitting there, I began to see Sara Mae as I had never seen her before. She didn't have on the tons of make-up I had been accustomed to seeing on her stout face. The moonlight that flooded our porch gave off a sort of hallowed glow to her. She didn't appear as stern as she did in times past. She almost looked *saintly!?*

"Did you go on a date this evening?" I asked, hoping to elicit a chance in a life time civil conversation from this woman who prided herself on being my mother.

"No, I decided to stay home and just enjoy me for a change. You know Anne, baby, for the first time in my life I've begun to hear, see, and taste things differently. How in the world can this be?" Sara Mae asked, running her hands softly across my face.

After that brief laying on of hands experience, Sara Mae got up and walked into the house. I just sat there in sort of a daze, wondering "what next Lord!" Sara Mae had never shown such tenderness to me before. LORD!

By now, Minnie had returned to the house. She was there to support me and be a part of my wedding. She had earned a graduate degree and was engaged to a successful medical doctor. Though she had not been home for many years, she and I interacted as though she had never left the house where she was lovingly reared and protected. All those years of sisterly rivalry seemed to have never existed. She appeared to be at my every beck and call. At times she was just too supportive, but I decided to take the high road and enjoy these few weeks she and I would be in this house together. So the old saying is true, "time and God will bring about a change in due time." Wow, here we were sitting together sharing jokes, photos, gossip, and having a great time. We were actually showing genuine concern about each other. Ooo wee!

The week before the wedding, Hori and I were nervous wrecks. At times he and I didn't say a word to each other. We would just stand or sit hugging or touching each other. And when we did speak, we would assure each of our love and promised that it would last forever.

On Thursday, two days before the wedding, Ant Boo and Sara Mae hosted a bridal shower for me. While gathered among the sisters there it appeared to me that only once, maybe twice, was a party ever given in my honor. Since none of my closest friends were classmates, it had been a while since I felt so honored. This gathering did much to settle my frayed nerves. For the first time in my life I felt as though I really belonged to the community as a whole. These sisters didn't spare any costs in making this a grand affair. Many pictures were taken at the shower. This project was the combined effort of Sara Mae, Jerome, Ant Boo and Deacon Henry, and Miss Peach. The affair lasted well into the cool June evening. After everyone had gone home, I telephoned Hori. Not getting an answer from him, I decided that his bachelor party must have been too much for him to respond, so I prepared myself for bed.

The next day didn't bring any better success in my contacting Hori. Finally, late Friday evening, Jerome and Charles called me. They had reached Hori. Their voices appeared strange; it was as though they wanted to say more to me than they did. My main focus being on the wedding didn't allow myself to get involved in anything too negative. After all, this was the day that I had prayed for all my life, surely "the All" would honor this once in a life time dream.

The warm sun beams made the day of my wedding an even happier day for me.

One half-hour prior to the wedding, Jerome appeared at the door where we all were stationed. He appeared upset as he began talking with Ant Boo. They insisted on speaking in whispered tones to each other. Shortly thereafter, Ant Boo stepped out of the room. When she re-appeared, she seemed as upset as Jerome. While Minnie and Rochelle were addressing some last minute touches on me, I noticed that Ant Boo, Miss Peach, and Sara Mae began to huddle in a corner.

Fifteen minutes before the start of the wedding, I was told that Hori hadn't made it to the church yet. Feeling a sense of love and trust in Hori being a responsible brother, I decided to quietly sit in a corner of the now somewhat heated-room alone. After a while, Ant Boo walked into the room for what seemed like the tenth time. As she walked towards me, a feeling of dread crept over me. I began to feel sick.

What could be the problem now? Surely nothing serious had happened to my Hori?

"Anne, what is Hori's work phone number?" Ant Boo quietly asked me. She then gave me a kiss, as if to assure me that all was going well.

"Why, Ant Boo? Isn't Hori here yet?" I asked, feeling more and more anxious as I looked into her face and saw the sad looks of others in the room.

"Now, don't go getting yourself into a tizzy child. It appears Hori hasn't gotten here yet. We want to give him a jingle and find...Well, what's his number Anne?" Ant Boo asked as she copied the number and exited the room again.

As Ant Boo stepped out of the room, I saw the expression on Sara Mae's face turn from that of a loving and proud mother to one of pure-hatred. And her pacing the floor did little to calm the rest of us in the pea-sized room. Miss Peach sat in a chair across from me and thumbed through her well-worn black Bible. The gaiety that had earlier filled the room was fading into something more somber.

Pastor Newbreed came into the room at five-forty and asked me to step out in the hall-way. As I followed him into that rather wide area, the pastor asked how long he should keep the folk in the sanctuary waiting. He said someone should speak with the restaurant about the reception. We might be at least one-half hour past our original time getting there.

I asked Jerome to entertain the audience for about fifteen minutes more. I was holding out against all hope that Hori would appear. What could have happened to him? Where was he? Had anyone heard about any accidents on the radio or television? I began to feel faint. I felt as though I was going to vomit at any moment. How could I face these people? What would I say to them?

"Anne, it's time you say something to the people waiting out there." Ant Boo said. "Anne, do you hear me?" Ant Boo knocked on the washroom door. "Come on honey, I'll stand by your side if you want, but it's way past time, those folk have been more than patient, Dear."

As I opened the door to the rear of the sanctuary, I could feel and see the disappointed, confused, and sympathetic expressions on the faces of family and friends in attendance.

Sara Mae and Ant Boo walked with me to the front of the church. Pastor Newbreed had just spoken to the people in attendance, requesting they remain calm. He then presented me to those several hundred in the room.

"Well, folks, it looks like I have to wait another day to rehearse for my wedding," I said, attempting to put some levity in this most embarrassing situation. "It appears that my husband to be has lost..."

At that very moment, we heard a loud noise in the hallway that led to the entrance of the sanctuary. Whoever it was appeared to be drunk. He was being helped down the aisle by two of the deacons. He could barely walk and had to hold on to the pews for support.

Hori's name spread like wild-fire from the back of the church to the front where I was standing. I began to lean on the Communion Table. I felt a pain shoot through my body. Jerome, seeing that I was about to fall, caught me and placed a chair quickly under me.

My deepest fear had come true and was taking me down into that dreadful depressed place. Hori was drunk and had the nerve to bring his drunken ass into the church on this of all days. Well, it was just too much!

I sat there in total disbelief, hopelessly spinning into that dreaded depressed hole; I could only hear the screams and total pandemonium filling the room. Between the floods of tears covering my face, I could see three deacons restraining Sara Mae as she attempted to beat Hori on the top of his head with her fists. I heard Pastor Newbreed yelling at Jerome, begging him not to hit Hori again. A few moments after the people had heeded the pastor's pleas and I had somewhat regained my ragged composure, my eyes then fell on poor Hori. His nose was bleeding. His sweatsuit was covered with mud and he smelled of stale liquor. His hair was uncombed and his shoes were covered with grass stains. Child, believe me, he was a total mess. He slowly made his way down the aisle toward me. When he got halfway towards me, he yelled some inaudible sound and then fell on the floor and began crawling toward the front of the church. My whole body became numb. I wanted to turn and run out the back door. But I also wanted to know what possessed him to behave in such a disgraceful manner. I wanted to hug my baby!

"Anne Marie, I've failed you," Hori began to mumble as he fell to his knees, sobbing.

It was at that moment that I turned and ran to the back of the church, through the hall and out the back door of the building. I ran down the alley to the back-yard of my house.

When I entered the gate, it dawned on me that I did not have the keys to the house. Icky Boo's loud barking did little to calm my worn nerves. Quickly I remembered where Sara Mae kept a spare set of keys. Finding them, I entered the house through the rear door. Climbing the stairs to my bedroom, I found that each step was one of dread. I felt as though I was walking toward a prison cell. My breathing became labored as I navigated the stair-well. Arriving at the second floor and inches away from my room, I had to stop and hold on to the wall in order to support my exhausted body. My head felt as though someone was hitting me with some large object. Between the flood of tears streaming down my face and the shear determination to win, I entered my room. I barely made it to the chair and ottoman before the loud ring of the telephone startled me. There I stood in the middle of my bedroom, just staring at the swirling walls. My iron-jawed will not to answer the phone was in place. No one could enter *my world right now.* That dreaded gray-green mist of emotions that had over-taken me years ago, was drowning me. May "the All" help me!

After too many failed attempts to get me to come out of my haven of safety, all those whom I loved so dearly, decided to leave me in the hands of "the All" for a while.

On the eighth day of self imposed isolation, I shed my cocooned life and re-entered civilian life. Thanks to "the All" and the prevailing prayers of the righteous, I was given the strength to contact my assistant at work and informed her that I was taking a vacation. After I had taken care of all other business concerns, I arranged to stay at a motel in the Detroit Area. All of this was done with the full knowledge that my physical health was rapidly deteriorating. The cab ride to the airport was one of shear physical pain for me. Only some two year old prescribed pain medicine gave me any kind of relief.

"Excuse me Miss Palermo, are you alright?" the man at the motel desk asked me.

"Yes, of course I'm okay, why would you ask me such a stupid question?" I snapped, in a sorry attempt to dispel my anguish.

"Okay ma'am, I didn't mean any harm," the desk clerk retorted as he continued processing my registration.

After checking into my room, I turned the radio to a late-night blues station. The D.J. announced that "Little Minnie Mama" was about to sing the next selection-"No More Blues":

"I told the meat man, I'd have no more of his over-priced beef

I told the ice-cream man, I'd have no more from his big dipper

I told the insurance man, I needed no more of his kind of protection

No more blues, no more blues, no more blues

No more blues, no more blues, no more blues

I've got the No More Blues from my head down to my red painted toes..."

I immediately began to undress and prepare for a shower. As I was sitting on the edge of the bed, I noticed that my upper thighs were covered with blood. A surge of panic and doom began to consume me. I quickly walked into the washroom and turned on the shower. I began to feel too weak to complete this process. I ached all over, especially in my vaginal area. I dragged myself to a chair that was placed under a small desk and sat down. Lord have mercy on me!

My mind began to swirl and I began to write. The pain was becoming too much to tolerate. I began to cry as I attempted to jot down some of my dwindling thoughts.

Dear Mama,

Please tell Jerome, Roger, Rochelle, Ant Boo and Deacon Henry, Miss Peach, Charles, and Pastor and Sister Newbreed, I love them and that the pain of this life..."

MEMORIES/THE HOMEGOING

And the peace of God, which transcends all understanding, will guard your hearts and your minds in Christ Jesus – Philippians 4:7 NIV

This was the first Bible verse Anne Marie recited at church. We were so proud of her that day. I will never forget the day of her failed wedding, memories, how they linger…

After convincing Jerome and Sara Mae to remain calm, Henry and I rushed to the aid of Hori. As we were attending to Hori, I saw Pastor Newbreed giving comfort to Anne Marie. Poor Anne was crying her heart out. Despite Hori's impassioned screams down the now crowded sanctuary aisle, Anne Marie was refusing to let Hori near her. The many years of distrust, emotional, physical, and even spiritual disappointments were too much for her to tolerate. The stress of the wedding did little to help Anne's shattered state at this time. How could Hori become such a disappointment?

Henry and four other deacons began to carry Hori out of the church. Jerome stood at the end of the sanctuary coldly staring at Hori. If looks could kill, Hori would be dead by now.

Collecting myself amid a now almost empty church, I couldn't help but notice how the room was filled with all sorts of exotic flowers. Sara Mae told us she was responsible for these most expensive floral arrangements. The sanctuary was draped entirely in a Fairy-Land Motif. Those of us who knew Sara Mae doubted her ability to afford such an elaborate staging. The place reminded you of a ball-room setting in some fairy land. The place was worthy of being placed in some interior design magazine.

Jerome and I were among the first to contact Anne Marie after the emotionally draining wedding fall-out. Our many attempts to get Anne Marie to come out of her bedroom and talk with us were met with constant refusals. Sara Mae, Miss Peach, and others were only allowed to set Anne's food outside her bed-room door. Anne stayed in that room for a little over a week. We were most fearful she would do something to harm herself. We made her promise she wouldn't do anything...well, foolish!

Reluctantly Anne's children, sister, Jerome and Charles returned to their respective homes. All this was done with Anne assuring us she was okay via notes, phone calls, and verbal exchanges. Miss Peach and I took on the assignment of looking in on Anne when Sara Mae was not in the house.

When the news of Anne having left town for a "vacation" got around, well, we were just beside ourselves with worry. Had Anne Marie not contacted us from what we now know to be the Indigo Motel, none of us would have known her whereabouts. Those few calls from Anne assured us that she was at least alive.

Hori had moved back to Savannah, Georgia. He didn't take the job with the Centers for Disease Control. His frequent phone calls to us inquiring about "his Anne Marie" were only met with second-hand information from us about Anne's well-being. Child, talk about a total feeling of helplessness at this time in my life! Ooo wee!

When the manager of the Indigo Motel contacted us about his discovering Ann's body lying in a pool of blood-well, you can just about imagine the depressed state we all found ourselves in. The coroner said she had been dead for about two days. It was concluded she died from cervical hemorrhaging. What a tragic, senseless death.

What is life worth, when love is just not enough?

When Jerome was told about his beloved Anne staying so close to him in a motel, he had to be given several days leave of absence from his job in order to deal with the news.

Sara Mae fell into a prolonged silence when she got the news of "her Anne's" death. The partly written missive addressed to *Dear Mama,* did little to calm Sara Mae's nerves. As a matter of fact, the note appeared to have sent poor Sara Mae into a further state of conflict. Sara Mae felt that on the one hand, Anne's note to her was a long awaited recognition of the obvious, but on the other, "the bitch had gone off and caused so much hardship." Poor Sara Mae! Indeed!

Rochelle and Roger were devastated. Rochelle had to be sedated. We all feared the worst for her. Roger would not show any type of visual emotions during the whole ordeal. He would only stare at pictures of his mother and him taken at the time of his graduation from college.

Her college advisor hand delivered a letter indicating Anne had met all requirements in order to graduate from the college.

With an occasional bit of input from Sara Mae, Roger and Jerome handled Anne's home-going arrangements. Anne Marie's funeral was to be a closed-casket service. Roger and Rochelle couldn't be convinced to attend their mother's transitional service. They said they could not stomach the pain of seeing their mother dead.

After our Anne Marie Palermo was buried, her uncle Rocco Palermo met Jerome, Sara Mae and me at the grave-site. He was the white gentleman sitting in the balcony of the church during Anne's home-going service. As he walked us to the awaiting limousine, he told us that Alphonso Palermo was Anne Marie's father. Rocco Palermo said that as teenagers, Alphonso wanted to run-off with Sara Mae and live where their families would not bother them. The affair between Sara Mae and Alphonso saw the start of a mini-war between Spring Oaks and Roseland. Roseland was a predominately Italian Community. As a result of this fracas, many persons in each town were injured. The resolve of this dispute saw Sara Mae and Alphonse agreeing never to see each other again. Mrs. Pitts was rumored to have instigated the many injuries by paying some folk from Spring Oaks and other folk from the Westside of the city "to crush" the Palermo Family and rid the area of them all together. The situation got so bad that state troopers were sent to stop the growing tensions.

Alphonso loved Anne from the time he first saw her at the hospital until to the day of her failed wedding. It was Mr. Palermo who was supplying all those flowers to Anne's shop, hospital room, and washed out wedding. See, I knew Sara Mae didn't have enough money to decorate the church on poor Anne's *that lying Sara Mae!* I mean, after all!

Rocco informed us that Alphonso died the day after Anne's failed wedding. He had made provisions for Anne in his will. The will stated that should something happen to Anne, her children would become the beneficiaries. Besides Anne, Angelo was Mr. Palermo's only other child.

Angelo and a cousin of his walked up to the limousine. He expressed his sympathy with regards to

P. Nelson Byrd

Anne's death and promised to help in any way he could in the future.

Sara Mae didn't say a word to Jerome and me on the way back from St. Catherine's Cemetery. She just kept staring out the car window with a blank look on her face.

Arriving home and getting out of the limousine, Sara Mae looked at Jerome and me.

"I'm sorry ya'll, I just didn't know how to…"

At that moment Miss Peach walked up to us, hugged Sara Mae and walked her into her house.

Jerome and I followed Miss Peach and Sara Mae. When we got to the porch, Jerome stopped and looked at the house. He glanced up and down the length of Church Street and tearfully whispered-*Anne Marie!*

A novel by P. Nelson Byrd

June 2002

ABOUT THE AUTHOR

Prentiss N. Byrd is a Christ-like African-American. He is professor emeritus of the Guidance and Counseling Department at one of the City Colleges of Chicago. Prentiss is an involved church member in Chicago, Illinois. He is a member of the American Counseling Association, the past proud co-founder of two black book/media groups, a past member of a research group at the Howard Brown Clinic, and NEST. He is the proud son, brother, uncle, cousin, nephew, and friend to a wonderful supportive family. Prentiss promotes holistic health; spiritually, physically, and emotionally.